The Belt

Books by Dale E. Lehman

Howard County Mysteries

The Fibonacci Murders
True Death
Ice on the Bay
A Day for Bones

Bernard and Melody Capers

Weasel Words
Rooftop Sonata

Science Fiction

Space Operatic
The Belt
Penitence

Short Story Collections

The Realm of Tiny Giants
Found by the Road
Manifest Secrets

THE BELT

Dale E. Lehman

Chase, Maryland

Cover art by Proi
https://99designs.com/profiles/proi

Book design by Dale E. Lehman
Book set in 12-pt. Callisto MT
Chapter headings set in 18-pt. Consolas

Published by Red Tales, 2023
Baltimore, Maryland
United States of America
https://www.DaleELehman.com

Trade paperback: 978-1-958906-04-0
Ebook: 978-1-958906-05-7

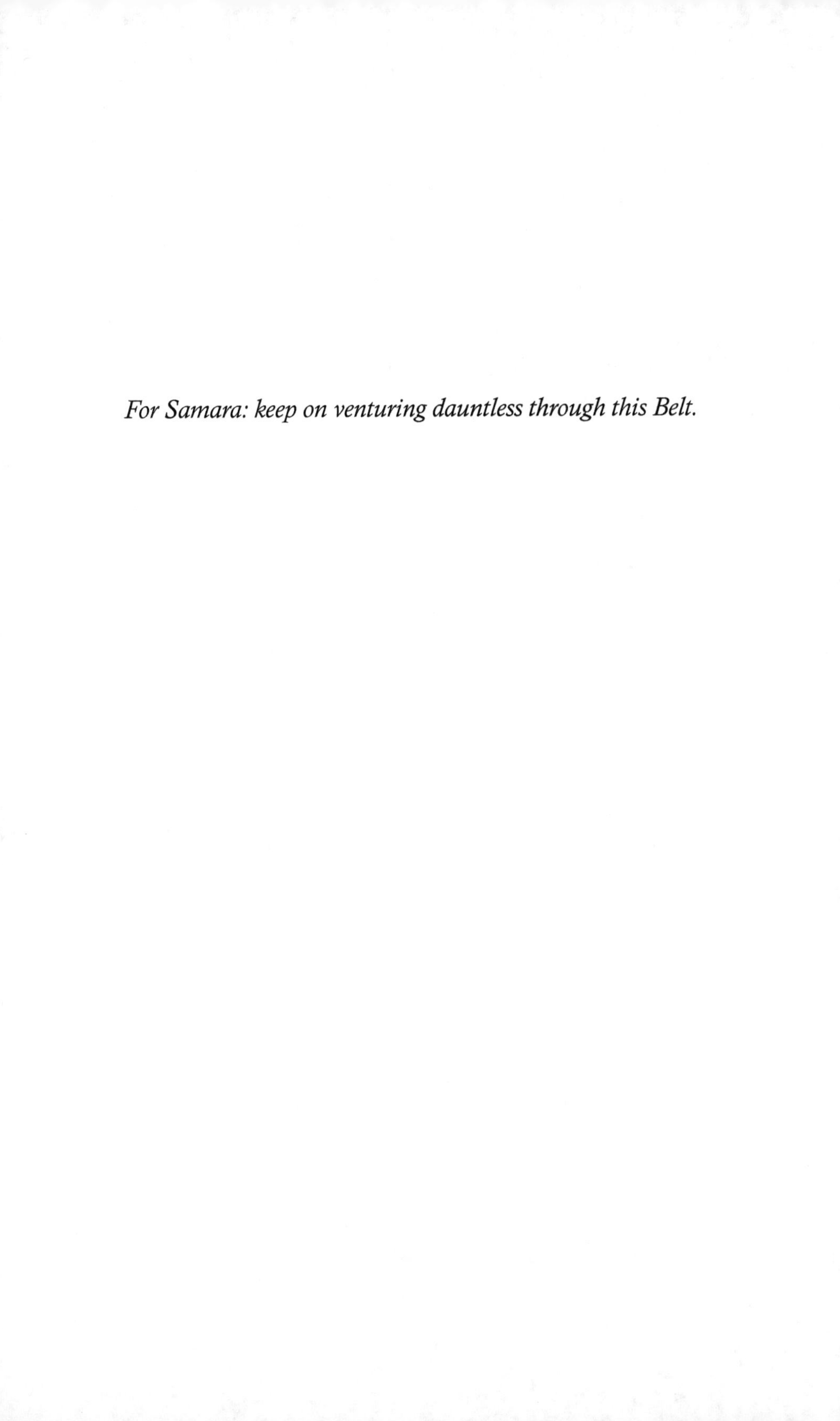

For Samara: keep on venturing dauntless through this Belt.

No AI tools were used in the crafting of this story. Seriously, where would be the fun in *that*?

Chapter 1

Target acquired.

Someone big wanted this, someone rich, someone hiding behind a trail of shadow contacts and laundered currency. He knew but didn't care, not until he saw the target. Now he cared. A lot. Because it made no sense. He hesitated while crimson lights blinked in the darkened rover and fire control chirped at him, awaiting his command.

Target acquired.

His contact—a radical environmentalist, she claimed, although he knew she wasn't—hadn't told him about the target. She'd only given him coordinates and equipment and a simple instruction: destroy what you find. But a drone could have torched this structure with less risk, certainly with less expense. Why offer Alejandro Carrasco—a cut-rate Belt mercenary, an outlaw who hadn't dared set boot on Mars in thirteen years—cash enough to buy a whole damned asteroid for *this*?

Target acquired.

Half a kilometer distant, a chrome sphere gleamed in the sun, a metal star fallen to the rocky red plain of Acidalia Planitia. Enlarged on the vid panel before Alejandro, black figures branded on the structure's curvature identified it: HYDRO STATION 68N 44W.

Why hire *him* to roast a hydro station?

Target acquired.

It had to be a trap. But why? The bounty on Alejandro's head wasn't that impressive. Who would go to such trouble just to nab him?

Nobody, that's who. This was paranoia, probably, but he locked his faceplate and pressurized his bulky white envirosuit anyway, just in case. The vid panels arrayed before him showed his surround, fore and aft, port and starboard, overhead. Nothing moved, nothing breathed, nothing bore witness but the hydro station and the dead surface of Mars. He couldn't even see himself on the interior camera. His smoky black faceplate obscured his visage. He might have been a robot.

Target…

"Fire." He spoke as much to shut the machine up as to complete his mission.

On screen, a dart of white smoke lanced the structure. An instant later, the hydro station erupted in scarlet flame. Brilliant light illuminated Alejandro's visor, revealing a flash of his face, lean and bearded, before lack of oxygen snuffed the flames, leaving a pillar of black smoke rising above a pile of ruin.

He eyed the panels, tense, wondering when the ambush would come, from where, what form it would take. If they wanted the reward, they wouldn't immolate him. They'd need a body part or two for DNA samples, which meant boots on the ground, at least to collect the evidence.

He stared at Mars and the sky and the smoke spreading on the thin wind. Still nothing.

Maybe the job was legit, after all. He wouldn't celebrate prematurely, but if he made the thirty-eight kilometers to the extraction point without incident, he'd leave Mars behind, this time for good. He'd collect his fortune, disappear into the Belt, maybe change his name once more, and retire to a life of ease on some affluent station. Not bad for uttering a single word.

Fire.

The soft arch of the Milky Way streamed above the transparent dome, riven by dark lanes. Where the heavens touched land, starlight framed shadows of distant hills. Beneath the dome, yellow and orange flickers of artificial fire illuminated the faces of the five seated on the floor about it, four mid-twenties, one mid-forties, all immersed in meditative silence.

The young, having feasted on success and their host's generous table, settled into companionable peace to contemplate their futures. Their elder let them savor the feeling a moment longer. They'd completed the initial analysis of their find and knew what it meant: their one small rock would change humanity's view of the universe forever.

If word ever got out.

It might not. A warning whispered in Dr. Miguel Hernandez's ear three hours before made it unlikely. He stood on the edge of a precipice, escape routes cut off. He could only jump and hope for the best. He'd come to terms with that. His fears tonight were not for himself but his students.

The moment passed, and he spoke. "I miss real fire."

Three of the youth looked amused, the other bemused.

The latter, Ricard Fulbert, said, "Rapid exothermic processes are dangerous, not to mention a waste of oxygen." He wasn't joking. Tall and wiry, Ricard never quite got humor, particularly not his own inadvertent variety. How could a Frenchman be so serious? But then, he wasn't truly French, was he? None of them were quite what their parents had been.

The others snickered. Quan Linh joked, "Then you'd better throttle back your brain, Ricard." Lihn was the sun to Ricard's shade, a Vietnamese woman barely five foot high clothed in smiles and laughter.

Ricard raised questioning eyebrows.

Grinning, Martin Ulenga explained. "Linh means you're thinking too hard, which is a problem she doesn't generally have." Martin was black velvet, the son of Namibian diplomats who had foregone Earth's shriveled politics for the newness of Mars.

"Be nice, Martin," his twin sister Petrina said. She'd led the way into the world when they were born and never let him forget her slight seniority.

Miguel smiled and smoothed his beard. He would miss this. That was the main reason he'd invited them to his home tonight. They were his fountain of youth, preserving him against encroaching age, a wine that dulled the aching memory of another child, long lost to him. But this was his last draught. Time settled heavy upon his shoulders, and the cup must pass from his hands.

Ricard parried the ribbing. "Ignore the children, professor. What's so special about real fire?"

Miguel gazed into the false flame. "Fire is alive, a dance of light, a crackling symphony. The sting of wood smoke in your nostrils forges new memories and summons old ones. It's more than chemistry. It's magic. No, more than magic. Fire—real fire—is spirit."

Petrina laughed. "Who stole Dr. Hernandez and left us a mystic?"

"Not you, too," Linh chided. "Ignore her, Professor. Your lectures are brilliant."

Miguel wanted them to go on and on. Let them pepper each other with foam darts, let them be young all through this final night. But time grew short.

"You've never seen real fire," he said. "You're first-generation Martians. I'm just an invasive species." *A species*, he didn't tell them, *slated for eradication*. "But more than that, you're the brightest minds I've ever taught."

The students beamed at each other. Ribbing aside, they knew their brilliance, and each other's.

Miguel's gaze swept over them. "Always remember that. But remember, too, that it comes with a cost. I must ask something of you."

Petrina leaned forward, eager to prove her worth. "Anything, Professor. Just name it."

"Something you won't like."

Martin seconded his sister's enthusiasm. "We trust you."

They were sprinters poised for the starter pistol, unaware he was dispatching them to Marathon and might die ere they arrived.

"Leave Mars. Go out beyond the Belt. Ganymede, Callisto, Titan. You know the most likely places. Go while there's still time."

The thin Martian wind brushed the transparent dome.

Ricard found his voice first. "What about our paper? The research preserve?"

"There won't be a research preserve."

"But…the Meridiani microfossils! How can you…" Ricard looked to the others, but none could finish the thought. Miguel's command had been a knockout blow to their skulls.

Miguel leaned toward the fire and stretched forth a hand to feel its feeble warmth. "I'm not abandoning our research. This find is too important. But the truth is, nobody cares right now. Nobody but us. Mayor Rand's ambition takes no account of scientific values. A colonization wave will soon break upon Mars, and it won't stop here. There's still time to look for evidence of life farther out, but for how long? Maybe only a generation or two. That's why I want you to go. You're the best-qualified to do the work."

He watched them chew on this news and find it bitter, but there was worse to come.

On the verge of tears, Linh asked, "Aren't you coming with us?"

"No. I've been fighting this battle longer than you know. Metaphorically speaking, I've broken Rand's nose one time too many. Dr. Lloyd sent word that come morning, I'll be branded an outlaw."

They all knew what that meant. Outlaw. Outside the law and its protection. No due process, no trial, no nothing, just a bounty anyone could claim by killing Miguel on sight. Rarely used, the brand had only ever been applied to the worst of the worst, the few thugs who threatened the existence of the colony. Thugs like…

No. Miguel wouldn't think of him. Not here, not now.

"On what charges?" Ricard demanded.

"Charges aren't necessary. That said, someone destroyed a hydro station this morning. They claim I did it."

"Where were you at the time?" Martin asked. "You must have an alibi."

Miguel dared not reveal that. He came to Mars to escape his sins only to fall again. He'd rather face life in exile, even death, than demolish his students' faith in him. Soon, that might be all they had. "I'm afraid not."

Petrina shivered and hugged herself as though the deep cold of the Martian wilderness had infiltrated her bones. "What will you do?"

"The only thing I can," he said. "Hide."

Ricard ran a hand through his wavy brown hair. "There's no place to hide on Mars."

Everyone always said so, but Miguel knew otherwise. He could but hope he was still welcome.

A safe house waited along the way.

Two and a half hours east of Lowell Colony, isolated, built into the side of a rise, the house's rusty façade blended with the slope, rendering it all but invisible save to those who knew where to look. The rising sun had just kissed its face when Miguel arrived. He paused to admire this epitome of architectural art, knowing the treasures he'd find within. With twice the space of the average Martian dwelling, this home could have been an art gallery, appointed with the finest furnishings, exotic plants, paintings, and sculptures, all lit by unseen light tunnels that set the place aglow. And the owner? She was a work of art, too.

Miguel knew the access code. Stashing his rover in the garage beneath the main floor, he entered, dodging the cleaning robots humming about the soft green and blue gathering room. He needn't announce himself. She'd know he was here. He clasped his hands behind his back and stood in contemplation before a twisted sculpture of pure silver that pulsed with light. He hadn't noticed before, but in outline the piece resembled…

"What the hell are you doing here?"

Yes. Her.

"Hiding," he said.

"Not here, not anymore. Andre might find out."

Miguel didn't mind her theatrics. She was a politician's wife, after all. *The* politician's wife. He turned and smiled at Carmen Rand, first lady of Lowell Colony, first lady of Mars. "How? I won't tell him, and neither will you."

He gathered her into his arms—or tried to. She pushed away and crossed to a small bar on the far side of the room. Crystal rang as she set out two glasses and poured a pale rose concoction. Keeping one for herself, she offered the other to Miguel. "I ought to alert him right now."

"While you're at it, tell him where I was yesterday."

"Bastard."

He drank to that. "Please, Carmen. Just one night." He kissed her on the lips.

She indulged him a second before backing away. "You've ruined your career. You're not ruining mine."

He laughed. "My *career*?"

"I was being gentle, but fine. Your life."

"Which is why I need to drop out of sight."

Carmen sat on the sofa and crossed her perfect legs. Her mouth signaled severity, her eyes humor. "Just because Andre never stages events here doesn't mean he won't find you."

"How? This is your hermitage, not his. Isn't that why he built you the place? So you could be alone?" Miguel sat close. Their thighs touched.

"The house might be bugged."

"For God's sake, Carmen."

"Don't you know what's happening?"

How could he not? He and Andre Rand had been on collision course for a decade. Miguel drove hard to sequester Sinus Meridiani for research, but the qualities that made it the place to seek evidence of life also made it the place to live. Neither man had taken evasive action. Inevitably they'd crash, and only one could survive. Odds were, it wouldn't be the scientist.

Miguel took a drink. Carmen leaned her head on his shoulder. Her dark hair lay soft against his cheek. "The agreements funding Schiaparelli Colony were concluded yesterday. A year from now, Meridiani will be half buried in concrete and steel. Why do you think Andre picked today to brand you outlaw?"

"That explains the timing," he said, "but it's not a total surprise. Word of my status upgrade leaked out yesterday. I'll only stay the night. I promise." He touched her cheek. "I don't want you in trouble."

She stroked his fingers before pushing his hand away and sitting upright. "You don't get it, do you? You think he doesn't know about us? He'll use me to take you down."

Miguel didn't doubt it. "He set me up."

"Damn right he did. Brilliantly. A half-second vid clip of your face, or somebody similar. It was convincing." She ran a finger along the line of his jaw. Her eyes said she wanted him, until she slapped him. Hard.

He flinched but didn't protest. He deserved it. "I heard. But you know where I was."

She shrugged. "Maybe, maybe not. Either way, Andre knows you'll come to me."

"Then why isn't Security hiding behind the sculptures?"

"I don't expect he figured you'd show so soon. Whoever leaked the info, Andre will have their head on a spike."

Miguel figured Dr. Lloyd knew how to keep his mouth shut. At least, he hoped so.

"And," Carmen added, "once he knows you're here, he'll have me distract you until his thugs can rush in and truss you up."

"Would you?"

"Hell, yes. That's why you're leaving. Death doesn't appeal to me."

"Come on, Andre wouldn't kill you."

"Damn idiot, aren't you?" She took his head in her hands and kissed him long and hard. He about drove her down onto the couch, but she pushed him away before he could. "It's been fun, Miguel. I don't regret a minute of it. But we both know it was greedy sport, and now the game's over. Get out of my house before I call the cops." She rose, took his half-empty glass from him, and vanished into the kitchen.

Water swished and glass clinked.

He left before Carmen could return.

Crouched on a plain in the south of Acidalia Planitia, far from the craters and ancient mud volcanoes of the region's interior, Lowell Colony hosted most everything human on Mars. The colony had grown over thirty-seven years from a single lab to a city of more than twenty-five thousand. Sealed walkways and transport tubes connected a hive of hexagonal, cylindrical, and spherical structures, some burrowed into the rust, some perched upon it, some half buried. Where they protruded, the low, broad profiles of the older structures flowed into the ruddy soil. Within the hive's warrens huddled the hospital that birthed you, healed you, and eased you into death; the fields and orchards and stockyards that fed you; the schools that prepared you for a life of service to spacefaring humanity; and the university that, if you were deemed sufficiently gifted, offered a chance at something more.

Otherwise, Mars remained pristine, or nearly so. A few adventurous souls, Dr. Miguel Hernandez for one, built homes beyond the colony's reach. Some ranged as far as a full day's journey, but never farther. The Martian wilderness was a deathtrap. Miguel's home stood a mere hour away by rover, a small but comfortable dwelling where he invited none but his most gifted students, and then only on occasion. The students lived and studied in the safety of the colony, venturing out only to visit him or accompany him on research expeditions. For them, leaving Lowell was an adventure, leaving Mars all but unthinkable.

And to leave Miguel alone in such circumstances?

"I can't," Petrina said. She dropped her fork on her plate. The clank drew attention from nearby tables. "He needs our help."

The breakfast crowd in the university cafeteria hummed about them. News from Lowell and off-planet chattered on wall-mounted vid panels for those caring to know. Few bothered to watch. Morning people chattered about classes, research projects, relationships, and pranks. Others stared at their food or at nothing, eating and drinking mechanically, waiting for the caffeine to kick in.

"What can we do?" Ricard demanded. "Shoot security when they show up?"

"There must be something."

Linh rearranged her imitation scrambled eggs. "He asked us to leave, not get involved in—"

"We're already involved," Petrina snapped.

Martin pushed his plate away, his meal only half-eaten. "Ricard's right. If Dr. Hernandez is outlawed, nobody can help him."

"You should be on my side," Petrina scolded.

"I just mean, we need to be careful. Think it through. This isn't a fossil hunt."

A lull in the buzz silenced them. The crowd's attention had been drawn to the news vids where a still of Dr. Hernandez smiled at the gathering as the anchor declared with excess gravity that the scientist, having destroyed a public works installation, had been declared outlaw. "A reward of five thousand obols will be paid for his capture," the anchor added with extreme gravity. "Dead or alive."

When Hernandez's face vanished and the next news item began, attention drifted away, and murmured conversation resumed.

"And there you have it," Ricard said. "Render him any aid, and we're outlaws, too."

"Drop it," Martin said. He nodded to the far side of the room, where a quartet of armed security guards had entered. "The cops are here."

Chapter 2

Damn her!

Alejandro should have questioned this deal from the start. Instead, he let the environmentalist's dark eyes and the prospect of wealth hypnotize him. That's how he'd meet his end someday. Some rich beauty would beckon him into the void, and he'd jump.

Take this one. She was no environmentalist, no radical. She cared not at all for the barren wastes of Mars, lost no sleep over strip mining or sprawl. Nobody did. Mars was carrion. Leave it to the human vultures who'd found it. No, likely she was a spotter for some fringe political or militant organization, which was fine. Such groups were his daily bread, and she sure did offer nourishment. She even threw in this skiff as a bonus. He'd never had a ship of his own. It was a dessert too sweet to refuse.

Or to be true.

Deep down, he knew that. He even had his moment of doubt in the sands. But with payment received and no sign of pursuit, Alejandro relaxed and set course for Itokawa Station in the inner Belt. Semi-comfortable acceleration provided stable gravity as he poured himself a scotch and watched the news vids leaking into space from Lowell Colony. Only then did the truth smack him upside the head. She hadn't needed his skills. She'd needed his face.

On panel, the reporter pumped the devastation for all it was worth. The hydro station blossomed into smoke over and over while voice-overs predicted immanent attacks on other facilities. Intercut with the destruction, an image boosted from his rover's interior camera showed Alejandro's face, misty and blurred behind his visor but clear enough to name the culprit.

Exobiologist Dr. Miguel Hernandez.

Alejandro killed the vid. A set up, all right, but he wasn't the target. Miguel was. Question was, should he care? No, that wasn't the question. Why the hell were they after Miguel?

Not that the scientist didn't deserve it. Alejandro nearly offed Miguel himself, once. As children on Earth, they walked divergent paths. Miguel excelled at science and math, Alejandro at mischief and mayhem. Miguel thought he could steer Alejandro onto the straight path, but he was no saint, either. Ambition got the better of him. In a bid for recognition, Miguel fabricated evidence to suggest the seeds of life originated in the Belt. When the fraud was discovered, he scurried off to Mars. His wife Mona begged him to stay, make amends, tough it out until he rebuilt his reputation, but Miguel couldn't stomach the shame. Rather than follow, Mona left him, taking their infant son Sef with her.

Alejandro thought himself free of Miguel until he, too, fled to Mars. Hunted by the authorities for a legendary chronicle of insurrections, he had no choice, but all he left behind were arrest warrants. Those, he could do without. Alas, he and Miguel were thrown together again. Lowell Colony wasn't big enough to keep them apart. History played a variation on its old theme as Miguel pressured Alejandro to go straight, get a legitimate job, become a vegetable. When reckoning day came, it left Miguel half dead while Alejandro escaped to the Belt, cursed with outlaw status. Rage and regret morphed into apathy as Alejandro built yet another life that, if not easy, at least suited his temperament. Miguel faded to irrelevance, like a vid of a forgotten neighbor.

Until now.

Alejandro stared into his drink. He shouldn't care. Whatever Miguel had done, he probably deserved this. Still, it felt wrong. The environmentalist hadn't hired him at random. She knew his past. She should have given him the choice. But no, the bitch used him, knowing he'd realize it once his face made the rounds. Why would she assume Alejandro wouldn't care?

She wouldn't. She wasn't an idiot. She knew he'd be a nuke poised to go critical. You don't let one of those choose its own trajectory.

Alejandro put down his drink. The cold of space crept up his spine.

Bolting from the pilot's seat, he combed the skiff for explosives.

The instrument pressed to Quan Linh's neck felt like a frozen dagger and hissed like a snake. Pain throbbed in her flesh. "What was that?" she gasped, barely able to speak through her terror.

The woman holding the instrument didn't answer. She pulled an alcohol wipe from a container on a cart jammed with medical supplies and wiped down the unit's tip. Dressed in a dark blue coverall, she might have been a security guard or a maintenance worker, but not likely a nurse. Or human, even. She packed up her gear and pushed her cart from the room. The metal door clanged shut behind her.

Linh trembled like a cornered mouse. Everything in this four-square-meter room was metal. Floor, walls, the chair to which she was strapped, all metal, all white save a bluish light emanating from the top of the walls. She sat alone in the whiteness for five minutes, maybe ten, maybe an hour. Who could tell? Eternity might have passed, and nothing met her eyes but the white, nothing filled her ears but the silence.

The door creaked and another woman entered, identically dressed but with gold and silver bars perched on her right shoulder. She frowned at a glossy wafer cradled in her right palm. "Quan Linh," she said, "age twenty-five, native-born, exobiology doctoral student at Lowell Colony University. Parents, brother, other useless shit." She pocketed the wafer and stared at Linh.

Linh looked away.

"You were with Miguel Hernandez last night."

Trembling, she locked her jaw. *Don't speak*, she told herself. *Don't speak, don't speak, don't…*

"You and three other students. What was it, an orgy?"

"*What?*"

"What did you do?" The woman spaced the words as though talking to a small child.

A few words tumbled out on their own. "Dinner. Talk. Nothing."

"What sort of talk?"

"Science."

The interrogator closed in, bent down, put her face in Linh's. "Insurrection."

Linh shook her head.

"Liar."

Memory failed her. She knew no past, no future, only this moment.

The interrogator straightened. "Petrina told the truth. Eventually."

Oh God, what did you do, what did you do to Petrina? Linh imagined the others strapped to cold metal chairs, frightened, minds clouded, bodies bloodied and broken. What would they say? What would she say?

The interrogator raised a small black stick and regarded it with a twisted smile. "Ever see one of these?"

She hadn't. She couldn't say so.

The woman placed the tip of the stick against Linh's bare forearm. Electricity tickled her skin, spread across her shoulders, down her other arm, along her spine, into her feet. Strange sensations followed in its wake: heat and cold, pressure and prickles, pleasure and pain, all at once. She tasted sugar and lime, salt and quinine, smelled roses and death. The jumbled sensations persisted, not overwhelming yet strange and unpleasant, until the interrogator lifted the stick.

"That's ten percent charge. Fun, yeah?"

Fun wasn't the word. She didn't know what was.

"Let's try twenty-five."

Panicked, Linh struggled against the restraints. The stick touched her skin. Fire erupted in her flesh. It roared through her body, consuming her. A chaos of sensation assaulted her, needles jabbing, knives slashing, hands and knees scraping over concrete, the ecstasy of sex, fire and ice, a barrage of tastes and smells that made her retch, accompanied by bombs exploding overhead, engines roaring, people shouting, and over it all her own nonstop scream.

And then nothing.

Linh gasped for air, shook, cried. Tears blinded her, and she couldn't wipe them away.

"Soft," the investigator said. "Petrina didn't fuss like that until we got to fifty percent. Fifty would probably kill you. Shall we find out?"

"No!" Linh pleaded. "Please, no!"

The interrogator laughed.

"Please stop, please, please let me go, please, what do you want?"

"What did Hernandez say?"

"I don't know! I can't remember!"

The black stick touched her flesh. She screamed under the assault of conflicting sensations. Her brain overloaded, and she lost consciousness. She only knew because she woke as from a nightmare, sweat-drenched, shaking, telling herself it was just a dream, just a dream, just a dream.

"No, Linh," the investigator said. "It's real. And I can make it go on and on and on."

She sobbed and pleaded and swore she knew nothing, nothing at all, *nothing*!

"But you do."

"What, like what, I don't *know* anything!"

"Where is Dr. Hernandez?"

"He didn't tell us, please, please, he didn't, I don't know!"

Fire consumed her body while she sank in a pool of ice water as a lover caressed her and an enemy flogged her and sounds of war and music echoed in her brain and her mouth was filled with sugar and salt and…

She raised her wet face to her tormentor. She no longer had a voice, not even to beg for mercy.

"Dr. Hernandez," the demon said.

Linh's eyebrows arched, just.

"He wanted you to join his insurrection."

Too big a word. Linh didn't know what it meant. She barely knew her name. She nodded anyway, not knowing why.

"He plans to destroy the colony's infrastructure."

Who? Linh saw the black stick hovering a centimeter above her wrist. Her body convulsed in terror.

"Answer the question, Linh."

She'd forgotten the question. She only knew she had to get away from that thing. She nodded, praying that would make it vanish.

"Do you give this testimony of your own free will?"

Linh blinked away her tears. More flooded her eyes. The black stick brushed the fine hairs on her arm. She didn't know what was being asked, only what the answer was.

"Yes."

"Next time you're asked, make sure you say so." The stick passed before her eyes, swept across her eyelashes. A tingle ran through her, a pleasant, terrifying reminder of what they could make her feel. She struggled against the restraints and wailed for release.

The door squeaked. Footsteps clattered on the hard floor. Someone said, "Wuss," and several others laughed. Someone grabbed her hand and pressed her fingers to a cold surface. More clattering, then the straps were undone and she was dragged, because she could barely stand, and thrown onto a hard floor.

When she opened her eyes a minute or a month or a decade later, she was lying on a rumpled bed. Petrina Ulenga sat beside her, gently stroking her hand. She tried to sit, but dizziness overwhelmed her. She whimpered.

"Shh," Petrina whispered. "Rest. You're safe."

Safe? *Safe?* She would never be safe again! Unless…

"God," Linh muttered. She pulled her hand from Petrina's grasp and set it to her forehead. "Was that a nightmare?"

Petrina touched her shoulder. "Yeah," she said. "A nightmare."

Another damn ribbon cutting.

Andre Rand, mayor of Lowell Colony, smiled his false suave smile and snipped the red and white ribbon with sterling silver scissors. "Let's all get rich!" he proclaimed. The small, overdressed crowd cramming the transport station laughed and hooted and clapped and pressed into the pristine Casino Acidalia, all but Andre and his beautiful wife Carmen. He put his arm around her, pulled her close, and smiled for the videographers vying for the best lines of sight. They ate the couple up.

Andre and Carmen were a work of art. A head taller, the mayor had a celebrity smile, a strong chin, a wrinkle-free black suit. Carmen had a model's body, a tight black dress, and a smile that could melt the polar caps. They maintained their pose before the brilliant lights of Mars' first casino while the videographers swarmed. Reporters cried questions but got no answers. Andre wasn't in the mood. Once the excitement faded, arm-in-arm the first couple gave themselves a tour of the facility, beaming and waving at patrons and not once risking their own money.

"It's rigged, of course," Andre whispered. He grinned.

She matched his grin. "Could you beat the house?"

"No, but they know to throw me a bone. Otherwise, they'll allow just enough wins to keep the crowds in thrall without impacting profits."

"Business is too complex for me."

The floor rang with bells and flashed with light. People laughed, called numbers, ordered drinks and food.

"Hardly. Your clever brain is full of schemes." He tapped a finger on the back of her head.

She smiled. "You wouldn't want a stupid wife."

"How long has he been banging you?"

"Who?"

"Hernandez."

"Does it matter?"

Andre put a hand on her shoulder and steered her to the bar. "Two rum and colas. On my tab." The bartender mixed and slid the drinks with practiced efficiency.

"It depends," Andre told her.

"Ah." Carmen lifted her drink, settled her back against the bar, watched the gamblers. Several of the men caught her eye and watched her right back. She winked at them. "Long enough to know not to trust me."

Andre turned, too. "Pity."

She leaned against him. "Why, what's he done now?"

"You know him. He's a mosquito."

"We didn't bring mosquitos to Mars, Andre."

He glanced at her in irritation.

"That was a joke."

He still didn't laugh.

"So squash him. You're the mayor. He's just a professor."

Andre took a drink while his eyes probed her face. "That wouldn't bother you?"

"Why should it? I can always find another toy. Maybe even one who doesn't want to suck your blood."

He laughed and tangled his fingers in her hair. "I think you enjoy crossing me. Is that how you get even, or do you just want a front-row seat for the knock-out?"

With a little shrug, Carmen said, "Bit of both."

"When do you see him again?"

"Never."

He took her chin in his hand and made her look at him. "You sent him away?"

"No, Andre. He did the leaving."

He squeezed just enough to hurt.

"Stop that or I'll walk out. Your media sycophants would have a field day with *that*."

Andre grinned, released her, waited for an answer.

She obliged. "It's the truth. I invited him to stay, but as I said, he doesn't trust me."

"Nor do I."

"Smart man."

"You wouldn't want a stupid husband." He settled against the bar again. He drank, shook his head, smiled and waved at a group of happy gamblers passing by. "Damn it, Carmen. Now I'll have to find him the hard way."

"It can't be that hard," she said. "There's no place to hide on Mars."

They both drank.

"Actually," he said, "there is."

Billows of rusty cloud obscured the southern horizon as a small sandstorm tracked across the distant Chryse Planitia. Miguel, his envirosuit caked with dust, watched from the crest of a low ridge. It had been a long day's drive, and the sun now hovered on the western horizon. Below the incline, his rover sat silent and obvious, as obvious as he. He wanted to be seen but had to trust to luck that the people living here would admit him. No doubt they already knew he was outlawed.

At least he was a familiar face. His fossil-hunting expeditions ranged across fifty degrees of Martian latitude and fifty of longitude. Along the way, he'd discovered something nearly as astonishing as the Meridiani microfossils: people lived out here, scattered across the wilderness, isolated from Lowell Colony. These were fiercely independent folk who, embracing the danger, had built concealed shelters using local resources and stolen or smuggled tech. Miguel didn't know how many explorers had struck out on their own, but he guessed there could be fifty or more homesteads within a month's journey of the Colony plus a few small bases used by smugglers. He established a rapport with a handful of these rogues after encountering them by accident. At first, he saw them as curiosities, and they saw him as danger. Once he cultivated friendships, some sprouted into valuable assistance on his research outings. Now, they might save his life.

Or kill him.

Miguel hoped the couple living beneath this ridge still counted him as friend, but they took their time deciding. He waited an hour and more while the distant sandstorm blew itself over the horizon and a tide of doubt slowly rose. He checked his oxygen level. The tanks held a sixteen-hour supply, but accidents happened. You didn't take anything for granted in the Martian wilderness.

"Come on, Metzler," he mumbled. "You know it's me."

There would be no radio communication with Carl Metzler. Carl's receiver was tuned to Lowell Colony's government frequency to keep tabs on the authorities. He had no transmitter and kept in touch with others through occasional face-to-face contact. His home was entirely underground, within the ridge, sustained by a homemade hydro station tapped into a subsurface ice reservoir. Regardless, Carl knew everything moving above ground. Miguel figured cameras were hidden about the ridge. An interloper loitering near the camouflaged entrance wouldn't go unnoticed.

Another half hour passed. Miguel about gave up before the ground vibrated and a hatch covered with rock and soil rose above the surrounding regolith three meters in front of him. It slid open to reveal sufficient passage for a pressure-suited man. A blaze of light ascended from the interior of the ridge, illuminating a ladder attached to a rock wall. Carefully, Miguel climbed down. The hatch sealed above him.

At bottom, he stood within a circular glass chamber. A light glowed red by the door until the airlock pressurized, then it winked green, and the door hissed open. Miguel moved through and waited for the door to shut before removing his helmet. The air had a dusty smell. This room was circular, too, equipped with storage cabinets and doorways sixty degrees to either side of the airlock.

As Miguel undid his envirosuit, Carl Metzler entered on the left, set his fists to his hips, and snarled, "What the hell are you doing here?"

That must be the way to greet him now. Miguel opened a cabinet. It already contained an envirosuit, so he closed that and opened the next, which he found empty. He stuffed his suit in and clanked the door shut. Turning, he extended a hand to Carl. Carl glared. He was a big man, two meters tall and solid muscle. He had sandy hair, a bushy beard, and eyes that could burn a hole in you.

"What do you think?" Miguel asked.

"Did you do it?"

"No."

Carl gave no sign of believing him.

"How's Jane?"

Jane Bonsell slipped in, her dark hair spilling over her shoulders, and put an arm around Carl's waist. She stood a head shorter than her companion. "Jane is good," she said. "Opinions on you are mixed."

"I'm not staying," Miguel assured them. "Just passing through."

Carl and Jane regarded each other in silent conference, then Carl nodded. "Come on."

They led Miguel into the interior of the dwelling. The rooms were rounded, carved from the rock. The furnishings looked like any other found on Mars: metal and plastic with padded synthetic coverings. They came to the kitchen, where a meal was in preparation. Miguel took a chair at a small table in the center of the room and watched the couple work. They could set a hearty table thanks to a substantial garden housed in a cavern at the far end of their complex. Carl had once shown it to Miguel. An impressive setup. Miguel never did learn how Carl obtained all those grow lights, but he doubted legitimate merchants were involved.

"Where will you go?" Carl asked as he diced an onion.

"South. Sinus Meridiani. We did it, Carl. We found microfossils in one of our samples, just like I said. I hope to collect more before construction destroys them."

"That again," Jane said. "You can't even see them without a microscope. What good are they?"

"They prove life evolved on Mars. That we aren't alone in the universe."

"Look where you are, Miguel," Carl said. They were here, the three of them, buried in the rock of a dead planet. "We're alone, all right."

Jane opened a cabinet and took out a large plastic bowl. She scooped up a handful of chopped vegetables and dumped them in. "Meridiani's the first place they'll look for you."

He didn't have a choice. The find bore too much weight, for science and himself. People had speculated about life in the cosmos for millennia, had systematically sought it out for over a century, and now he held the proof in hand. Real proof this time, not like the chemical signatures his younger, more foolish self had implanted in asteroid samples to suggest the seeds of life had originated in the Belt. That cost him his home and his heart. Mona. Sef. As gone as if they had died, as if he had killed them. The Meridiani micro-fossils weren't just a discovery. They were his penance and salvation. But he had little time left. Andre Rand, in his quest for power, had claimed Meridiani for his own and would soon blast any remaining fossils into oblivion. Miguel had to play the thief, slipping in and stealing what he could find. Once he had them, his contacts in the Belt would get him off planet, where he could process and publish at leisure.

Carl came to the table carrying the knife he'd been using on the onion. "You're going anyway, huh?"

Miguel nodded. "Have to."

"You can't take your rover. It'll give you away."

"It's a long walk, Carl."

"So you need fresh transport." He turned and called, "Jake!"

Another man, bigger than Carl, his face marred by scars, lumbered in from a darkened doorway. He eyeballed Miguel before nodding to Carl. Miguel didn't like the look of him.

"I asked Jake over in case you showed up with some idiot plan," Carl explained. "He'll get you where you need to go. Stay the night, leave at dawn, but don't get on his nerves. He's got a temper."

Miguel nodded. "Hello, Jake."

Jake grinned a creepy sort of grin, like he was enjoying the thought of murdering someone.

"What about my rover?" Miguel asked.

"Don't worry," Jane said. "We brought it inside. We'll cannibalize it for parts."

Chapter 3

Ricard Fulbert's apartment smelled of bacon. Real bacon, which wasn't cheap, but their troupe needed help displacing the memory of their supporting roles in Dr. Hernandez's war with the authorities. Ricard spent his meager savings to procure a full breakfast—eggs, bacon, pancakes, orange juice, coffee—all real. He didn't mind the expense and enjoyed the work. Cooking was part of his normal, and the others promised to pay him back. The twins did, anyway. Quan Linh was another matter.

"How is she?" Ricard asked when Martin Ulenga shuffled in and inspected the proceedings. Last night, government thugs had stuffed them into envirosuits and dumped them in the darkened Colony's seediest sector, a crime-ridden stretch of old shelters occupied by the poorest colonists. Ricard and Petrina had no more than one brain between them at that point. Martin contributed only a dazed stare, and Quan Linh was a babbling liability. Ricard and Petrina flagged down transport and ordered the driver to Ricard's apartment. The driver figured they were hopped up on drugs and insisted on payment in advance, but he delivered them safely.

Student apartments consisted of no more than a gathering room, a bedroom, and a kitchen, all equipped lowest common denominator. Still, it was Ricard's place, safe and familiar. Once there, they collapsed into restless sleep.

Martin shrugged. "Petrina said she had a long night." He leaned over the pan of frying bacon and yelped when a pop of grease hit him square in the forehead. "What the hell are you doing?"

"It's called frying."

"Can't you use the microwave, like everyone else?"

Ricard pinched his lips. He didn't want to cook like everyone else. When he moved in, he'd taken out a loan to upgrade to a convection oven and an electric stovetop. The university had qualms about modifications to student housing, but he offered to pay extra for the privilege. That convinced them.

Martin set a finger to the burn. "What?"

"This is a classic technique. When you taste it, you'll melt with ecstasy."

"Classic, hell. Maybe on Earth, but in case you hadn't noticed, this is Mars."

"Grease pops on Earth, too, just not as high. Stand back and let me work."

Martin stood well back. After a moment's hesitation and an ungraceful clearing of his throat, he asked, "What did you tell them?"

Martin focused on turning the bacon so as not to think about it.

"I tried to keep my mouth shut, but…" Wobbling as though seasick, Martin grabbed the back of a chair to steady himself.

"Selective nerve induction," Ricard said. "The idea's old, but the application…" He transferred the bacon to a plate and removed the pan from the stovetop. "I've never heard of anything like it."

Martin closed his eyes and took a few deep breaths. "How did it feel?"

Like every neuron in his body had fired simultaneously. Pain and pleasure, heat and cold, pressure, itching, scraping, clawing… Best not to go into detail. "Overwhelming. Utter confusion." Ricard heated and greased a new pan for the pancakes.

"I don't even know how it felt."

"I didn't, either, at the time."

"What did you tell them?"

Ricard didn't care to dwell on that, either. "What do you think?"

Martin dropped into a chair and stared at his shoes. "I betrayed him."

Petrina came into the kitchen, hair every which way, eyes sunk. "We all did."

Ricard refused to give guilt quarter. He couldn't, especially not if the others were drowning in it. "Don't blame yourselves. Nobody could have withstood that. Besides, nothing we said counts. Statements given under torture aren't admissible in court."

Martin turned on him. "Admissible! You think they care? Dr. Hernandez won't get a fair trial."

"He won't get a trial at all," Petrina said. "He's an outlaw. Anyone can kill him."

Ricard flipped the first pancakes. "He might. That's why they needed us."

Martin spread his hands at Petrina, who copied the gesture.

Linh's voice intruded, quiet, shaking, but insistent. "We're leaving. Today." She stood in the doorway, propped up by the jamb, hugging herself.

Petrina hurried over and hooked her arm through Linh's. "You okay?"

"My brain's inside out." She was staring at something only she could see. "Dr. Hernandez told us to leave Mars. We should. Today."

"It'll take a few days to make arrangements," Ricard said. "And money, which nobody will have after paying me back."

"You will," Martin snapped. "But we aren't leaving."

"We have to," Linh insisted. "*I* have to. I can't stay here."

Petrina guided Linh to a chair and settled her in it. "We'll take care of you. Dr. Hernandez needs our help. We can't abandon him."

"He didn't want our help," Ricard said. "He told us to go."

Martin slapped the counter. "We can't!"

Ricard hated to use scare tactics, but they needed to face facts. "If we make trouble, we'll be right back in those chairs. We might not get out alive."

Linh retched. Petrina kept an arm around her until the dry heaves passed. "Stop scaring her," she said. "Martin and I are staying. To clear Dr. Hernandez before he gets killed."

Ricard poured out more pancakes. "I'm following his instructions. For Linh's sake, if nothing else."

Linh detached herself from Petrina and tottered to Ricard's side. She grabbed his arm for support. "Thank you. I can't do that again." She turned pleading eyes on the Ulengas.

Martin and Petrina here, Ricard and Linh there, they stared across the kitchen as though on opposite rims of Valles Marineris. Ricard put a protective arm about Linh's shoulders.

Petrina looked away. "You'd better eat first," she said.

Jake wasn't a talker, which suited Miguel. Jake's rover suited him even better. A monster of a vehicle, it bore armor plating and enough weaponry to qualify as an assault vehicle. It could seat ten but more resembled a warehouse. Spare food, water, oxygen, ammo, and replacement parts for the rover's engine and support systems filled most of the seats and floor space, with good reason. Jake drove like a racer, bouncing over the rough Martian terrain at sixty kilometers per hour, grinning like a maniac. He must not have been a stranger to accidents.

Rough ride aside, only one thing concerned Miguel: Jake was going the wrong way. Sinus Meridiani, where Miguel had found his microfossil-bearing rock, lay southeast of Carl Metzler and Jane Bonsell's homestead. Jake bore due west, according to the rover's GPS. Miguel pointed out the discrepancy early in the journey, but apparently it wasn't an accident. Jake's reply was a more intense version of that grin.

Although the cabin was pressurized, they kept their enviro-suits on, face shields raised. In the event of a mishap, they could be sealed and safe in a matter of seconds. But Jake knew the route. He dodged boulders and craters like a running back weaving through opponents on his way to the goal. The day passed without much conversation. When darkness fell, Jake brought the vehicle to a halt and shut down all unnecessary equipment. Miguel broke out packets of beef and vegetables that heated themselves when the seals were broken, and they settled in to eat.

Only then did Jake speak. "How you likes the trip?"

"Scenic," Miguel said. "But not the direction I expected."

"Carl tells me what you expects. Invisible fossils, huh?"

Miguel nodded.

"Carl says you thinks one little rock stops the new colony." He laughed and shook his head.

"Delays it. Maybe relocates it. It's a special little rock."

"Must be. Where is it?"

"Someplace safe."

"You gots it on you? I can sees it?"

Miguel did, but he wasn't about to flash it. Increasingly, he didn't know who to trust. He wasn't sure he even trusted Carl. Where was Jake taking him? Maybe Carl and Jake expected to split the bounty. "I left it at home," he said.

"Pity." Jake ate in silence for a time, a thoughtful look replacing the grin. "Meridiani isn't safe for you. I takes you somewhere safe."

"Where?"

"You'll see."

He hoped he wouldn't regret seeing. "The longer I wait, the worse the odds I'll find more fossils."

"You gots your rock. Why you needs more?"

Science lecture time. Miguel held up his food packet. "I found this in your rover. Does it tell me all about you?"

Jake grinned and shook his head.

"My rock is like a food packet. It's insufficient for understanding a species, much less an entire ecosystem. I need more data."

They finished eating and tossed the containers in the trash chute. Jake returned to the pilot's seat, Miguel to the only open passenger seat in the back row.

Jake reclined. "Jake is easy to understand. So is Dr. Hernandez. Both only wants one thing."

Miguel hadn't gained much insight into his guide and doubted he'd given much away, but curiosity got the better of him. "What's that?"

"To be remembered."

Jake snapped the cabin lights off.

In the perfect dark of the Martian night, Miguel listened for the sound of an impending attack, but it never came. An hour later, he slept. He dreamed of lying with Carmen and woke in a cold sweat when, brandishing a knife, she stabbed him through the heart.

His skiff on autopilot, Alejandro flopped on a bunk on the lower deck, exhausted. A thorough search of the ship had revealed nothing. If the environmentalist—or whatever she was—wanted him dead, she at least hadn't chosen a crude execution method. No sabotage, no explosives accessible from the cabin, no abnormalities the computers could detect in any of the systems. Maybe she counted on his antipathy toward Miguel, after all. Very well. If she let him live, he'd forgive her chicanery.

He slept several hours and woke to a headache and a nonstop chirp issuing from the upper deck. Acceleration was still on the high side. He hated feeling this heavy. He dragged himself up the steps, boots clomping on the metal deck, and tapped a light flashing on the control console.

"Incoming message," the system said.

He pulled himself into the pilot's seat. "Play."

A vid filled the panel. The environmentalist's dark, mysterious eyes widened with delight. She was too beautiful for her own good. "I hope you are well, my friend, and happy with your reward. Your service is much appreciated."

I'll bet, he grumbled to himself.

"I wish you all happiness. You are now free. You may even return to Mars. Every impediment has been removed in thanks for your service."

Alejandro gaped in surprise. Did she have that much pull? He'd never heard of an outlaw being rehabilitated. Or maybe that was her way of disposing of him: he returns to Mars thinking he's free but is captured or killed the moment he debarks?

You are so damned paranoid, he told himself.

With good reason, he answered.

"However," the environmentalist continued, "if you purpose to remain in the asteroid belt, you will no doubt find ample accommodation for your every desire. Moreover, we would be pleased to employ you as an occasional consultant when the need arises."

Ah, so they meant to buy his silence. Sure, he could live with that.

"Specifically, we would appreciate information regarding the activities of four young insurrectionists." The woman's face was replaced by a collage of four other faces: a black man and woman, an Asian woman, and a grim white male. Each enlarged momentarily as she provided names. "Petrina Ulenga. Martin Ulenga. Quan Linh. Ricard Fulbert. They may be posing as graduate students from Lowell Colony University."

Not posing, Alejandro guessed. *Miguel's students.*

"You need not make contact. We only wish information regarding their whereabouts and activities. Once again, our deepest gratitude. Please signal your willingness to continue our association. Thank you."

The images faded and were replaced by a green circle and a red x. Alejandro about tapped the x. He was a mercenary, not a spy. But maybe this wasn't what it seemed. This environmentalist played a twisty game. Maybe the green circle meant life, the red x death. Push the wrong button, and he destroys his own ship?

Definitely paranoid, he told himself.

He tapped the circle anyway, just in case.

"A wise choice," the environmentalist said as the panel went black. "You will be richly rewarded."

By Earth's calendar, the Rands had been on Mars eleven years, seven months, and twenty-three days, which was a year and three quarters Martian, but nobody used local time. Seasons were meaningless inside Lowell Colony, where temperature and humidity remained roughly constant, barring the occasional glitch. In the colony's infancy, ordering life the Gregorian way injected a measure of familiarity into the alien experience of the red planet. As Lowell grew to adolescence, nobody thought to change the calendar any more than they thought to take up breathing carbon monoxide.

But Carmen had made one change. Once, she had lived full-time with Andre in Lowell. Now she only stayed with him on occasion. She only felt at ease in her private home outside the colony. Andre had built it for her six years ago as a retreat, a place to escape politics when it threatened to overwhelm her, which was often. He never visited. He had no need. Politics was the oxygen in his blood. Yet she increasingly suspected his minions had dropped by in her absence with some unwanted gifts. No surprise he'd known about her affair with Miguel, but his familiarity with dates and times was another matter.

"Every Tuesday and Friday for the past six months," Andre groused over breakfast in their joint residence in Lowell Colony. Servants had set out the meal in the circular private dining room, a room of chrome and smoked glass and mirrors. "Dinnertime through noon the next day."

"And your point?" She raised her coffee mug to her lips and inhaled the dark aroma. She knew his point. He wanted her to know he was watching. If Miguel came back, she'd have no choice but to betray him.

"You're not that stupid."

"Your games bore me. Just say it."

"If he hadn't bolted, nabbing him would have been easy. Now not even his apprentices know where he's gone."

"Apprentices?"

"His top graduate students. His picks for the future of his field. Some future. Two running away, two trying to rejoin him."

Again, so she'd know he had eyes on everything. "Then you know which two to follow, don't you?"

Andre studied his plate as though the answer were hidden among the eggs and sausages. Picking up his utensils, he attacked the food.

She took a sip and set the mug down. "But why bother? You got what you wanted. He's out of the way."

"You can't kill the mosquito you can't see. It'll circle 'round to bite you again and again."

Carmen found that amusing. He liked that mosquito analogy entirely too much. "Why must it end in death?"

Andre stared at her, face stone, eyes betraying nothing.

"I'm just saying," she added.

"You care about him." He spat out the accusation.

"No, Andre, I care about you." She turned her attention to her meal. "Your obsession with Miguel is unhealthy."

He continued to stare while she ate and gave up when she didn't flinch. "It's not an obsession. It's business. Each day Schiaparelli Colony doesn't break ground, costs jump."

"Let them. You're not paying for it. Celia Fundichely is, and she can damn well afford it." Carmen said it lightly but cringed inside. Celia's wasn't a name on which she cared to dwell. Thank God the woman— or psychopath or demon or whatever she was— lurked far off in the Belt.

"She only signed on because I agreed to her insane schedule."

"You'll whip the contractors through it."

"If Hernandez stays out of the way, but that bastard doesn't give up."

True, Miguel had acquired considerable finesse over time. He knew almost as many legal tactics as bedroom maneuvers. But Andre had the lower regard for rules. He beat Miguel's lawsuits with judicial bribery, then he cowed the Colony Council into rejecting Miguel's proposal for a research preserve. She mentioned the latter.

"That wasn't my doing," Andre said. "Best I could do was convince Bess Zwick to push for further study."

Bess was the only woman Carmen knew with stronger libido than herself. "In exchange for who?"

"Some no-talent understudy at the theater. I didn't ask, I just made the arrangements. When she floated the proposal, Hernandez went critical and threatened to blow something up. That lost him everyone's support. I wish I could say I planned it that way, but his loss of control surprised even me."

Carmen hadn't heard about that. Had Miguel lied to her? Maybe he was the culprit after all. Not that he could have done the deed, but maybe he hired help, timed the attack for when he was with her. "So Miguel's a serial loser. So what?"

"The key word is 'serial.' An outlaw brand won't stop him."

"It might. He bolted as soon as he heard."

"Before the news was out. Who told him?" Andre was focused on his plate, but she knew who he suspected.

"It wasn't me. I told you before. He already knew when he came to me."

Andre gave no indication of doubt or belief.

"What's your next move?" she asked.

"I don't have to move." He looked up, smug. He was always smug when plans were in motion. "His students do."

Chapter 4

"I have an idea," Petrina told her brother.

Martin, wrapped in a gray blanket, was scanning news vids on his portable panel, missing more than he picked up. The words blurred before his eyes, his splintered mind racketed through past, present, and possible futures without aim. Three days had passed since…

Since *that*.

He couldn't even name it. Three days during which he couldn't concentrate, punctuated by inexplicable rages that Petrina bore with limited patience. What was *wrong* with him?

Ricard and Linh were gone. Ricard had used those three days to secure leaves of absence from the university, arrange passage to Itokawa Station in the Belt, and compile a short list of academic contacts who might help them once there. Their departure for the spaceport sent Martin into another of his rages. His bedroom was all but destroyed: clothing strewn about, drawers ripped out by their roots, dents in the walls, a broken mirror hanging cockeyed with glass strewn beneath. Petrina cowered in the gathering room during the demolition. When he shuffled out, bleeding from a cut on his hand, she said in their mother's tone, "Done?" She cleaned and dressed the wound and left him to himself for a time.

Eventually, he grabbed his panel and searched news vids from the past few days for any mention of Dr. Hernandez. He found nothing. Anger built once more when Petrina, who had done nothing but sit cross-legged in a chair the whole time, spoke.

"I said, I have an idea."

They needed an idea. Why should finding one after three days trigger his rage? Maybe because he hadn't formulated one himself. Maybe because it had taken Petrina three days. They were both smarter than this. Martin took a steadying breath. "Like what?"

"Dr. Hernandez said Dr. Lloyd warned him."

"You think Dr. Lloyd knows where he went?"

"Maybe. It's worth a shot." She uncrossed her legs and sprang to her feet. "Let's talk to him."

Martin set the panel aside. "He won't appreciate me trashing his office."

Petrina reached for his hand. Reluctantly, he took it and stood. "You won't," she insisted.

He stood two inches taller than his sister. He looked down at her, she up at him. They both looked like hell, like they hadn't slept for a Martian year. But Petrina, at least, was in control of herself. "Why didn't it affect you?" he asked.

"You think it didn't?"

"I explode. Linh collapses into terrors. You and Ricard…" The mere thought irritated him. How could he and Linh suffer so but Martin and Petrina remain unmoved? He focused on his breathing to ward off the anger. Breathing seemed to help.

Petrina looked away. "It must affect everyone differently. Ricard told me he detached himself from the experience, whatever that means. I guess he shoves it aside, pretends it didn't happen."

"What about you?"

"I…I can't talk about it." Her voice cracked, and a tear dribbled down her face. She swiped at it in annoyance. "Not yet."

If their torturers had been in the room, Martin would have killed them without thought or regret. He focused on his breathing so as not to imagine it, not to act it out and put Petrina in danger.

"Let's go see Dr. Lloyd," Petrina said.

And so, they went.

The transport departed on time with a four-member crew, seven passengers, and as much cargo as it could lift into orbit. Ricard Fulbert had ushered Quan Linh aboard, his arm about her as she tottered on the edge of emotional meltdown. The other passengers kept an uneasy eye on them. "Death in the family," Ricard told them, which earned Linh a measure of sympathy.

The passenger compartment pretended luxury, with well-padded recliners in rows of three. A few were empty, allowing Ricard and Linh to hide in the back row by themselves. He massaged her hand during ascent. Tension consumed her while they powered into orbit. She buried her head in his chest until the pilot announced deorbiting, putting them en route to the Belt. Meals were then served by automated cart. She ate mechanically, as did Ricard. Afterward, he couldn't say what he'd downed. Linh finally slept and didn't stir when one of the passengers, a balding fellow with a salesman's smile, slipped into the seat beside Ricard.

"Death in the family, you said."

Ricard nodded and wished him away.

He didn't go. "I lost my wife three years ago. It's rough."

"Yes."

"Oh, I'm Bob Wreyford." He stuck out his hand. Ricard stared at it until Bob withdrew the offer.

"I have a thing about infection," Ricard lied.

"What is that, a phobia?"

"Roughly."

Bob nodded. "Yeah, my wife had one of those, but with her it was crowds. We had to live outside the colony. She wrote software. I taught mathematics. What about you and your wife?"

"She's not my wife," Ricard said. "We're just traveling together. Exobiologists." Too late, he regretted having said it.

"Oh, scientists. Wonderful. Lovers?"

"Colleagues," Ricard snapped. "What business is it of yours?"

Bob took no offense. If anything, he looked amused. "What would a couple of young exobiologists want in the Belt? You'll find no life there. Even most of the people aren't living." He chuckled at his joke.

"We're going to Ganymede." Damn it, why couldn't he keep his mouth shut?

"Really. I was there once. Rough place to live. They say only those with something to hide go to Ganymede."

Ricard hadn't heard that one, nor did he care. He glanced at Linh. She slept on, oblivious to the men.

"Say, did you know that Hernandez fellow, the guy that blew up that hydro station? He was an exobiologist, wasn't he? If I were him, I'd make straight for Ganymede. Nobody'd find him there. It wouldn't be much of a life, but he'd be safe."

Maybe this guy needed help shutting up. "What did you have to hide?"

"Me? Oh." Bob waved it off. "Youthful indiscretion. She had rich parents. Powerful people. You can guess the rest. The sad thing is, I'm not sure she was worth it."

Linh moved and made a small sound. Ricard protectively put his arm about her.

Bob smiled. "Whatever the relationship, she's lucky to have you. Let me guess. She's the one running from trouble."

"You can guess all you like. Leave us alone."

Bob leaned back as though Ricard had thrown a punch. "Whoa, there's no need for that tone. You want me to leave? Just say so."

"I did."

Rising, Bob held up his hands in mock surrender. "On my way." He returned to his own seat near the front of the cabin.

Lihn made a little noise and pushed against Ricard. He held her close and vowed that nobody would ever harm her again.

Three damn days. That's how long Jake zigged and zagged the rover westward, carrying Dr. Miguel Hernandez farther and farther from his destination with no explanation but, "I takes you somewhere safe." Miguel didn't want safe. He wanted Sinus Meridiani.

The land rose, pockmarked with more and larger craters, and still Jake drove until, reaching a crater wall soaring ten meters over their heads, he slowed, maneuvered up the rim, and made a cautious descent into the bowl. Miguel was white knuckled, expecting the vehicle to flip. He exhaled in relief once they reached the bottom.

"Here it is," Jake said. "A very safe place."

They secured their envirosuits, depressurized the rover cabin, and stepped onto the rust-red surface. The late afternoon sun kissed the lip of the crater. Jake led him north to an airlock built into the crater wall. Once inside, they stowed their suits in a long row of lockers.

"The complex," Jake said, "she runs way around the crater." He raised an index finger and traced a great circle in the air. "Airlocks at zero, ninety, one eighty, and two seventy. We comes in at ninety."

Degrees, obviously. Miguel hoped there would be signage.

They passed into a corridor that swept along the curve of the crater rim. "Palm prints and sometimes access codes opens things," Jake said as he led Miguel along the corridor. They passed sealed doors left and right, their booted footfalls echoing in the deserted ring.

"What's this place for?" Miguel asked.

Jake grinned. Miguel mistrusted that grin and was beginning to fear it, even though Jake had done no worse than ferry him to nowhere.

Numbers over the doors marked their location on the circle in degrees. Counting down from ninety, they reached the mid-eighties before Jake stopped at location eighty-four and pressed his right palm against the wall. The door opened. He motioned Miguel in.

Once Miguel passed through, the door closed behind him. Jake hadn't followed. Great. He slapped various spots on the wall with his palm, but the machinery refused to obey.

Trapped. Was there any other exit? Where the hell was he?

The place had the feel of a student apartment: a small gathering room furnished in blues and yellows, cheap plastic end tables, abstract art on the walls. What was he supposed to do, set up housekeeping? Two doors, one left and one right, stood open. Probably a bedroom waited behind one, a kitchen the other, neither concealing exits.

"Dr. Hernandez. What a surprise."

A young woman in a gray coverall slipped in from the left. A redhead, her hair was cropped short, her eyes intense, her mouth amused. Not afraid, certainly, but mistrustful. The feeling was mutual.

"Haven't made yourself popular, have you?" she asked.

"Old habit," he replied. "I can't seem to break it."

She crossed the room and sat in one of the chairs. "Might as well be comfortable. You'll be here for some time."

He sat as far from her as possible. "I don't have time for comfort. I'm already three days in the wrong direction."

"Fire your driver." She smiled, just a little.

"I didn't hire him. Carl did. Since you know me, I'm guessing you know Carl."

She nodded. "This was Jane's idea. Carl wanted to throw you back to the dogs at Lowell."

Then he owed Jane one, he supposed.

"You're quite the man, a danger to everyone on Mars. Everyone important, anyway. The government. Developers. Homesteaders. Me."

Miguel didn't see how he was a danger to homesteaders, but he didn't argue the point. As for her… "Who are you?"

"Nessa O'Clery."

"And what do you do?"

"I don't do anything. My people are miners and transport engineers."

A crater far beyond Lowell Colony seemed an odd place for either occupation. "Your people? You run the show?"

She smiled again, more than a little.

At least he was talking to the boss. "Why am I here?"

"Staying safe. Naturally, there's a price."

"I don't dare access my funds. If they're not frozen, they're being monitored."

Nessa leaned forward. "My price isn't money."

Of course not. Miguel didn't care to ask what it was.

"Join my people. We need your expertise."

"I'm no expert in mining or transportation."

"You know some geology, I'm sure. And unlike a certain politician, I don't care if you pick up an interesting rock here and there, so long as you find me useful ores."

"A mining operation must have geologists," Miguel told her.

"Only one, and I'm afraid he's not well at the moment."

"Lowell has a great hospital."

Nessa smirked. "They'd rather kill us than treat us."

"You're outlaws?"

"Not technically, but as good as. I said miners and transport engineers. In cruder terms, claim jumpers and smugglers."

Aimed for Phobos, crashed on Deimos, as the saying went. This association would seal his doom, even if it had utility. "Can you get me to Meridiani?"

"No, Dr. Hernandez. Can I call you Miguel? Call me Nessa. I dislike formality."

"You can call me whatever you want if you'll take me—"

"We have no facilities there. We principally work the Tharsis region."

Tharsis. A volcanic plain rich in minerals but lacking enough ice deposits to support a colony. Hardly the best candidate for a fossil hunt. "Then I can't help," he said. "Time's my enemy. I need to get to Meridiani."

Nessa stood. She had the stance of a warrior and the demeanor of a queen. "You'll work for me, Miguel, or be put out without an envirosuit." She cocked her head. "That's no choice, is it? If you preferred death, you wouldn't have run from Rand."

Put that way, joining the family sounded like a temporary plan. Besides, she must have rovers. If he could grab one…

Nessa eyed him. "Scheme all you like. What's your answer?"

"What's the pay?"

"Room and board." She motioned at the furniture. "This is your apartment. Jake's keying your prints to the door and other necessary facilities. Welcome to the family, Miguel."

"Thanks," he muttered. "Nessa."

Chapter 5

The stonecrafter had earned his pay. The rust-orange rock in Dr. Gene Lloyd's hands matched the scans perfectly, or as perfectly as his old eyes could tell. He compared it to the scans displayed on his desktop panel once more, just to be sure. One hundred forty-seven millimeters long, fifty-three millimeters wide, thirty-seven millimeters thick, the irregular block could have been the original. It needed only explanatory text to become a museum piece. And who knew? Maybe someday the old fraud would be.

He turned it on its back to examine the series of tiny pits marring its surface. These pits, the museum info panel would explain, marked where samples had been scraped. A vid would show the process in quick glimpses: collection, disaggregation, treatment, picking, examination. Laborious but not difficult work. Then would come the inevitable disappointment. No microfossils were found in this sample. Because Mars, it seems, never harbored life.

Gene transferred the rock to a sample box, closed it, and shelved it in the storage room down the hall from his office. A number identified the box: 374866. Just another rock, nothing special, awaiting further description and analysis.

There was, however, a difference. This was Dr. Miguel Hernandez's find, or a facsimile thereof, a specimen he claimed contained a wealth of microfossils. Likely both Miguel and the stone would fade from memory, but if they didn't, if someday his findings must be contested, this fabrication would be pulled, analysis performed, papers written. The conclusion would be inescapable:

mineralized pseudo-fossils, possibly formed in proximity to ancient hydrothermal springs.

Sorry Miguel, Gene thought. *I did warn you. Several times.*

Upon returning to his office, he found a pair of familiar faces waiting. He knew them, slightly: Miguel's students Petrina and Martin Ulenga, the brilliant twins. They hardly looked brilliant now. Seated with their backs to the wall, they might have been awaiting execution. Petrina jumped when Gene entered the room. Martin gripped the arms of his chair as though to tear them off. The news about Miguel and his disappearance must have devastated them, but at least they weren't double agents like Gene, flanked by Miguel on one side and Andre Rand on the other, defying the dictator one moment, stabbing a friend in the back the next.

He smiled for them. How quickly he'd become adept at lying. "What brings you here?"

"Dr. Lloyd," Petrina began, but she stalled out.

Without drawing attention to the images on his desktop, Gene sat, locked the screen with a quick tap, and folded his hands. However they phrased the inevitable questions, he had but one answer: he didn't know. He rehearsed it in silence to ensure he believed it.

Martin might have been a compressed spring awaiting release. "Where's Dr. Hernandez?"

Gene replied with an exaggerated shrug. "He didn't confide in me." That much was true.

Leaning forward, Martin pointed a shaking finger, but Petrina set her hand to his wrist and pushed his arm down. "Calmly," she ordered. The quiet command had some effect. Martin huffed and leaned back. "We know you warned him," she told Gene.

His smile froze. How could they know that?

"He's your friend. He must have told you something."

"I'm sorry, Petrina. This is as much a surprise to me as it is you."

"Surprise, hell!" Martin shouted. "You knew what was happening! You warned him!"

Damn. Rising, he closed the office door and spoke in a whisper. "Forget whatever you heard. If Dr. Hernandez had advance warning, he didn't get it from me, nor do I know where he went."

Petrina studied his face. "You're afraid."

"I'm afraid for you," he lied. "This kind of talk will get you in trouble."

Martin slammed his fist on the desk. "We're already in trouble! We've already been—"

"Martin," Petrina warned.

He crossed his arms over his chest and threw himself back in his chair.

Memories long buried emerged from the shadows to torment Gene. He grabbed for the desk to steady himself. "You were questioned?"

Petrina nodded.

"Oh, God."

"You, too?" she guessed.

"No."

"Don't lie."

He fumbled his way to his chair and dropped into it. "Go. I can't tell you anything. Don't come here again."

Petrina rose and planted her fists on his desk. Leaning toward him, she looked more dangerous in her self-control than Martin in his rage. "We aren't leaving until you tell us."

How could someone so intelligent be such an idiot? "For God' sake, Petrina, forget Dr. Hernandez. He's an outlaw. You can't help him. You'll end up dead."

Martin stood at his sister's side, a volcano on the verge of eruption. "He said you warned him!"

Damn you, Miguel! And double damn you, Martin! Gene put his head in his hands.

"Tell us what you know," Petrina insisted. "The door's closed. Nobody will hear."

"You think closed doors keep them out?"

"Who?"

Somebody had to warn them. They were only students. Young, clueless, students. Just fools, nothing more. Andre Rand wouldn't concern himself with them. Or would he? He'd interrogated them. He'd…

"Before they questioned you," Gene asked, "did they inject you with something?"

Petrina and Martin glanced at each other. "How did you know?" she asked.

"It's dangerous to be friends with someone like Miguel. His enemies know how to use his friends."

Petrina squeezed her eyes shut, shook her head, grabbed Martin's hand. "They…" she started. "Damn it," she muttered. "I almost had it."

Martin put an arm around her and drew her close. "What's wrong?"

"Nothing. They…" She looked at Gene. "They got you, too."

Martin's anger. Petrina's confusion. Gene recognized the signs. With him, it had been a plague of fear that had never entirely faded. "Before," he said. "Long before."

"What did they make you do?"

Too much, he thought. "Nothing that matters now."

Martin's anger sublimated into fear. "What did they do to us?"

"Biomech nanobots. Some facilitate the nerve induction process. Some…"

Gene cradled his head in his hands. He might as well tell them. He'd outlived his usefulness anyway.

"Some are trackers," he said. "And some listen."

Claim jumpers and smugglers, Nessa O'Clery had said. Claim jumpers were outside his experience, but Miguel had befriended a few smugglers. They worked over the horizon from Lowell Colony where law enforcement didn't, connecting with runners who brought stolen goods from the colony and returned with ill-gotten imports and contraband. The runners took the planetside risk, and the smugglers dealt with the Space Force, which was fine by them. Stretched to its limit, the Space Force was hardly an obstacle. Miguel wasn't above trading with smugglers when they had something he needed. Their wares came tax and duty free, and sometimes they supplied materials he couldn't otherwise obtain. But joining their team? That stripped him of all pretense to innocence.

On the plus side, Nessa proved a generous host. She'd gifted Miguel a private four-room apartment, including an office with top line electronics and dark net connections to data sources in Lowell Colony. Her organization maintained their own digital resources, too, some far surpassing the colony's. Her people had developed more detailed geologic maps of the Tharsis region than any Miguel had seen. She'd also given him a mandate: conduct surveys to develop similar maps of the region around this facility. It wasn't his field, but she didn't care.

So Miguel planned and made his best guesses. She restricted his target area to no more than three days out. He doubted this was prime mining territory, but when she dropped in at the end of his first day on the job, he presented her with an initial list of candidate sites. She approved.

"How do I get there?" he asked.

Nessa examined the map displayed on his desktop panel. "You'll be assigned a rover and all the supplies and assistants you need."

"You trust me that far?"

"Take charge, Miguel. I told you, I don't do anything."

What was to stop him from turning a research outing into a one-way expedition to Sinus Meridiani?

Displaying her uncanny ability to guess his thoughts, Nessa smirked. "I want you to meet someone."

She led him on a long walk around the circular corridor, passing zero degrees and venturing into the high three-fifties.

"This is our medical section," she said, pressing her palm to the wall beside door three hundred fifty-seven. Inside, the air had an antiseptic smell. They passed through a cluster of offices, exam rooms, procedure rooms, and a single operating theater slumbering in the dark. A strange quiet filled the section. "It's not Lowell's hospital, but it suffices, should the need arise."

She palmed another door open. Beyond, a man lay in bed, a white sheet pulled to his chin, monitoring devices winking and chirping his status. With gray hair and a wrinkled face, he seemed asleep.

"This is Emil Sarkozy," Nessa said. "Our geologist."

Miguel watched rising and falling lines trace Emil's heartbeat and breath. "What happened?"

Emil's mouth curled up in an ironic smile. "Pride," he said, "goeth before a fall."

Miguel started, then laughed. "You knew we were here."

The patient's voice was surprisingly strong. "It's a small room. I know everything that happens in here."

A sense of humor, too. He couldn't be that bad off. "I gather you had an accident," Miguel said.

"Several, but I wouldn't be here if I hadn't tried to go home."

Nessa rounded the bed and stood by Emil's side. Reaching under the sheet, she drew out his hand and caressed his fingers. "Emil joined us four years ago," she said. "That was his first accident. He came from one of the Belt universities to collect samples for a research project. He inadvertently crossed paths with some of my people."

Emil picked up the story. "They don't like random encounters, but they gave me a choice. Join them or die. What could I do? It wasn't so bad. They treated me like family, and the work was interesting. Besides, I figured once I earned their trust, I could escape. How hard could it be for a Ph.D. to outsmart a gang of outlaws?"

Nessa touched his cheek. "Poor Emil." If her expression was genuine, she pitied his naïveté.

"I never questioned why Nessa let me wander Tharsis unsupervised. It seemed a gift. But once I strayed into forbidden territory, the rover died. I was stranded five days. Life support degraded. I got frantic and tore the machine apart, trying to make it run again. Got a nasty electric shock, cut myself bad. Ran out of food and water. Nearly ran out of oxygen by the time they rescued me. I'd been semi-conscious for ten hours." Emil finally opened his eyes and blinked at Miguel. He looked befuddled. "I thought they'd left me to die."

"Oh, Emil," Nessa purred. "We wouldn't do that. You're family."

He squeezed his eyes shut and took her hand in his. "I know." His voice cracked as he said it.

Nessa caressed his fingers. "Thank God you're strong." To Miguel, she said, "Once he's on his feet, he'll be your boss and geology mentor. But now…" She bent down and kissed Emil's forehead. "…you need some sleep. And do sleep this time, okay? Let's go, Miguel."

Miguel followed her back toward his apartment, mulling over the story. "You didn't warn him about straying."

"No."

"But you're warning me."

"So it seems."

"Why?"

"Because you're more stubborn and less shrewd. That's a dangerous combination. Look where it put you."

He didn't care for her characterization, but he couldn't argue with the conclusion. "I'm stubborn with good reason. I've made the most important scientific find in history, and—"

"Oh, Miguel!" She laughed. "We should write your name in the stars!"

"I'm serious. I have proof life evolved here eons ago."

"And died here eons ago. How exciting. Miguel, listen." They had come to his apartment. She stopped before him, set her hands lightly on his shoulders, and peered into his eyes. She was half a head shorter but oddly felt far taller. "*We* are the proof that life exists in the cosmos. Us. Your fossils are just flecks in a rock. Rocks want nothing. We do. You know what I want, Miguel?"

"Gold," he guessed.

Her eyes sparkled. "Hell, yes! But you'll probably never find that in useful quantities, so I'll take aluminum and titanium and every other good thing Mars gives us. Look for your microscopic corpses if you must, but find me the good stuff." She released him and vanished around the curve.

He understood how Emil could forgive her. She was strong, beautiful, and infectious, not unlike Mona before—

No, Miguel told himself. *Don't think it.*

But memory refused to obey his command. He heard once more Mona pleading with him to weather the storm, start over, rebuild his reputation. People would forget once he put in a decade or two of solid work. He was yet young, he could still be a star. He already was to her. Couldn't that be enough? Earth was home. Familiar. Safe. They had family and friends here. What was Mars but an empty promise? She couldn't live there. She couldn't. Please don't ask it. Please…

But fear and despair ruled him, and ask he did, and pleaded and insisted and demanded until whatever was left of him died when she walked out with their infant son Sef in her arms.

All he ever had was dead to him now. Mona, Sef, even his students—his surrogate children—gone. They lived on somewhere, but nothing remained to him save their fossil imprints in his memory. And the fossils he'd held in his hand? The planet's memory, dead to everyone but him. He wouldn't let Nessa or Andre Rand or anyone steal them away. Nessa had erred in showing him the harness she'd placed on him. Somehow, he would slip from it. He had to, even if nobody on Mars cared, even if nobody in the whole damn solar system cared. Greed would not bury this discovery. He owed a debt to humanity, to Mona and Sef, to Petrina and Martin and Ricard and Linh.

Besides, who wouldn't want his name written in the stars?

To unlock secrets, you needed money or a credible threat. Riding so often the edge of insolvency, Alejandro Carrasco relied on threats, but things had changed. With money in his account, bribery offered an easier path. He knew a woman at the Space Force with access to ship manifests, passenger lists, and station records, a woman who, like himself, had operated under a succession of aliases to hide an unwholesome past. In her present puritanical incarnation, she called herself Aarohi Dayal.

Aarohi didn't like the sound of Alejandro's voice, not even on a secure private link, not even after four months of silence. "You nearly got me fired," she said in an angry whisper, suggesting she might be overheard. "Bully me again, and I'll push you out an airlock."

Which was justified. He hadn't been kind to her. "What say we kiss and make up?"

She made a retching sound. In case he didn't understand, she added, "Hell, no."

"I came into money," Alejandro told her in a rush before she could disconnect. "This one's on me."

That silenced her.

"Aarohi? You still there?"

"How much?"

He'd let her name a price and talk her down. "I'm looking for anything you got on four people." Aarohi could do that in less than a minute if the students had left Mars. Even if not, it entailed no significant effort. Alejandro knew because she'd done it before, several times.

"A million," she said.

Everybody started there, didn't they? "Come on, Aarohi, that's stupid."

"Yeah? So what's not?"

"You tell me. Just don't be an idiot."

"You're one amazing kisser, Alro." She'd been calling him that for two years. He didn't mind so long as she delivered. "Give me the names."

Alejandro did so.

"Wow, they sound important," she quipped. "Ten thousand."

"One," he suggested.

"It's not for the job. It's for the hell you put me through."

Alejandro had to give her that. "Two, then."

"Living hell," she emphasized.

"All right, all right. Five."

"Eight."

"It's just four names, Aarohi."

"I thought you wanted to kiss? Eight's barely a handshake."

So much for negotiating. Alejandro didn't realize she had that much spine. Or was she faking it? He gave it one more go. "What say we call it six and be done with it."

"I guess you don't really want those kids, then."

"Who said they're kids?"

"Me. I got the details right here."

"What's it say?"

"It says, 'Alro gives me eight thousand, and if he makes one more trash offer, the price is ten.'"

"Fine, you win. What's it say?"

"It says, 'Transfer the money.'"

Using his panel, Alejandro generated the transfer and told Aarohi to transmit her acceptance code. She sent a long string of characters. The panel initiated the transaction, after which the code expired, and a confirmation appeared.

"Damn, Alro" Aarohi said. "You actually did pay."

"What did I buy?"

"Half of what you wanted. Ricard Fulbert and Quan Linh are en route to Itokawa Station. If their ship doesn't blow up, they'll arrive in four days. I got nothing on Petrina and Martin Ulenga."

Which meant they hadn't left Mars. "Send me the first pair's room number when they check in," Alejandro instructed. "And contact me if the other two show up."

"If I think of it. Love ya, Alro. Kissy, kissy."

Aarohi cut the connection before he could reply.

"I liked you better when you were groveling," Alejandro told nobody.

Chapter 6

"It's so good to see you, Yago." Carmen Rand took Yago Moncayo's dark hands in her pale ones and gave him a light peck on the cheek. "It's been, what, six months?"

"Five," he said with a broad smile. "Too long, no matter the number."

Everyone important on Mars knew Yago. He was the scion of a Founder Family. His grandparents Oleos and Aurelia Moncayo had been the only Ecuadorans on the first colony ship thirty-seven years before, selected because the couple had designed and constructed award-winning public buildings across South America. The Moncayos created the architectural DNA of Lowell Colony: low, broad buildings that blended with the planet's rust. Builders paid homage to them in later designs, but as the colony grew, mutations proliferated.

Yago preserved the pure genes. Abandoning colony construction to lesser architects, he looked to the land beyond, creating homes for those wealthy and daring enough to live on the edge of the wilderness. Of those homes, his most celebrated was the private residence of Carmen Rand, Lowell's first lady. Its façade, laser carved from a cliff, hardly appeared to be of human craft until you looked closely, and then the whole of the bluff morphed into intentional design. A beautiful illusion, and not the only one. Inside, natural light filled the rock-bound space, gathered at the top of the rise and poured into the home through scores of hidden optical channels. While buried in the ground, the room was so bright it might have been floating in the thin Martian air. Whenever he visited, Yago felt a deep pride and satisfaction, but also sadness. He would never top this design.

"Then you must have a drink with me," Carmen said, still holding his hands, "and dinner, and long, rambling conversation."

"Of course. That's why you invited me. Although..." He arched his eyebrows. "I suspect you have other motives."

"Me?" She hooked her arm through this. "Come on, my hard-working staff has everything ready." She led him into the dining room, a circular space ablaze with chrome, faux glass, and rose-colored accents. She sat at the head of a long table surrounded by twenty-six padded chairs. He took the seat on her right.

"Do you ever fill this table?" Yago asked rhetorically. "Why did you let Pavani talk you into it?"

"For the same reason I married Andre. It makes me look important. How is Pavani? She could have come, you know."

"Still the same. Always working. She's bidding on the Schiaparelli Colony courthouse and mayoral residence. She'll probably sell them tables just like this." He patted the tabletop. "But they won't be so alone when they use them."

A domestic robot fluttered in to serve drinks, then withdrew.

"Alone has its charms. I sit in a different chair every meal. The view changes with each one. Different light and shadow, different artwork, even the sounds are different. How many people get to know a room that intimately? Who else appreciates your work so deeply?"

Very few. He toasted her devotion. Small talk consumed them for a time as Carmen asked after his son and daughter, his business, his thoughts on Schiaparelli Colony, and why he wasn't designing the buildings Pavani planned to furnish and decorate.

("Too many contractors, too many conflicting ideas. And your husband wants everything yesterday. A Moncayo must never be rushed.") The domestics served Caesar salad, roasted chicken and vegetables, and for dessert, blueberry cheesecake. Yago felt a long nap lying in ambush once the robots trundled out with the last of the dishes.

Carmen crossed her arms on the table and leaned forward. "As to my other motives..." Her eyes sparkled in the light.

"I knew it. You want an addition."

She laughed. "No, sorry. I just need advice."

"Can I charge a consulting fee?"

"If I can pay under the table."

"Oh, that kind of advice. What's your problem?"

Carmen didn't answer immediately. Her gaze strayed about the room. "Andre's watching me."

Suddenly jittery, Yago searched, too, but saw no glint of light from hidden lenses, no subtle modifications to his work. "Watching?"

She nodded. "He knows who visits. In detail. Dates, times."

"What they say? What they do?"

"No. At least, I don't think so."

Hell. He had nothing to hide from Andre Rand, but he'd heard stories from someone who did. "What makes you think so?"

"He told me, in his roundabout way. He described the comings and goings of..." She shrugged. "A friend."

A lover, more likely. She and Andre flirted for the videographers, but Yago suspected they played less in the bedroom than the boardroom. Although none dared speak openly, rumors of the first lady's affairs slithered like vipers through private conversations. "Then I advise being careful."

"This isn't a joke, Yago."

"I wasn't joking."

She toyed with her napkin. "I'm so rattled, it took me five days to realize you'd know someone who could fix this."

Security wasn't his forte, but yes, he knew people. One or two might even enjoy crossing Andre Rand. To Yago, though, it was a terrible idea. "Simplicity's best. Conduct your trysts elsewhere."

She blinked at him. Then she grinned. "My trysts aren't the issue, only certain playmates. Andre's concerns are purely political." Her look darkened again. "This is my home, Yago, not his. I won't be told who to welcome in my own home."

He knew better than to get in her way. She could be as ruthless as her husband when motivated. "All right, but please don't put me in the middle of this, Carmen."

"Of course not. I invited my dear, long-absent friend to dinner. We had a wonderful time catching up, and as he left, he promised to bring his lovely wife next time. Maybe in two months instead of five or six?"

"I'll try to twist Pavani's arm," he promised. "She did want to come." Not that he would return. Pavani would win the contracts. She always did. Two months from now, they'd be living in the infant Schiaparelli Colony, too far for a casual visit to the north. This might be his last time seeing Carmen, his last time seeing her home, his greatest design. Both thoughts saddened him.

Her eyes softened with understanding. For the remainder of the evening, they spoke only of the inconsequential.

Ricard Fulbert and Quan Linh debarked into swirling crowds, disorienting illuminations, and the cacophony of Itokawa Station.

Currently the closest to Mars of twelve co-orbital inner Belt stations circling the sun, it was thronged. Ricard read the station's specs on the last day of the voyage. Serving as port of call for ships passing between Mars and the asteroids, the great wheels of Itokawa and its eleven sister stations rotated to create Mars-equivalent gravity. Each consisted of three decks accommodating a thousand residents and five hundred transients.

But the numbers hadn't prepared him for the chaos. The port complex befuddled Ricard from the get-go. A jumble of boarding gates, shops, restaurants, customs stations, and info terminals, it had no logical organization. The signage bombarded them with a confusion of colors and arrows and flashing lights. Linh clung to his arm, eyes glazed and mind useless while he searched for the baggage claim.

After two full circuits of the complex, he located it annoyingly close to their arrival gate. They had packed light, one bag apiece, and now trailed their luggage into an uncrowded eatery with low lighting and faux wood furnishings. Ricard picked a table tucked into a corner away from the few other customers. In the relative quiet, Linh's brain came back online.

"Hungry?" Ricard asked. He scrolled through the menu on the vid panel in the tabletop. "No wonder the place is empty. Look at these prices."

Linh gave the restaurant a prolonged examination. "I don't know why, but I don't feel…"

"What?"

"Safe."

Ricard felt a vague unease, too, like someone had poked the back of his neck with a blunt knife. Aftershocks from the torture, probably. He could deal with it. But could Linh? The ordeal had turned her personality inside-out. Would her cheerful nature ever come out of hiding? He hadn't realized it before, but she was the sunshine in their collaboration. He hoped the clouds might soon disperse.

"Once we're en route to Ganymede," he said, "you'll feel better."

"Maybe."

"So, are you hungry?"

"No."

"We should eat something. We have a lot of work ahead of us."

Linh sighed and fidgeted with the menu. "Root beer float."

"Seriously?"

"Yeah."

What the hell. She deserved something frivolous. He tapped in the order: a roast beef sandwich for himself and two root beer floats. A timer counting down minutes to delivery replaced the menu on the panel. He wondered if the roast beef would be real or imitation. Lowell Colony raised some livestock, but he suspected Itokawa Station didn't have the facilities, not with all these people to house.

"What happens next?" Linh asked.

"We find lodging. Then we find our contacts. Dr. Hernandez had friends here. First on my list is Dr. Craig Snyder. He's a minerologist, supposedly well-connected."

Linh leaned on the table and stared at nothing.

"Are you okay?"

She shrugged. "Just don't leave me alone."

"I won't. We'll stay together, no matter what."

"We'll share a room?"

Ricard hadn't considered that.

She looked up, pleading.

Again, what the hell. "Sure."

She stared at the tabletop. "I hate this."

"Hate what?"

"Being such a mess."

"It's not your fault. You just need time. You'll feel better tomorrow." That earned him a quirky smile. It was almost the old Linh, readying a playful jab. "What?" he asked.

"After a night with you, huh?"

Ricard blushed. "I didn't mean—"

"Oh, shut up. I know what you meant." Linh sighed and shook her head. "I don't know, Ricard. I'm sure they did something to us. It scares me."

"It was just selective nerve induction."

"Something else, I mean. Something we don't know yet."

He recalled only the torture. "If so, it can't be worse than what we do know."

The food arrived on an automated faux silver tea trolley. They transferred it to their table. Lihn scooped a bit of ice cream from her root beer float and tasted it. "Non-dairy," she pronounced. "Figures."

Alejandro Carrasco hated conflicting instructions. The environmentalist and her superiors must be clueless. Or fighting among themselves. Or both. Whichever, it signaled trouble.

The kids had arrived and rented a room. Aarohi Dayal deigned to send him their room number, thank God, and he dutifully relayed it to the environmentalist—pseudo-environmentalist—who returned wishes for a long and happy life, which together with a large deposit to his account signaled mission accomplished. Minutes later, the transaction was reversed. Another communication followed, instructing him to watch room two seven three eight on Itokawa Station, where the students were holed up. When they emerged, he was to follow. He was halfway there when the environmentalist rescinded that instruction and directed him to the research section, specifically the office of one Dr. Craig Snyder, where he was to take the good doctor's place.

Take his place. How politely she put it. Just as politely as when she gave Alejandro the choice between cooperation and immolation. How was he supposed to pose as a scientist? Give a lecture? Alejandro's forte was hardly scientific. But orders were orders, and as before, he saw no choice.

Gaining entry to the research section on the third and innermost level of the station took only patience and a little luck. Access was via five secure doors widely spaced along the central corridor. The doors employed two-factor authentication: a subcutaneous chip embedded in an authorized person's forearm, and a palm print. Alejandro didn't have a chip, but these offices weren't high security. People had grown lax. He posted himself opposite the main entrance and pretended to read from his panel, hoping the environmentalist wouldn't change her mind again. Within a few minutes, a young woman approached and pressed her hand to the wall. As the door opened, Alejandro slipped into her wake. She didn't notice.

Inside, he wandered a maze of corridors and offices. The place was flooded with brainy people rushing to meetings, conferring in offices and open doorways and corridors, grabbing snacks from vend stations. Alejandro checked door labels, but the numbers meant nothing. Not one read "Craig Snyder," or any other name, for that matter. Fifteen minutes of fruitless search left him all but seething. He grabbed the arm of a bent old passerby and snapped, "Where the hell is Dr. Snyder?"

The fellow shook his arm loose and pointed. "Three intersections down, left, two more, left again. That general area. I think."

"Thanks," Alejandro grumped, wondering how general.

Two similar encounters later, he found it. Dr. Snyder's door stood open, his office dark. The lights came up when Alejandro entered. Maybe the environmentalist had removed the scientist herself?

Cramped, bare, and grey, the office felt like an interrogation room. A gray desk with an embedded panel filled the space, leaving little room for the chairs that accompanied it. Maybe Snyder spent most of his time in a classroom. He'd go nuts in here. Alejandro would, anyway, already was as he squeezed into the chair behind the desk.

Now what?

As if in answer, the panel activated.

We are gratified all went well, Dr. Snyder. Your guests will arrive momentarily. Be kind. They have had a trying journey.

What the hell did that mean?

The message vanished. Half a minute later, an unseen woman in the corridor said, "Dr. Snyder's in here." She didn't show herself, but an unlikely couple stepped into the doorway, he tall and European, she far shorter and Asian. He looked wary, she spooked, as though Alejandro had materialized from thin air.

He waved them in, but they didn't move.

"Somebody kosh you on the head? Come on, sit down." Probably that wasn't a Dr. Snyder line. Alejandro didn't give a damn. This business was getting weirder by the minute.

The man took gentle hold of the woman's arm and escorted her in. They sat, eyeing him like a potential enemy.

"So?" Alejandro prompted.

The young man did the introductions. "I'm Ricard Fulbert. This is Quan Linh. We're students of Dr. Miguel Hernandez."

Yeah, he knew. How would Dr. Snyder react? Hell if he knew. "You don't say."

"He sent us…" Ricard looked like he'd bitten into a rotten onion. "Who *are* you?"

Fair question. Alejandro wasn't sure he knew. "Dr. Craig Snyder, apparently."

Linh was shaking so bad she had to clasp her hands to hold them still. "Why do you look like Dr. Hernandez?"

"Do I?"

"You know you do," Ricard stated flatly. "Enough to be his brother."

Alejandro forced a laugh. "Must be a cosmic joke on one of us."

"Explain it to us."

If the environmentalist was after his past, she was in for a disappointment. He wasn't about to tell this pair, or anyone else. "Explaining's your job. Why're you here?"

Ricard waited for a real answer. The deflection hadn't fooled him. Linh might not have had a mind left to fool. Her whole body quivered. She couldn't look Alejandro in the eye.

Trying journey, the environmentalist said. A gross understatement. "Linh," Alejandro said. "I won't hurt you. What do you need?"

She grabbed Ricard's hand and looked at it. "Dr. Hernandez sent us. We're going to Ganymede. We thought you could help."

The panel displayed a message. *Where is Hernandez?*

Oh, that was sweet. The environmentalist set Miguel up, then failed to capture him. He must have gone to ground, and now it was up to Alejandro to trick Miguel's students into betraying him. Fine, he'd do that. But it had better end there. "Where is Miguel? Didn't he come with you?"

Lihn shook her head. "He stayed on Mars. He's—"

"Involved in important research," Ricard said quickly. "He suggested you might help us."

The message on the panel changed. *Where?*

He couldn't ask that. Ricard was already suspicious. "Shuttered himself in his lab, did he?"

"Maybe. "

"And that's all he said? Go to Ganymede?"

Linh leaned into Ricard and squeezed her eyes shut. Tears dribbled down her face. As gentle as a breeze, Ricard wiped them away. "We'd appreciate your help," he said.

"Miguel should've been more explicit. Where is he? I'll send him a message and—"

"We don't know where he went, only that he's unavailable."

This guy was good. He might even be telling the truth. "Okay. We'll do without him, then."

A new message displayed: *Keep them in the Belt. Sell them. The profits are yours.*

For God's sake, why didn't she just tell him to shoot the couple?

Ricard leaned forward. "What are you looking at?"

Tapping the panel, Alejandro entered a one-word reply: *No.* The message vanished before Ricard could read it. "Staff meeting alert," he grumbled. "Damn nuisance. What do you need to get to Ganymede?"

Although suspicious, Ricard answered. "We're short on funds. And we need an academic contact. Exobiology, paleontology, someone on-site who can help us get set up."

I am saddened by your decision. It will cause hardship and much suffering. Will you not reconsider?

Damn it, she'd scatter his body parts in the void if he didn't play along! He'd have to worm out of this the hard way. He tapped back, *Fine.* Then to Ricard he said, "Give me an hour or two to unfurl the solar sails. Where're you staying?" He knew already, but they didn't know that. "I'll contact you there."

"Two seven three eight."

"Got it. Go home and relax. I'll set you up."

Yeah, he'd set them up, all right. He hoped Ricard would get the message and the environmentalist wouldn't. She couldn't blame him if they bolted on their own. Unfortunately, Ricard gave no sign of understanding, and the environmentalist…

Don't lose them, the panel warned.

Okay, she could blame him.

But he was done with defense. From here on, he'd play offense.

Their bodies were spying on them. Biomech nanobots, Dr. Lloyd had said, some aiding in torture, some tracking their movements, some listening. That's all he told them before fleeing in panic, probably to hide. But there was no place to hide on Mars, not when your bloodstream signaled your every move, transmitted your every word.

Petrina's mind froze in terror while Martin exploded with hot rage. She escaped to the corridor, sank to the floor, and shivered against the wall. She hoped Martin wouldn't injure himself. He emerged fifteen minutes later, sweat-soaked, fingers bloodied, face bruised. He slid to the floor, knees pulled up, head buried in his arms, and wept. Thank God nobody passed by.

Petrina wrapped her arms around him. They wouldn't live long as such damaged goods. They had to figure this out, only she didn't know how. She didn't suffer Martin's rages or Linh's terrors, but she couldn't *think*. Every time she tried to focus, she fell into a mental whitewater cascade that dashed her against rock after rock until, battered and exhausted, she was thrown onto the riverbank. That was worse than any torture she could imagine. She neither knew how to tell Martin nor could she bear hiding it from him. Worst of all, Lowell Security was listening, so she dared not speak openly.

"Martin," she whispered. "I need your help."

He shivered, examined his hands, balled them into fists.

"We need to talk. Just you and I."

His eyes, sunk into his flesh, narrowed in concentration. He looked like a vampire down a couple of liters. "Remember Ricard's kitchen?" he said. "He's into retro."

She'd never been more glad to have a twin. Nobody would have understood the exchange, nobody but them. They couldn't talk openly, couldn't message via panel, couldn't even hide. It was too big a problem for her damaged mind. But Martin had an idea.

Ricard gave them access to his apartment as a safe house before he left. He informed the Housing Authority he'd be on extended leave with the intent to return. The apartment wouldn't be assigned to anyone else, not until they figured out he was gone for good. Lowell Security, believing nobody in residence, wouldn't raid it. Ricard hadn't known about the nanobots, but Martin didn't intend to elude the authorities as such. He was looking for something.

He found it tucked in a drawer in Ricard's desk: a package of writing paper and a box of pens. Both were mint condition, unopened. Martin and Petrina sat at the dining table and stared at the antiques for some minutes before reluctantly breaking the seals. They placed a sheet of paper between them, and each took a pen. In rough, uneven letters because she had never written anything by hand before, Petrina gave it a go.

The value of this pen just went down eighty percent.

More for the paper, Martin wrote back.

Petrina then set forth the problem: *How do we lose nanobots? If we can't, how do we disable them?*

Talk to a doctor?

Can't talk.

Let's research it.

Can't use panels.

What can we use?

Don't know.

Why not? You always have ideas.

Petrina looked at Martin. Tears flooded her eyes, but she willed herself to silence. She wiped them away and wrote. *Just don't.*

He touched her cheek before replying, *Damn them. I'm sorry.* But instead of descending into anger, he suggested, *Dr. Lloyd knew about them.*

Of course. Dr. Lloyd must have been tortured in the same way.

Maybe he figured it out, Martin added. *Got rid of or neutralized them. But he's gone.*

We'll hack his account.

Petrina didn't need to ask how they'd manage that. Her astonishment broadcast the question.

Martin grinned. *I know a guy*, he wrote.

Chapter 7

For three hours, Quan Linh and Ricard Fulbert waited in their temporary apartment on Itokawa Station for word from Dr. Craig Snyder. Ricard didn't trust him. Linh didn't either, but she didn't know why. He stalked her through the dark alleys of her fear, caught her with fingers of ice, whispered death in her ear. She tried to push him away with thoughts of light and warmth. Her childhood. Her parents. Field expeditions with Dr. Hernandez. Anything.

Her brain refused to serve up memories. She had nothing left but here and now. The cramped, nondescript apartment, the white walls devoid of decor, the small, gray couch at the side of the room. The round chair in which she sat, legs curled beneath her body. Ricard, seated opposite her in an identical chair, flicking through displays on his panel, silently seeking God knew what. He must have felt her eyes on him, for he looked up and smiled half-heartedly before returning to his search.

Ricard the rock.

How had he escaped unscathed? In the days between the terror and Linh and Ricard's departure from Mars, Martin and Petrina had shown no overt signs of injury, but Linh felt something gnawing on their hearts and minds. Sooner or later, they would succumb. Only Ricard remained unimpaired, a marble statue daring time itself to erode him. He should have been the one to stay, the one to help Dr. Hernandez. Instead, he surrounded Linh with his strength, devoted himself to her safety. Why didn't matter. He just did. His presence comforted her. Just the sight of him sitting across the room drove back the horror.

Moved almost to tears, she rose and went to him. He looked up. Without speaking, she sat in his lap, put her arms around his neck, and leaned her forehead against his. He felt tense, unsure, but she didn't care. He was the only thing keeping her sane.

"Thank you," she whispered.

"You're welcome."

They sat unmoving for some time. She didn't want to ever move again. But Dr. Hernandez had sent them on a mission, and so long as they were together, she could see it through. "What's Ganymede like?"

"I don't know. I've heard the only people who go there are those with something to hide."

Linh raised her head and looked into his eyes. It sounded like one of those inadvertent jokes for which Ricard was semi-famous. She managed a faint smile for him, and for herself. "Where did you hear that?"

"From a guy on the shuttle."

"Who?"

"A retired academic named Bob Wreyford, or so he said. He was too inquisitive, so I told him to go away. You were asleep at the time."

She wished she hadn't been. It might have been amusing to see that. "I guess we'll fit in, then."

"I guess."

His tension melted, but he refrained from touching her. Linh felt unasked questions swirling through his mind. She laughed a little.

It felt good to laugh again. "You're probably wondering what I'm doing in your lap."

As serious as ever, Ricard replied, "I know why you're there."

"It's okay?"

"It's okay." Finally, he put his arms about her waist. His touch was surprisingly gentle. "But let's not fool ourselves, Linh."

"That would be bad," she agreed.

Before they could discuss what constituted being fooled, a chime sounded, signaling a visitor. "That'll be Dr. Snyder," Ricard said. Linh sighed and slipped from his lap. He took her hand, and they went together to answer. But no, it wasn't Snyder.

"Why, look who it is!" the caller said. Glowing with humor, he added, "Remember me? Bob Wreyford! We met on the shuttle. Well, you and I did." He smiled extra bright at Linh. "You were asleep, so I didn't have the pleasure."

Ricard maneuvered Linh back and stood between her and Bob. "I told you to leave us alone."

"He's the guy who told you about Ganymede?" Linh whispered. She clung to Ricard's arm in a vain effort to untangle the sudden knot in her stomach.

Bob held up his hands in mock defense. "Hey, Ricard, calm down. I didn't follow you. I didn't even know I was seeing you. Dr. Snyder sent me."

Warily, Ricard looked up and down the corridor. "How do you know Dr. Snyder?"

"He's an old friend from my university days. I'm in logistics now. Transportation, shipping, housing, all that. Takes a lot to keep scientists moving. If you're going to Ganymede, I'm your man."

"I thought you said you were retired."

"I didn't exactly say that."

Ricard eyed him with mistrust but then stepped aside and motioned Bob in.

Bob settled himself in one of the chairs while Linh and Ricard sat side-by-side on the cramped couch. "You're in luck," he said. "I found you passage on a small ship headed your way, but you'll have to leave in four hours. Can you be ready?"

"We need money," Ricard said. "And contacts."

"Already done. I arranged a small grant for you. It'll cover transportation and something to get you settled once you're there. I'll send you the transfer request shortly. You want separate housing?" He raised his eyebrows.

"No." Ricard's stone gaze dared Bob to comment.

Bob didn't have to. His grin said it all. "I'll have a place ready and waiting. Dr. Snyder will message you the contacts before departure. Anything to ship?"

"Just one piece of luggage each."

"Travelling light. Smart move. You can find sixty percent of what you want on Ganymede. The rest you can do without. You're leaving the comforts of home, but something tells me you only need each other."

Before Ricard could bite Bob's head off, Linh leaned forward. "We lived our whole lives on Mars. We don't know anything about Ganymede."

For just an instant, a look of pity flitted across Bob's face. "There's not much to tell. It's a big ice cube dotted with little research stations and a few mining outposts. You'll be fine there. I'll return in four hours and see you to your ship. Be ready."

Once he was out the door, Linh leaned into Ricard, who put an arm about her shoulders. "Four hours," she said. "I'm ready now. I want out of this place."

Ricard squeezed her. "I don't trust him."

"You shouldn't."

"Because?"

"You said he was too inquisitive. What did he want to know?"

"If we were married. If we were lovers. If we knew Dr. Hernandez."

Linh shivered. "Something's wrong. I can't think straight or remember anything, but I keep getting these…" She closed her eyes.

"What?"

"You'll think it's stupid."

"Never."

"Feelings."

Ricard stroked her hair. "That's your pre-conscious brain doing its job. Trust it. Let's not be here in four hours."

"Where do we go?"

"Anywhere but here."

Problem was, there were only so many places on a space station.

They wandered the broad public corridors on Itokawa Station's middle ring side by side, hand in hand, packing their meager belongings, seeking a place to vanish. Ricard wanted someplace accessible, easy in and easy out, but unexpected. They passed clusters of shops, rows of third-rate mining company offices, blocks of residences. Not a suitable hiding place could they find. While they walked, Ricard picked at the threads of their experience:

Dr. Snyder's uncanny resemblance to Dr. Hernandez; his peculiar behavior; the communication he carried on via panel while talking with them; Bob Wreyford's intrusion on the shuttle; his unexpected appearance at their door. Whatever those two were, they weren't good Samaritans. Both asked after Dr. Hernandez's whereabouts, and Dr. Snyder tried several times to elicit the information.

Ricard's grip on Linh's hand tightened.

She looked up, frightened. "What's wrong?"

He eased off the pressure. "Nothing. I was just thinking."

"About what?"

"Snyder and Wreyford. They're using us to find Dr. Hernandez."

"We don't know where he is."

"They don't know that."

She slipped a bit closer, held on a bit tighter.

"It's all right," he said. "We'll get to Ganymede on our own."

"How? We don't have money."

They didn't, but that could be fixed. A sign caught Ricard's eye, a green tree underscored by a green arrow. "Maybe that way."

They followed the arrow and came to a transparent door. Beyond, scents of soil and plants and moisture bloomed, scents they knew from the farming facilities in Lowell Colony on Mars.

"The source of your soy ice cream," Ricard said in all seriousness.

Linh smiled and leaned against him.

Just beyond the door were more pictograms: a gold coin, a corn stalk, another tree, a gray bin, a blue line graph. Ricard decided to follow the money. A walk of five minutes brought them to a small hive of clerks busy at desktop panels. The closest to the door, a woman with dark hair and pale skin, looked up at their entrance.

"New arrivals," she guessed. "Good timing. We have openings in clerical, monitoring, and harvest. What suits you?"

"What's the pay?" Ricard asked. Linh remained close, barely breathing.

"A hundred obols a week." The clerk shrugged as though it hardly mattered. "Plus a room in the ag section next door." She eyed their entwined fingers. "One room?"

Ricard nodded. "Monitoring is tech work, I suppose. We're qualified for that."

She laughed. "It's zombie work. You stare at panels all day."

"We'll take it."

"Can't your lady friend speak for herself?"

Linh swallowed and straightened. "Monitoring is fine."

Pointing to the wall beside them, the clerk said, "Enter your application there. It takes about an hour to be approved and assigned. You can wait in those chairs by the back wall."

At the panel, they confronted a form requesting personal information. "We should use aliases," Linh whispered.

Ricard thought for a moment then entered his name as Jules Berry. "They won't get the joke," he told Linh.

"Neither do I."

"A long-dead French actor who once played the devil." He finished filling in the data, fabricating all the way, and submitted the application. "Your turn."

Linh entered her alias without hesitation: Trung Trac. While she completed the form, she smirked the way she so often had before the torture. "I have a sister, Trung Nhi. She and I raised an army and drove out a cruel Chinese governor in A.D. 40. Then we established a state under my rule."

"Impressive," Ricard replied. "Our enemies don't stand a chance."

Applications submitted, they retreated to the chairs to wait. The clerk said an hour, but two passed before they were recalled to the front desk, given room and work assignments, and sent on their way with instructions to report for duty the following morning.

Their apartment proved barely adequate, with a gathering room only large enough to seat four and a narrow bed almost overflowing the bedroom. The place offered little storage. The kitchen was but a bank of undersized, overused appliances tucked with their filth into a corner. Ricard figured it would do until they had money for the voyage to Ganymede. "You can have the bed," he told Lihn. "I'll sleep in that chair." He indicated a gray recliner that looked like it had been the favorite of an ogre for the past half century.

"You'll never sleep in that thing," she said.

"I'll manage."

"You won't."

"It's better than the floor."

"I didn't suggest the floor."

"But where else— "

She took his hand and pressed a finger to his lips to silence him. "Take a wild guess," she said.

With the pen, Martin Ulenga inscribed nearly legible instructions on a semi-precious sheet of paper taken from Ricard's apartment. It took time, since writing wasn't a skill he—or anyone—acquired in school. Then he messaged a dinner invitation to his childhood friend Samuel Lasker. That evening, leaving Petrina alone in the apartment, he met Samuel at Lowell Colony's only Spanish restaurant, and the duo talked science, computers, and women.

Samuel, closing in on a Ph.D. in infosecurity, decried how weak most systems remained, even in this day. Given time, he boasted, he could break into anything. Good thing he was one of the white hats. Martin detailed everything that could and did go wrong on field expeditions in the Martian wilderness. Samuel told Martin about his latest romantic supernova and its subsequent collapse into a black hole. Martin reciprocated by describing his ill-fated relationship with a beautiful Japanese girl from the less wealthy side of the colony.

Somewhere someone listened, not knowing Martin had told Samuel that tale before, not knowing Samuel had told it to Martin a few times, himself. It was a pre-arranged code concocted during their teen years to signal a hush-hush scheme in the works. So, when over dessert Martin pushed the folded paper across the table to Samuel, Samuel took it with barely a raised eyebrow and tucked it away for later perusal. Just after midnight, Samuel messaged the logical question.

Where the hell did you *learn to write?*

Martin wasn't sure it was safe to answer. He and Petrina figured their accounts were being monitored.

Samuel understood the lack of response and gave assurances. *We're clear. I've secured the connection.*

I owe you, Martin replied. *Any luck?*

Skill, man, skill. Dr. Lloyd's account is one weird place.

Martin's note had asked Samuel to search Dr. Lloyd's files and messages for information on nanobots, particularly removing them from a human body. *Weird how?*

Mostly gibberish. Clear text written in code. Nothing I've been able to crack yet. Some encrypted files, too, likewise uncrackable. He was good. But then this one document, unencrypted, unencoded, too technical for me.

What's it say?

Samuel sent the file to Martin. It was a scientific paper on nanobot-destroying nanobots. Dealing heavily in the biochemistry of immunity, it was hardly Martin's field, but the gist seemed to be a proposal for what the authors called assassin bots capable of removing the zwitterion-based coatings used to render nanobots invisible to the immune system.

Does anyone make these? Martin asked.

Not on Mars.

Then where?

Don't know, Samuel replied. *Looked around, but they don't seem much in demand. Dr. Lloyd took a half-year trip to the Belt two years ago. If he got treatment, it must have been there.*

That wasn't an option for Martin and Petrina. Dr. Hernandez needed them now. They had to get rid of the damned things quickly.

You sure you're infested? Samuel asked.

Dr. Lloyd said so.

I'll prowl some more.

Martin appreciated it, but what could Samuel do?

He returned home to find Petrina sleeping on the couch. He spread a blanket over her and retired to bed, depressed at his failure, anger stirring in the recesses of his mind.

Over breakfast the following morning, Martin and Petrina spoke openly of putting this horrible episode behind them. They would focus on completing their Ph.D.'s and never think of Dr. Hernandez again. While they spoke, they passed notes. Martin told

Petrina of Samuel's findings, and Petrina fretted over not having the brainpower to assemble the information into a coherent picture. Her slide into despair angered Martin anew. Fists clenched, he willed himself into a steady breathing rhythm while Petrina ran her fingers over his and silently cried. He felt like he'd climbed a ridge, seeking passage to the land beyond, and found a sheer cliff instead.

It occurred to him that the nanobots swarming in his body might have the power to push him over the edge.

During his first five days in the crater-rim facility, Miguel had seen almost nobody. Jake had vanished, which was just as well. Although the temper Carl Metzler attributed to Jake hadn't flared, sometimes it seemed to be hiding behind that savage grin, longing for escape. Nessa O'Clery likewise hadn't shown herself since introducing Miguel to injured geologist Emil Sarkozy, who must still be confined to his bed in the medical section. The only regulars Miguel encountered were a pair of armed guards prowling the main corridor, and they weren't much on conversation.

So what purpose could this place possibly have? An all but deserted steel circle some hundred and sixty meters in circumference buried beneath a crater rim in the middle of nowhere. It made no sense. Nessa said she mined Tharsis. This place couldn't serve an operation so far away. Nor did it aid the smuggling side of her business. No people, no transports, no storage areas he could find. He tried all the doors within ninety degrees either way of his apartment, but those his palm print activated contained little more than food and basic supplies.

Miguel could puzzle over that until the sun burned out and find no answers, so he turned to planning his first survey expedition instead. He studied geology references, created a route and schedule, determined his supply needs. He almost felt he was back in his office at the university. Although he loved field work, in recent years much of his job entailed planning and administration. He had a surprising knack for it. Twenty years ago, he wouldn't have thought so, but even as he blundered into Andre Rand's gunsight, there'd been talk of appointing him department chair.

He decided to start close to the base and plotted routes of no more than a week's travel in each direction. He picked sites based on both mineral and fossil potential. He had little hope of replicating his Meridiani find—even that had required a healthy dose of luck— but it couldn't hurt to try. And besides, he had one other item on his agenda.

Escape.

Barring a lucky find, Sinus Meridiani remained his objective, and time was short. Once he reached the site of his original find, he could load up on samples and get off-planet with the aid of a friendly smuggler. He only needed one of Nessa's rovers. With a bit of study, he could disable the governors her people had installed.

By the sixth day of his captivity, he'd drawn up equipment and supply lists. Just as he submitted the requisition, piercing alarms shrieked in the corridor. Fire? Containment breach? He rushed the door and felt it for excess heat. Nothing. The alarms continued to scream, so probably the atmosphere hadn't much diminished. He slapped the senor to open the door just as a pair of guards rushed by, their boots pounding the floor.

Miguel pursued without thinking, all the way to the southern airlock where he found Jake grappling red-faced with an intruder. The newcomer equaled him in size, but Jake had him at a disadvantage. Left arm wrapping his adversary's throat from behind, Jake's right hand locked onto the man's wrist to prevent him from wielding the silver stun gun he was trying in vain to twist in Jake's direction. The guards flanked the intruder and immobilized him. Jake released him and delivered a bone-cracking blow to his jaw. The man's legs gave out. The stun gun clattered to the floor. One of the guards snatched it, pressed it to the intruder's chest, and fired. His body convulsed and hit the floor.

Jake kicked him in the ribs and wiped his mouth on his sleeve, leaving a red smear on the fabric. "You gets to kick the bastard, too, Miguel. He comes for you."

Miguel recognized neither the unconscious face nor the clothing, an orange coverall that could have blended with the Martian sand. It wasn't a Lowell Security uniform. "How do you know?"

"He's stupid. He asks for you."

"How did he find me?"

Jake motioned carelessly to the guards, who grabbed the limp form and dragged him, groaning, to the airlock.

"Wait," Miguel objected. "What are you doing?"

"He tells nobody about us."

"You can't—"

The guards retreated and sealed the airlock, depressurized it, waited in the red glare of the warning light, their faces taking on demonic aspects. Miguel felt as though the air had been sucked from his own lungs. Jake approached and poked him in the chest. The impact knocked him back a step. "Nobody finds us. Ever."

The guards snagged envirosuits from lockers near the portal and put them on. After repressurizing the airlock, they stepped in, sealed it, and depressurized it again.

"I don't likes funerals," Jake muttered. He lumbered away. Miguel trembled, hand on the wall for support. He slid to the airlock and looked out the window. The chamber was empty now, the body gone, the guards nowhere to be seen.

They'd killed a man because of him. He might as well have done the deed himself. Weak-kneed, he leaned against the wall and turned away. They'd killed a man because of him.

He tried to rationalize it. They'd had no choice. They were criminals, outlaws in all but name. Lowell Security would destroy them. Yet this might not have been Security. Maybe a friend or colleague had come looking for him. No, that couldn't be. Miguel hadn't recognized the man. Regardless, he was here for Miguel, not Nessa and her people. Miguel had led him here. The blood was on his hands.

A whisper of breath startled him. Nessa stood beside him, back to the wall, arms crossed over her chest. She stared at the airlock as though her gaze might incinerate it. "Good riddance," she said. She turned a sympathetic smile on Miguel. "Don't worry. You're safe."

He wasn't worried, not about that.

"You never saw a man killed before."

Jaw tight, he couldn't answer.

"Now you have. Next time won't be so hard. Should I say it's not your fault?"

Miguel shook his head, partly to clear it, partly to claim his share of the responsibility. "He followed me here."

"You think he'd be less dead if he blundered in by accident?"

"But he didn't."

Nessa took his hand in hers. "We protect our own. If you must blame someone, blame him. He shouldn't have come." She caressed his fingers, then let go.

"You didn't kill me. Or Emil."

Her eyes reflected the stark beauty of the Martian desert as she looked into his. "Because you're useful."

But for how long? She was a sandstorm, he a cliff in her path. Once the storm had scoured the cliff, the wind would fade. But the sand remained, waiting to be whipped into a frenzy again and again.

Nessa touched Miguel's face. "You're family. We protect our own. And we know our own. Don't think you can take me in. Or down."

Angered boiled in his gut. "I didn't ask to be brought or kept here, and I sure as hell didn't ask you to kill for me." He grabbed her wrist, twisted her arm, and tried to force her to ground. He wasn't much of a fighter, but he'd learned a few maneuvers, and she was smaller than he, weaker, a woman.

A smart woman, it turned out, and skilled. She pivoted, used his own weight to throw him off balance, jammed her knee into his gut as he fell. His face struck the floor. His grip on her slipped as his body slammed down, the wind knocked from him. She pressed her knee into the small of his back, grabbed a fistful of hair, and yanked his head up. He felt steel at his throat.

"Train up before you try that again," she said. She wasn't even breathing hard. She released him and stood over him, knife in hand.

Miguel rolled over and sucked in a few breaths before struggling to sit. "Point taken. Literally." He motioned at the knife. "In my defense, most of the women I've wrestled wanted to be taken down." A cheap shot, but it was out before he knew it.

Nessa slipped the knife into a sheath hidden in the right leg of her coverall. "For that, call a whore." She extended a hand to him.

Refusing her help, he clawed himself to his feet. "You have those in the family?"

"A few."

"Haven't seen any."

"Check our field bases. Where the men are."

Field bases. That explained a few things. What was this place, an understaffed headquarters?

She cocked her head and gave him a lopsided grin. "I thought you were a scientist. Don't you do research?"

Sure, but why would a criminal organization make operational details accessible?

Apparently, they did. Nessa shook her head. "Use the damn network," she said.

Chapter 8

"Children are forever underfoot. They are best relegated to caretakers." The faux environmentalist gazed on her white-clad form in a great oval mirror. Gold flecks glinted along the edges of the glass and in the fabric of her dress, sparkling like constellations in the heavens. Hers was the beauty and mystery of a comet sprayed among the stars. Men once thought comets omens of disaster or messengers from the gods. The environmentalist's presence might foretell similar fates. She turned to Andre Rand, mayor of Lowell Colony, the most powerful person on Mars, and showed no fear. Comet ice filled her veins.

She had come without appointment, giving security a name that, upon the mayor's standing instructions, unlocked the doors to his presence: Hitomi. The black of the eye.

She stood now like a statue, one adornment among many gracing his office: paintings and carvings, light sculpture, hand-crafted furnishings. Reporters branded it an art gallery, while videographers salivated for the smallest taste of the treasures within. But they had never seen Hitomi. They'd give their lives to record her. She would take them if they did.

"That's why I pay you," Andre said. "To play caretaker."

"Make me a drink. Hold the poison."

"Why would I poison you, Hitomi?" He flashed her his most charming smile and went to work at a wet bar beneath a window overlooking the colony's north side. The low, sand-colored buildings of the commercial district were spread before his feet, and beyond them the homes of wealthier residents. He mixed her a dry martini, then made one for himself.

She sipped, eyes peering at him over the rim of the glass, inscrutable as always. "You should have been a bartender."

"Thank you." He raised his glass to her and drank. "I'd rather be king."

"How disappointing to have your dreams demolished by an arrogant scientist and his gang of brats."

Had anyone else questioned his competence, Andre would have beat them with the iron poker stowed by the faux fireplace. But Hitomi was…special. Even so, his hands trembled with anger. He set his glass on his desk before he spilled it. "Hardly demolished. I just don't want further delays. But that's not why you're here, is it? What do you want?"

With a cool smile, she sashayed to a couch, sat, crossed her legs at the ankles, and drank. "Continuity."

Damn her. When she first approached him a month before, she offered to rid him of Dr. Miguel Hernandez. Andre would have brushed her off, save she knew too much. Everything, in fact. She knew Andre's ambitions for future colonies and political control of the planet. She knew Miguel's troubles on Earth and his desperation to redeem himself. She knew of the escalating conflict between mayor and scientist and even that Miguel was sleeping with Carmen. Andre should have killed her on the spot, if only to ensure that last tidbit remained concealed. Instead, he hired her. It seemed prudent at the time. And she had, indeed, delivered.

But then Miguel vanished, and Hitomi insisted on tracking his students, claiming they'd run straight to him. Except they didn't. And now she'd come for more.

Andre leaned against the desk. "You're getting paid. Excessively. That ought to be enough."

"Lesser operators may find your terms generous." She set her glass on an end table. "But you did not seek a lesser operator."

He hadn't sought her, either. "What constitutes continuity?"

"No doubt you will maintain the peace in Schiaparelli Colony with the same ruthless efficiency as here. Yet Mars will long remain a haven for outlaws. You have no reach beyond the colonies."

Andre took up his glass once more and joined her on the couch. He sat so close and scrutinized her face with such intensity that it would have embarrassed any other woman. Hitomi, though, never displayed her feelings. Maybe she had none to display. "What happens outside the colonies doesn't concern me."

"Then why not let Miguel Hernandez go? Why pursue him? And, not to be indelicate, what became of your expert tracker?"

What was she, clairvoyant? Andre tried to hide his surprise, but that hint of a smile tugging at her lips signaled his failure. "Hernandez is a special case," he said.

"With friends in the wilderness. You fear that."

"I don't. Those rogues chose their oblivion. They can have it." She smiled into her drink.

"Fine," Andre snapped. "Be my desert enforcer. Find Hernandez. Make sure he doesn't recruit any mercenaries. But you clear all operations with me in advance. I refuse to pay for random raids on no-account smugglers."

"Especially when they supply you with luxuries otherwise unobtainable."

He ought to slit her throat.

"We will require a base of operations," she said. "Lunae Planum would suit admirably."

"Damn it, Hitomi—"

"Unless you wish me gone?"

He did. He didn't. They weren't finished. "A small base of operations. And I approve all plans before any construction takes place."

"A wise arrangement, Andre. May we both prosper through it." She enjoyed mixing promise and threat, but she was wrong if she thought she could intimidate him. He would be rid of her. Eventually.

Andre stared into his glass. "What about the students?"

"Ricard Fulbert and Quan Linh appear ignorant of Dr. Hernandez's whereabouts. Their destination was Ganymede, but I have no reason to believe he is there, so I made them other arrangements."

"Such as?"

Hitomi picked up her glass, swirled it, and drank.

"Bring them back to Lowell. I want to keep an eye on them."

"Your eyes are myopic, Andre. We will use mine." She set down the glass and regarded him, emotionless, hypnotizing. "How thoughtless of me. I've repeatedly offended your sense of worth. Would bedding me restore it?"

Andre nearly threw his drink in her face.

"Then I shall take my leave." She rose and crossed the office, a queen concluding an audience with a peasant.

"What about the Ulenga twins?" Andre demanded. "I paid you watch them, too."

"They remain on Mars. An operation with respect to them is in progress."

"I didn't authorize that."

"You meant to. I forgive the oversight." She slipped out, a comet receding into the black of space.

Andre so wanted to kill her. The day might come when he would, but not today. She was too dangerous to touch until he found out how she knew so much, until he knew who held her leash. Someone stood behind her, someone with more resources than he. For now, he could only curse himself for hiring her.

They were endangering Linh. That's all Petrina could think about.

Samuel Lasker had constructed the equipment and planted it in the exobiology lab early that morning when nobody was around. Mid-afternoon, Petrina and Martin played at prepping samples collected over the past year. Two grad students doing their jobs, nothing suspicious, no matter that their mentor was on the run.

But they weren't so innocent. Petrina fumbled through the work, unable to focus. Time and again, she had to ask Martin to remind her what came next, and Martin grew increasingly irritated. She could see it in the set of his mouth, hear it in his clipped instructions. Rage had been his curse since the torture, as a scrambled brain had been hers. The fires of their handicaps threatened to burn to ash what little hope remained.

As they struggled to maintain a veneer of normality, Samuel's devices, secreted about the lab, scanned and triangulated. When they detected signals originating within Petrina or Martin's bodies, they informed tiny gray discs sewn into the collars of the twins' shirts. The discs jammed those signals. If Petrina and Martin couldn't rid themselves of the nanobots prowling their innards, they could at least stop them from tattling.

Assuming it worked. They wouldn't know until they tested it, and Petrina feared the test Martin had proposed, even though he insisted Linh would be safe. She'd gone to Ganymede—hadn't she?—and Lowell Security had no jurisdiction off Mars. Petrina saw no evidence that Security cared about rules, but Samuel agreed with Martin, and now a tiny vibration from the gray disc in her collar said they were go for the test. She pinched her eyes shut and tried to remember the script.

Martin had the first line: "I haven't found the Meridiani sample. Have you?"

She swallowed and shook her head but couldn't respond. The words swam away before she could catch them.

Martin motioned her to speak. Getting no answer, he pressed forward. "I wonder where he stashed it."

Petrina squeezed her eyes shut. *Concentrate*, she ordered her mind. *Concentrate!* They'd rehearsed this in writing. The words were in there somewhere. She just had to speak them.

"Petrina? He didn't give it to you, did he?" Forced to improvise, Martin pressed his hands to the lab table as he fought against a torrent of anger.

"No," she blurted out. Somehow, speaking that one word released the rest of them. "No, he didn't give it to me. Maybe Ricard has it. Or Linh." She nearly choked on the name, remembering Linh's terror in the wake of the torture. What if Samuel's toys didn't work? What if Martin was wrong and they found her and tortured her again?

"Ricard wouldn't risk it," Martin said, "but Linh would do anything Dr. Hernandez asked."

"Should we search her apartment?"

"Security might be watching."

Petrina shuddered. It wasn't an act. "How do we get it, then? We can't just leave it."

"We might have to, at least until things calm down. Better to play it safe, don't you think?"

Safe! she wanted to scream. *Nothing is safe!* But she stuck to the plan. "Okay. Maybe in a couple of weeks?"

"Maybe," Martin replied. "We'll see."

And it was done. They returned to their work and didn't speak of Dr. Hernandez again. The afternoon wore on.

In Linh's apartment, hidden cameras watched for any response to their seemingly idle chatter. None came, neither that day nor the next. Martin relaxed and put away the vintage pens and paper they had taken from Ricard's apartment. They could speak openly now.

Petrina didn't buy it. Something felt wrong. But she dared not voice her fear lest she rekindled her brother's anger.

Wind stirred the rusty sand, shifting it in waves down the ancient channel. The westering sun threw sharp shadows across the land. Just below the lip of the bank, Miguel carefully excavated the last of twelve rock samples. It was slow work in his white envirosuit. He had chipped his way from the riverbed to the lip of the two-meter bank, assembling a record of biological activity in the four-billion-year-old channel, if activity there had been.

Probably not. Miguel had collected thousands of samples from a wide swath of the Martian surface, and only one, a loose rock picked up in the Meridiani region, had revealed evidence of living organisms. Possibly life, having originated there, had no time to spread before the planet dried and cooled and became a tomb for its microscopic inhabitants. Mars then slumbered for billions of years, awaiting creatures from its neighbor planet to evolve sufficiently to bring new life to it. The humans at long last came, bringing their greed and thirst for power. That brief efflorescence of native life might now remain forever buried in the sand.

If he was to prevent that, Miguel needed considerable dumb luck or a clever idea. So far, he'd had neither.

Work done, he bagged his specimens and hiked to the rover, where Jake awaited his return. Miguel still wasn't sure what role Jake played in Nessa O'Clery's "family" of crooks, but he seemed to have his fingers in everything. When he heard about this outing, he invited himself along as driver, turning aside objections with his creepy grin. Now here they were, two days from base, Miguel working and Jake doing nothing.

Inside the rover, Miguel removed his dusty helmet and gloves and sat in the seat next to Jake. Together, they watched the sun dip below the rim of the bank. Darkness settled quickly over the land. Miguel stared into the void.

"Something wrong?" Jake asked.

"A lot of things, but you don't care."

"How you knows? Name one."

"I'm a prisoner."

"Why you thinks that?"

Miguel didn't know whether to laugh or punch him. He might have done both, except he'd seen Jake all but choke the life out of a man. Best not to antagonize him. "I'm as good as shackled. I need to get to Sinus Meridiani."

"Bah. You don't knows what you needs. Nessa knows. You listens to her."

"Where the hell did you learn to speak English, Jake?"

In the dark, Jake shifted his weight and cracked his knuckles. "You don't likes my English?"

Right. Don't antagonize him. "It's an unusual dialect, that's all."

"I gets it from a vid. I watches the first three parts of twenty. The others gets destroyed."

For three lessons, he wasn't doing half bad. "Destroyed how?"

Jake didn't answer. His breath came quick and shallow. It must've been a bad memory.

Opting for safety, Miguel dropped the subject. In the deepening dark, stars flooded the sky.

Jake tapped the console, and a dim light illuminated the interior of the rover. "I gets us some food," he said. He rose and lumbered into the back, where the supplies were stashed along the rear. He rummaged among bags and boxes before returning with a container for each of them. He tossed one to Miguel. Chicken stew. It heated itself when popped open. It tasted like salted plastic, but Jake downed it as though it was a perfectly grilled steak—the real thing, not a Martian imitation.

Jake might have sprouted from the Martian wilderness. He had its roughness, its wildness, and he was a survivor. If anyone was a true Martian, it was Jake. So why did he submit to Nessa's rule? Curiosity getting the better of Miguel, he asked, "What are you doing here?"

Jake finished his meal and discarded the container in the trash chute. "Making sure you doesn't kills yourself."

"I don't need a bodyguard."

"You needs a handler. You does stupid things, like tries to escape. Then you ends up like Dr. Sarkozy, half dead in medical and no good to nobody."

Miguel had to admit the possibility. The organization's network taught him not only procedures for requisitioning rovers and supplies from field bases but also details of the governors that prevented rovers from venturing beyond Nessa's designated perimeter. Should one exceed its limits, should its governor module be tampered with, all systems would shut down, current location would be transmitted, and any occupants could but wait for rescue or death. That wouldn't stop him from trying. Too much was at stake.

"I mean," he said, "why do you work for Nessa?"

"You asks too many questions."

"It's my job. I'm a scientist."

"Your job is to finds minerals."

"You said we both wanted to be remembered. What I want to be remembered for isn't finding minerals. What about you?"

Jake stared out the viewport.

"Come on," Miguel pressed.

"For that I kills a man."

He must have killed more than one already, but those would have been murders of necessity. People who got out of line. Interlopers. Those weren't killings to be remembered. Jake had his sights on someone important, but Miguel couldn't ask. The memory of that last murder remained too near.

Jake told him anyway, in a whisper. "The man who kills my sister." He turned, mouth quivering, hate radiating from his eyes. "Andre Rand."

Midnight. Miguel hadn't slept, nor had Jake. Reclining in their seats in the pitch black, they hadn't spoken for hours, but each knew the other was awake. Whenever he closed his eyes, Miguel saw anew Jake choking the trespasser, kicking his unconscious body, ordering him thrown out the airlock to asphyxiate. The first instance of the vision sickened him. During the second, he broke out in a cold sweat. He watched the third in numb detachment and realized that, having been unwitting party to one murder, he was capable of enabling another.

The thought should have horrified him. Instead, it sparked an idea.

"I could help you," Miguel said.

Jake didn't reply.

"I know Carmen Rand."

Jake made a sound, possibly a dismissive snort, possibly a laugh, possibly both.

"If you help me, I'll help you."

In the brief silence that followed, Jake must have considered it. But his decision was unequivocal: "Go to hell."

Chapter 9

Work done and assurances given, all that remained was to test the technician's claim of perfection. Fortunately, he was young, in awe, and not at all the master of his hormones.

Carmen didn't doubt his skill or the care he'd lavished on the job. She'd watched from an upper window while in his bulky envirosuit he wandered the rubble field half a kilometer from her door, pretending to photograph the residence and the cliff into which it was built. That was his cover while he took measurements—of what she didn't know—to determine the locations of hidden cameras. Once done, he retreated to his rover and trundled off, only to return later in a camo envirosuit, riding a camo hoverbike, tracing a convoluted route, sometimes near the cliff base, sometimes retreating until invisible, here and there pausing fifteen or twenty minutes. Following him was all but impossible. What he did during those pauses, she couldn't say, but after considerable flitting about, he arrived at her airlock and with a wide grin pronounced her safe.

Assuming the technician's self-assessment proved reliable, Andre would no longer know who came and went. His hidden cameras would show only the façade of her home unless she deactivated the new system. She could allow her husband to see what she wanted and hide the rest. Carmen wanted to trust the tech, but trust wasn't prudent where Andre was concerned, so she seduced the young man, which despite his surprise wasn't difficult. After he left the next morning, she showered and dressed and called for unannounced transport to the colony—no reporters to be informed. Upon her quiet arrival, she walked in on Andre and his advisors during their morning briefing.

Her intrusion caught him off-guard, but he hid it well. "Here for a shopping spree?" he asked.

"Came to see my husband," she countered. "I assume that's allowed?"

The advisors numbered five, three old men and two almost old women, all of whom Carmen knew. She ignored them, and they looked away in embarrassment.

"It's allowed," Andre said. "Just ill-timed, unless you're here to file some boring report."

"Don't be absurd, Andre. I'll wait in the reception room."

Now that he couldn't ignore her, she withdrew and took a seat in a spacious, well-appointed room just outside his office where he typically met with important guests among faux leather chairs, potted plants, a small bar, and a cherry sideboard imported from Earth. Carmen thought the sideboard looked forlorn. On it sat a small vase with white flowers and nothing else. She didn't often come here unless her presence was required for a reception, but on those occasions, the sideboard would be spread with twice as many hors d'oeuvres as needed for the guest list.

She listened for half an hour to indistinct talk leaking from the office, then all fell quiet, and Andre entered. He had a right to be angry, but he looked pleased with himself. One of those boring reports must have contained good news. She rose, took his hands, and pecked him on the cheek.

He laughed. "You're up to something."

"I'm always up to something. So are you. You go first."

He led her to a couch beneath a painting of Olympus Mons that reminded her of Hokusai's Mt. Fuji series. They sat and gazed into each other's eyes. Anyone watching might have thought they'd just fallen in love. It was part of the game they unceasingly played. Carmen thought it more fun than being in love, and she supposed Andre did too, else he would have long since rid himself of her.

"We break ground on Schiaparelli Colony next week. Equipment and supplies will be delivered a day ahead of schedule. Best of all, Celia Fundichely's first installment is in the bank, so everyone gets paid on time. No word of Hernandez, but she's taking that as a good sign."

"That's wonderful," Carmen breathed. "We should celebrate."

"I'd celebrate if you told me where the bastard went. He hasn't come to your place recently, I suppose."

"You know he hasn't, and I've been getting lonely out there."

Andre tangled his fingers in her hair. "Oh, is *that* why you want to celebrate."

She leaned into him. "It's a good reason, isn't it?"

"I'm surprised you haven't replaced him."

Carmen brushed her lips over his. "You won't believe this, but I didn't want to. For some inexplicable reason, I only want you of late."

Andre maneuvered her into his lap. "You've been all alone out there without even an old friend for company?"

Naturally, he knew of Yago Moncayo's visit. His cameras had been nominal then. "With one exception," she said in acknowledgement. "And you know his sensibilities."

Andre kissed her hair. "You've been such a good girl. We should do something about that."

"Please do."

He shifted her off his lap and said, "One moment." He vanished into his office. Door locks clicked into place, and she heard him give instruction to the outer office that he was not to be disturbed.

Carmen relaxed and stretched out on the couch, hair scattered, one arm behind her head, legs parted in anticipation of his return. Had Andre known of the technician or his handiwork or her dalliance with him, he would have dropped at least a hint, but he hadn't.

Her home was once more hers.

Four nights Linh and Ricard slept entwined in the little bed without making love; four days they worked side-by-side without fearing pursuit. Linh's terrors melted in the warmth of Ricard's embrace, and for the first time since the faux fire at Dr. Hernandez's she knew happiness. *We shouldn't fool ourselves*, Ricard had said. He'd been right, but she had changed; they both had. Stripped of fear, she no longer wished him merely for her shield. She wanted to be part of him in every way imaginable, and though he wouldn't say so, he felt the same. She knew he did. He couldn't hide his desire. The bed was so small, she inevitably felt his yearning against her as he held her in the darkness, yet he neither asked her to give herself to him nor turned away in embarrassment. In silence he refused his need rather than risk her further harm.

She admired him for that, but he could no more harm her than reduce the whole of the Belt to dust. If he didn't realize that, she'd have to tell him, today, before he spent one more night in hushed denial. At the end of their shift that day, she slipped her arm about Ricard's waist. He pulled her close, and they walked to their apartment as one amid the flow of workers coming and going. Linh wondered if she need say anything. Would he understand if she stopped him here, now, and with everyone watching pressed her lips to his?

They were almost home. She almost did it, but for the figure standing by their door. In an instant, her panic returned, and all thought fled before it.

Ricard stepped before her, once more her shield.

Leaning against the wall, arms crossed over his chest, Dr. Snyder watched with the same pride they'd so often seen on Dr. Hernandez's face. "You guys are good," he said. "I nearly lost you."

"What do you want?" Ricard demanded.

"You came to me, Ricard."

Ricard waited for a real answer.

"Why don't you invite me in?" Snyder asked.

"Why don't you leave?"

"It's either me or my boss, and she's the last person you want in your face."

With Linh clinging to him, Ricard palmed open the door. Snyder pushed through and took in the apartment. "I see why you're so hot to get to Ganymede. This place is a dump. Not that ice moons are any better."

"Start talking," Ricard snapped.

Snyder took the recliner and motioned the students to the couch. Only when they were huddled together there did he speak. "They say you're both smart," he said. "What do you know about nanobots?"

Linh clung to Ricard, unable to halt her trembling. Not even the torture session frightened her as this news had. Worst of all, she could see no escape. She could only trust that Ricard would think of something.

Ricard kept an arm about her and faced down Dr. Craig Snyder—or rather, Alejandro Carrasco, a mercenary of modest renown, as he now claimed to be. "Why should we believe this?" Ricard demanded.

"You shouldn't. Believing Miguel is what got you into this. But it's true."

If so, their bodies were full of biomech nanobots, injected to prep them for torture. When activated by the black sticks, some of those nanobots created sensations of intense pain and pleasure, while others were trackers and bugs. With the nanobots active, neither Ricard nor Linh, Petrina nor Martin could avoid surveillance or escape the possibility of further torture.

"So why tell us?" Ricard asked. "Whoever's listening will know."

"Good," Alejandro said. "You *are* as smart as they say. Here's the answer." He dug in a cargo pocket at his left hip and showed them a small gray box. "This detects and jams transmissions. I find it useful in some of my…" He smirked. "…activities." He stuffed the box back into his pocket.

Ricard gave no sign of his thoughts or feelings. He might have been a machine running a program. "And your point?"

"You're in big trouble. Bigger than you know."

"We have a pretty good idea. You had Wreyford on us before we even got here."

Alejandro grimaced. "Wreyford isn't my man. I suspect my boss hired him in case I couldn't deliver. Or wouldn't."

Still a blank slate, Ricard said, "So even your boss doesn't trust you."

"With good reason. Regardless, she's not keen on Ganymede. She wants you here in the Belt. I'm supposed to sell you into slavery."

"Like hell."

"You're already acquainted with hell. You can handle it."

"You have no idea."

Alejandro laughed. "Spirit and brains won't change anything. I have the stun gun." He patted his right hip, where Linh only now realized a weapon was holstered. His smile slipped as he continued. "I gotta follow orders, but I don't like it. So let's make a deal. You play along, and I'll get you out as soon as I can."

"You mean you want us to be happy little slaves, at least until next Tuesday?"

"I don't know about Tuesday, but yeah."

Ricard leaped to his feet, but before he could make another move, Alejandro drew and aimed. "These things hurt, kid, and your girlfriend would probably die of fright before you came to. Sit down."

Linh grabbed Ricard's shirt sleeve and tugged. "Please," she whimpered. "Please let us go. We haven't done anything wrong. We just want to get to Ganymede."

Pointing the gun at the ceiling, Alejandro's expression softened. "That's what bothers me. I do what I do for money. Most days, I don't care what constitutes justice. I certainly don't care about the boss's motives. Ask too many questions in this line of work, and you end up dead. But this job's been weird from the get-go. I find myself wondering what's behind it, and until I figure that out, I gotta pretend to love it. I got nothing against you. If it was up to me, you'd be on your way to Ganymede and oblivion. Good riddance.

But someone's using me. So…" He aimed at Ricard again. "We'll do this my way."

Linh squeezed her eyes shut and buried her face in Ricard's shoulder.

"You won't believe this." Samuel Lasker looked like a puppy anxious for a walk. He bounced on his toes when Petrina admitted him to her apartment. Making for Martin, he clapped his old friend on the shoulders, grinning from ear to ear. "No wonder Dr. Hernandez was branded an outlaw. He's been a very naughty boy!"

Petrina followed Samuel, and the trio stood in the middle of the gathering room, the twins anxious, Samuel giddy. Nobody spoke until Martin snapped, "Well?"

Petrina took his hand. "Calmly," she whispered. "We're all friends here."

He shot her a look of irritation. "I'm not melting down," he said. "Not yet. Out with it."

"Dr. Miguel Hernandez, your beloved mentor, Mars' very own Albert Einstein—or was it Superman?—was screwing Mayor Rand's wife."

Martin nearly choked. Petrina whispered, "Damn."

"Wait," Martin said. "Wait. How do you know?"

"I hacked into his account and—alakazam!—found messages to her. Not many and all encrypted, but easy enough to decrypt once I had his credentials. Smart people can be such idiots."

Petrina flopped onto a chair and put her hand to her forehead. Carmen Rand! Why would Dr. Hernandez have been so stupid? Had Andre Rand found out? How did the Meridiani fossils figure in? Why had the students been shot full of nanobots and tortured?

There were too many variables swimming through her brain, darting about with no coordination. Nothing made sense. She pounded her fists on the chair arms in frustration. Why couldn't she *think*?

Martin shoved his hands in his pockets and stared at the wall. "You mean," he said, his voice rumbling not unlike a lion's, "we suffered all this because he couldn't keep his damn pants zipped?"

"Sure looks like it," Samuel answered.

"I thought it was about fossils. About Sinus Meridiani. About…" Martin thumped his fist against the wall. "Damn it!"

"Don't break your hand," Samuel said. "I'm sure all that figured in. Dr. Hernandez had high-powered lawyers and activists in his pocket. An impressive operation, well organized. Seems he's got a genius for that as well as for—" He smirked. "—biology. For years, he's spent his free time shooting Andre Rand in the ass. But so what? Our illustrious mayor had him outgunned the whole time. Rand knows more dirty tricks than Satan himself. So outlawing Hernandez…" He shrugged. "That's the nuclear option and so unnecessary. Rand doesn't just want to beat Dr. Hernandez. He wants him dead. Sure sounds like jealousy to me."

Petrina barely listened. No explanation could change the basic fact: Dr. Hernandez had doomed them. Fossils, development, power struggles, none of that mattered. He'd endangered them all through reckless passion and hadn't had the courage to admit it.

Martin stalked to the kitchen. Petrina jumped when something crashed. A moment later, he returned with a cut on his right hand. He pressed a finger against it to stop the bleeding. "I know, I know, that was stupid," he said. "We have to talk to her."

Petrina took his hand to examine it. "Talk to who?"

"Carmen Rand."

"Why would she talk to us? If we accused her of…" Shaking her head, Petrina went to the bathroom for an adhesive dressing. She returned and pressed it onto the wound. "She won't talk to us."

"If she was banging him, she'll know where he went," Martin insisted.

"What's the point?" Petrina snapped. "Everything's changed. We should leave, like Ricard and Linh did. Why chase after Dr. Hernandez now?"

"Maybe to cut off his balls."

"Carmen Rand won't talk to us, Martin!"

Martin's visage took on a murderous cast. "I'll make her," he said.

Chapter 10

One didn't learn the art of control—gauging a subject's fears and desires, enticing without promising, threatening without overt cruelty—from books and lectures but from experience, and as with all art, masters possessed an innate superiority. Hitomi was a master almost without equal, but now she stood in the presence of one greater. Here, her instincts were for naught. Her superior, her commander, her mistress, lurked in the shadows, unseen and unreadable. An awe bordering on love filled Hitomi's soul.

She had no choice in her feelings. Everything was calculated to elicit them. The wall swept about her in a great, dark circle twelve meters in diameter, dead black save glitters of gold tracing its junction with the floor. A waterfall of concentrated illumination poured down from on high. It crashed upon Hitomi's elegant body, drowning her in white, blinding her. She stood at the center of the universe witnessing its creation, while its creator looked on, a shadow moving in the dark. She felt that shadow study her, possibly curious, dangerous of a certain. Hitomi knew the watcher's power, even knew her name, a name she'd been forbidden to speak until the time of revelation.

That time was coming. Soon.

"Oh, Hitomi," the watcher sighed. Her filtered voice sounded metallic and distant. The words were clear, but no true feeling animated them, only an electronic sigh of pleasure, a false emotion born of a randomizing algorithm. "You're a gem."

The praise may have been genuine or sarcastic. Hitomi, hoping for the former, conjured a vision of sunlight glinting on water.

She had known that sight once, long ago as a child. She called upon it whenever she needed detachment. "Thank you, madam."

"A gem polished to perfection, revealing the fire within." The voice dipped into the bass and echoed from the encircling wall, twisted and malignant.

"I only desire to please you, madam."

"Hmm." A fragment of laughter accompanied the sound. A soft, gentle finger slipped along Hitomi's left cheek. She pushed aside the instinct to flinch and the desire to melt with pleasure. "You do, indeed. But now I require nothing short of magic."

"I shall perform it."

"I want Mars."

Had it been Hitomi's to give, she would have delivered it at once, but Mars remained wild, untamed. Not even Andre Rand's tiny slice had been fully subdued. "What must I do?"

"Reunite what has been scattered."

Hitomi bowed. Magic, indeed! So much had been scattered, and some remained lost.

"You seem dismayed," the shadow said in a voice like the twitter of birds.

"No, madam. I am humbled by your faith."

"Do you doubt yourself?"

Rising, Hitomi said, "I will do whatever you ask."

The shadow withdrew. From a great distance, the voice replied, "I know. And don't fear. I'll be with you. Always."

The light in which Hitomi stood failed, leaving her in darkness. Then a glare of white flooded the great room, momentarily blinding her. As her eyes adjusted, through half-open lids she glimpsed a door slide open and a dark figure slip through. Before the door closed, the figure glanced back, and Hitomi saw a beautiful jet-black face, the face of a dark angel with smoldering eyes and a hint of brilliant white teeth glistening behind dark lips parted in amusement.

The half dome stood empty now, no furnishings, no décor, nothing but Hitomi. Tears filled her eyes. She'd been blessed with a glimpse of the unseen. She would do anything for her dark mistress now. She *could* do anything. Because that shadow, that vision, that angel of power stood guard over her. How could she fail?

"Don't split up the set."

Short, overweight, wearing a grimy jumpsuit and a tangled beard, the buyer laughed. "Set, huh." He leered at the woman, oblivious to the ice in her companion's eyes.

Alejandro Carrasco clapped a hand on the man's shoulder and squeezed until the fellow winced. "I mean it. That girl's brains are cracked glass. Separate 'em, and you'll have to fry 'em both, her to stop the screaming and him so he don't rip out your liver. A waste of good money just to save your worthless skin."

The buyer knocked Carrasco's hand away, calculating how badly he'd been ripped off. "Why didn't you say that before?"

"*Caveat emptor*, friend. A pleasure doing business with you." Carrasco saluted and sauntered off.

The buyer glared after him, then set his hands on his hips and frowned at Ricard Fulbert and Quan Linh, seated on the floor with their hands bound behind them and ankles shackled before them. "Fine," he decided, "but no trouble, or I *will* fry you. Stefan! Get the hell over here and in-process these two. They're yours. They work together."

Stefan, a towering bundle of muscle, stopped before the students and gave them a peeved examination. "You're kidding, right?"

"Do I look it?"

"This girl won't last a day on the crew. What the hell you expect 'em to do, sweep the floors?"

"The seller said they're smart. Give 'em something brainy to do." The buyer waddled off, no longer interested.

"Brainy," Stefan grumped. "You'll crack rocks, like everyone else. But don't get yourselves killed, or he'll take it outta my feed. Think smart thoughts for a bit. I'll be back."

Linh leaned into Ricard and whimpered. They were alone now in a small cavern, backs against the rough rock wall, all but immobilized by the weighted manacles. The air smelled of rock dust. Ricard wondered if it was safe to breathe. Their new owners hadn't worn filters, but he wasn't sure that meant anything.

Nor did he know what to tell Linh. Alejandro had warned them to keep silent about their earlier conversation. Once he had them in tow, he could no longer risk jamming the nanobot's signals, so whoever was listening would hear everything they said. Play dumb, Alejandro ordered. They'd been captured and sold into slavery through greed, and as far as they knew that was the end of their careers, if not their lives. They would never see Alejandro again, never reach Ganymede, never return to Mars, never be free.

Alejandro had declined to mention what they would be, other than slaves. Until now, they hadn't even known slavery existed in the Belt. By all the laws they knew, it shouldn't.

"I can't do this," Linh whispered. Her voice quivered in his ear.

"You can," Ricard insisted. "I won't leave you. We'll face it together."

"But what if—"

"Don't speculate. We don't know anything yet." He kissed her hair to reassure and calm her. His touch worked its magic; she relaxed a little. If they hadn't been manacled, he would have wrapped her in his arms and kept her safe from…everything. Linh was all he cared about. He should have told her so, should have shown her so. He'd wasted the past few nights overthinking their relationship.

She closed her eyes. "Maybe we don't want to know."

"Don't worry."

"Why am I such a mess? Am I permanently damaged, or is it those damned—"

Ricard kissed her lips to stop her mentioning the nanobots. And because he wanted to. Her eyes widened with surprise. "You just need time," he said. "Stay positive. Make jokes, like you used to."

Linh gave him a crooked smile. "Is that your prescription, Doctor? Jokes and kisses?"

"It is."

He'd been serious, but as so often happened, she laughed, and he couldn't help but smile in return.

"I'll do my best," she promised.

A shadow passed over them. Stefan had returned, still irritated. Maybe it was them, or maybe he was always angry. "Glad you find this funny," he said. "We're gonna indoctrinate you now, then you'll be as miserable as everyone else. Listen up. Rule number one: do what you're told. That goes for where you stand, where you don't stand, when and what you eat, when you sleep, and every other damn thing you do." He leered at Ricard. "Including jumping her."

Had he been able, Ricard would have wrapped the chain around Stefan's neck and hung him.

"Rule number two. Break rule number one, and you get a taste of this." Stefan thrust out his right hand. In his curled fingers, he held a small black stick much like the torture devices Lowell security had used.

Linh's eyes widened in terror, and she tried to push herself through the rock. "No, no, no," she whimpered. "Please, no, please!" Ricard all but threw himself at her to block her view of the device, but the chains yanked taught and dug into his flesh.

Stefan pocketed the stick. "I guess we won't have any problems, will we?"

"No problems," Ricard said, "unless you keep frightening her."

Stefan kicked Ricard in the ribs. Ricard grunted but continued to face down his captor. "I got other ways of keeping you in line," Stefan threatened, "but that stick is always waiting. Trust me, you don't wanna give me an excuse. Death comes slow when I'm motivated. On your feet." He took another device from his pocket, this one a small silver disc, and pressed his thumb to its surface. Linh and Ricard's shackles disengaged and fell off with a crash.

Ricard stood and helped Linh up. She leaned heavily on him, vacant eyes trained on the ground.

"What the hell's her problem?"

"Allergies." Ricard put his arm around her to hold her up.

Stefan sneered but must have decided killing them before they'd done any work wasn't the way to impress the boss. "Keep in mind," he snapped, "you're on a smallish asteroid with few pressurized facilities, cameras everywhere, and no way off. Come on." He struck off deeper into the cave, moving at a pace Ricard couldn't hope to match with Linh leaning on him.

"Not so fast!" Ricard called.

Stefan's reply was nearly inaudible. "Keep walking. You'll know when to stop."

"Ricard?" Linh whimpered.

"It's okay. That device wasn't …" No, he couldn't even hint that he knew about the nanobots. "They don't know what happened on Mars. They couldn't. They're just miners."

"I'm going to throw up."

He guided her to the side of the cave and held her up until the retching stopped.

Samuel Lasker improved his design and delivered to Petrina and Martin pocketable devices that handled both scanning and jamming. Warning them not to lose the units, he removed himself from the affair so as not to become a target. Petrina couldn't blame him. If Lowell Security cared to know, they'd have no trouble figuring out why the signals stopped.

Complicating matters, Martin was on a mission. He rented a rover from a low-end dealer on the outskirts of the colony and drove his sister to the most famous residence on the planet: Carmen Rand's private home. Petrina tried to dissuade him. The first lady might not be there. If she was and by some miracle admitted them, she might not know anything. Mentioning Dr. Hernandez would be dangerous. Just being there would be dangerous.

Martin wouldn't listen. "She's his lover," he insisted. "If anyone knows where he is, she does. And she's damn well going to tell us."

"Let's not add assault and battery to our profile," Petrina scolded. "Or murder."

He grimaced at the red sands. The rover rolled on.

In due course, they arrived before the façade in the cliff. Petrina had to admit, it was a stunning piece of work. It blended so well with sand and stone, it was all but invisible unless viewed from the right angles, and then the whole of the cliff seemed of human design.

"Where's the airlock?" she wondered aloud.

"It's there somewhere. Suit up. We'll bang on the rock until we find it."

"Fine, but if we get inside, I do the talking."

"You can't even think straight."

"At least I don't demolish the furniture. Her footstools probably cost more than we'll make in both our lifetimes."

"You always have to give the orders, don't you?"

"Because I'm way older than you. Twelve whole minutes." Petrina gave him a sarcastic smile. He didn't appreciate it.

Guests didn't just drop by, and if they did, Carmen only admitted those she knew. This pair, though, proved stubborn to the point of idiocy. They wandered the base of the cliff for an hour, one knocking on the rock here and there, the other trailing like a useless appendage. Whatever their story, it must be interesting, or at least unusual. Giving in to curiosity, Carmen activated a voice channel. It scanned their communications and picked up the frequency on which they were talking.

"Who the hell are you?" she said, lightly so as not to startle them. It didn't work. On the vid, they jumped and caught at each other to avoid falling. Carmen laughed.

"We want to speak to the first lady," a female voice said. She sounded young and unsure of herself.

"Why?"

"It's about Dr. Hernandez," the other said. A man, equally young but with a rough edge.

"Martin!" his companion scolded.

"She's his lover. We know she is." One of the figures looked toward the top of the cliff. "We know you are!"

Subtle bastard, Andre was, sending a couple of kids to do his dirty work, knowing they'd be as delicate as a bomb blast. She was supposed to think they couldn't possibly be his agents. Fine. She knew how to play. "What interests you? Quality? Technique? Size?"

"Oh, God," the woman said in a half-whisper. "Just stop, Martin. Please." Louder, she added, "We just want to talk. We're his students."

Students, sure. Students would be the last to know about Miguel's dalliances. "I caught Martin. What's your name?"

The long pause suggested either she hadn't made one up yet or her comm link had dropped out. "Petrina," she said. "Martin's my brother."

Carmen knew that pair of names. Miguel had indeed mentioned them somewhere along the line, but she couldn't recall details. On the vid, the suited figures waited, faces tilted toward the cliff top as though they honestly didn't know the location of the airlock, as though Carmen's voice had floated down from on high. Who *were* they?

She tapped a control, and the airlock slid open. "What the hell," she said. "I like a bit of surreal in my day."

They entered. She cycled the outer door shut, pressurized the chamber, and opened the inner door. Still on comm, she instructed,

"Suits off. Hang them on the hooks in the airlock. My staff hates dust." Or at least, it clogged their filters something awful.

Carmen made them wait fifteen minutes before making her way to the huge gathering room. She found them awestruck among the soft greens and blues, the *objets d'art*, the elegant furnishings. They didn't notice her at first, and she smiled at the wonder in their eyes. That, anyway, was genuine. It was nice to be appreciated for a change.

"Petrina, Martin, how wonderful to finally meet you. Miguel often spoke of you."

"Did he," Martin said. "He never once mentioned you."

"No," she agreed. "He wouldn't. Care for a drink?" She motioned to the small bar at the side of the room. "I'm always serving drinks, it seems, so I'm always drinking, probably too much."

"No," Petrina said a bit too quickly. "But thank you." She glanced at Martin before adding, "My brother has a medical condition."

"Oh? That must be inconvenient. But let's at least be comfortable." Motioning to a couch, Carmen sat in an opposing wing chair and waited for her guests to be seated. Once they were, she added, "If Miguel never mentioned me, how is it you know about us?"

Martin leaned forward to speak. Anger and mayhem flashed in his eyes until Petrina put her hand on his. He leaned back, miffed but without voicing objection.

"That doesn't matter," Petrina said. "We just need to find him. It's important. We hoped you'd know where he was."

If she was lying, she was good at it, but no matter. Carmen was comfortable speaking the truth about Miguel. "He didn't tell me where he went, and honestly, Petrina, he had good reason to disappear. Don't chase him. You'll only get hurt."

Martin slapped his thigh. "She already got hurt! We all did! They arrested us and tortured us and dumped us on the street!"

The outburst surprised Carmen, but she was practiced at hiding her reactions. With a sympathetic bow of her head, she rose and went to the bar. "Are you sure I can't make you a drink? I think you need one. I sure do."

She could hear Martin's ragged breath and Petrina's whispered pleas for calm. Since neither requested anything, she poured white wine for herself and returned to her seat, setting the glass on a table at her side.

"I'm sorry," she said. "But then, you see how dangerous it is to even talk about Miguel, much less associate with him. I liked him, but he always was a dangerous man, the sort who doesn't know how or when to give up, the sort who becomes either an emperor or a martyr." Taking up her glass, she gazed into the pale liquid. "Believe me. I've had both."

While Martin struggled to contain his rage, Petrina stroked his fingers and studied Carmen's face. Gauging the first lady's truthfulness? Wondering if she posed a threat? Whatever the young woman sought, her frown said it eluded her.

"You don't trust me," Carmen suggested. "I'm not shocked."

"That we were tortured doesn't shock you, either," Petrina said. "It should."

Carmen took a drink before answering. "Andre's ruthless when he wants something, and he wants to find Miguel as badly as you. He's even keeping an eye on me."

Martin was still shaking despite Petrina's ministry. "Then he knew about you and Dr. Hernandez?"

"Of course. He didn't care about the affair, but nobody stands in the way of Andre's ambition. He's the same as Miguel, really. That's the problem."

"He knows we're here?" Petrina turned to Martin. "I told you we shouldn't have come!"

"He knows you're here," Carmen acknowledged, "but not why or what we're saying. He'll ask me soon enough."

"What will you tell him?"

"The truth. That you were worried about Dr. Hernandez, but I couldn't help you, so you left disappointed. Naturally, he'll want to know why you thought I of all people could help." She raised her eyebrows to prompt them, knowing full well they wouldn't oblige. No matter. She'd already guessed. Miguel must have left some incriminating bit of evidence hanging about, probably in his electronic files.

"You like telling the truth," Petrina replied evenly. "Say you don't know."

"There, see? You know the game." Carmen took another drink. "Forget Miguel. That's what he wanted. He left us in the dark so we wouldn't get hurt, which was decent of him, don't you think?"

"We can't forget him," Petrina insisted. "We must find him. For several reasons."

Carmen stared into her wine. "I drink too damn much," she mused. "That's probably why I can't remember what you just said."

Chapter 11

Watching Martin pilot the rover back to Lowell Colony, Petrina experienced a minor revelation. Whenever Martin's rage rose, his breathing slipped into deliberate, forced cadence, and the tide reversed. Of course. Breathing exercises were used in stress, anxiety, and anger management. Why hadn't she thought of that before? Could the practice help with her mental fog? It was worth a shot.

Back in Martin's apartment, she sat at the small kitchen table, eyes closed, hands folded on the tabletop, mind empty, each breath measured. At first, she found it hard to maintain focus. Her thoughts flitted about like a starving insect desperately searching a field of wilting flowers for one still offering nectar. Impatience nearly convinced her to give up, but fear spurred her on, fear that if this didn't work, she'd never find herself again.

Time passed without her knowing. Her mind stilled until the mental fog dissipated. Then, like the sun emerging with the passing of a sandstorm, something occurred to her, something so simple, so obvious, the realization nearly knocked her from her chair.

She opened her eyes. "Martin?"

Martin was flopped on the couch, his dark form sprawled without care, his gaze on the ceiling, his fingers twitching. "Huh?"

"I know where Dr. Hernandez went."

He rolled onto his side and craned his neck. "What?"

"Remember what he said about having friends in the wilderness?"

"No."

"About a year ago, the west Meridiani expedition?"

Martin sat and gave her a "you're cracked" look.

"Settlers and smugglers. He knew some of them, and sometimes they helped him. That's what he said. He said they knew we were there, they watched us pass by, but he didn't dare introduce us."

"I don't remember that," Martin said.

"I do. At the time I thought he was joking, trying to scare us. But it wasn't a joke. That's where he's gone."

"Of course it was a joke, Petrina."

"It's the only place. Carmen Rand said he didn't want anyone to know where he went, but there's no place to hide on Mars. He couldn't stay in Lowell or at his house or even at hers. There's no place he couldn't be found other than the wilderness. Think about it. Who in their right mind would look for him out there, even if they thought to look?"

Martin squeezed his eyes shut as though in pain.

"What's wrong?" Petrina asked.

"You want to go."

"Yes."

"So, you're saying we're not in our right minds."

That didn't deserve an answer. Petrina had found her mind for the first time since this began.

"Great," Martin said. "All we have to do is search the whole damn planet."

"Just our expedition routes. Remember? He said he wasn't abandoning the research. He must be trying to get to Meridiani. If we can find even one person who's seen him, we can track him down."

Martin came to the table and sat across from Petrina. "Cross the wilderness to find someone he didn't dare let us meet. Great plan, Petrina."

"Actually," she said, "it's brilliant. We're doing it."

"Brilliant? You said you couldn't think. Ever since..." He choked back the words.

"Breathing exercises. I saw you doing them."

He thought about that. "That was only half intentional, but you're right, they do work."

Reaching across the table and taking his hand, she squeezed his fingers. "Let's do this."

"I guess I can't say no, but do we want to find him? What he did..." Martin shook his head.

"It wasn't what we thought. Andre Rand knew and didn't care."

"I don't mean that. Dr. Hernandez knew what was coming."

Petrina felt a flush of embarrassment. "He told us to leave. We ignored him."

"Yeah, but he wasn't honest about it. Not fully. He could have warned us, but he didn't. And here we are."

Petrina had to give Martin that. Dr. Hernandez hadn't been the role model any of them thought. "When we find him," she said, "you can deliver his performance evaluation." She hoped that would make him laugh.

It didn't. If anything, his gloom increased. "I wish we'd gone with Ricard and Linh," he said. "We'd all be on our way to Ganymede in blissful ignorance."

Petrina squeezed his hand again. "We've lost our innocence," she agreed, "but maybe that makes us stronger. And yes, I do want to find him. I want to know the truth."

"What truth?"

"Who the hell he really is."

Rays of sunlight filtered into the office, muted by the roof's dusky transparency. Beneath, uniformed security monitors swarmed in a compact honeycomb of walled compartments as they tracked, analyzed, reported. This was Lowell Colony Security's brain. Data poured in and was processed into operations designed to impose order on a disorderly citizenry.

The Commercial and Criminal Divisions occupied the bulk of the space, with the tiny Political Division huddled in the core. PoliDiv may have looked insignificant, but Subcommander Leah Leaf and her three subordinates held more power than the other two divisions combined. Every monitor longed to work for her. These were Mayor Andre Rand's wolves, and he fed them well. Leah herself had been tapped as Security Commander for the soon-to-be-built Schiaparelli Colony. Beneath the transparent roof, she basked in suns real and metaphorical.

But today, a dust cloud overhung her future. The threat algorithm had dropped Ricard Fulbert and Quan Linh off the political hotlist and deleted them from monitoring. As indentured servants in the Belt, they posed no further danger to Lowell Colony. That was good. But simultaneously, Petrina and Martin Ulenga rocketed to the top, raising more alarms than even Dr. Miguel Hernandez. That shouldn't have happened. Leah felt her promotion sinking in the Martian sands.

She studied the system's explanation on her panel. Dr. Gene Lloyd told the Ulengas about the nanobots. Afterward, their trackers and listeners suffered sporadic outages. Possibly a technical flaw.

It happened sometimes, and the Ulengas did nothing noteworthy while the devices worked. But coupled with their outing to Carmen Rand—when the nanobots conveniently failed—Leah had reason to assume the worst: the Ulengas had learned to jam the devices.

She couldn't touch Carmen Rand. She could only escalate that incident to her husband. But Martin and Petrina were hers, and they appeared hellbent on sabotaging Leah's future. After nine years as subcommander, promotion lay in her grasp. The Ulenga twins would *not* steal it from her. She ordered a sandstorm of actions to take them down.

Search the Ulengas' apartments. Confiscate all electronics.

Detain and interrogate all known contacts.

Arrest anyone suspected of tampering with their nanobot transmissions.

Arrest the Ulengas.

Subject them to full physical searches, mental probes, and nano-assisted interrogations. And when all was done…

…execute them.

They would *not* sabotage Leah's future!

Part one was done. Alejandro had intercepted the kids and sold them into slavery, where they'd be uncomfortable but forgotten until he returned. Now for part two: convincing the environmentalist to forget Alejandro, too.

This was the important bit. Everything that came after depended upon it. With her gaze fixed upon him, Alejandro could do nothing but her bidding. She was a ghost, slipping up unseen and whispering an arctic breeze through your soul. Alejandro therefore behaved like a well-paid but terrified minion. Fleeing Itokawa Station, he piloted his personal skiff further into the Belt to Vegas Station and there blew obscene amounts of money on a luxury apartment, rich food, high-stakes gambling, and high-end prostitutes. Twelve days of excess later, having detected no sign of the environmentalist's attentions, he pre-paid his rent for a further six months to signal his intent to continue a life of debauchery, then quietly—with the aid of a few bribes—set course for Mars.

Aside from his recent in-and-out mission to destroy the hydro station, he hadn't set foot on the planet for thirteen years. His career on Mars hadn't made him popular. By the time he fled, the list of enemies thirsting for his blood was impressive even without his outlaw status. Thank God at least one smuggler had been willing to exchange cash for safe passage. He didn't know what to expect upon his return. Like the Belt, Mars changed people, made them forget who they were and where they'd been. He might find himself welcomed, forgotten, or hunted. And if the environmentalist had lied about fixing his status?

Somebody would die.

Regardless, he had two solid possibilities, a pair of old acquaintances who might yet look on him with favor. The first, strange as it seemed, was the daughter of a good friend and sharp smuggler. His friend had been killed in a firefight with authorities a month before Alejandro fled. The young woman had her father's fire and drive. It was all Alejandro, her honorary uncle, could do to talk her out of a suicidal act of revenge. Nessa, she was called, Nessa O'Clery. Alejandro hoped she hadn't flown blind into the sandstorm after his precipitous disappearance.

The other was a self-styled prospector boring holes in Mars beyond the fringes of Lowell Colony. Speaking no English, Jarek

Zoric—a.k.a. Jake—kept himself apart from most people. When necessary, he relied on his pretty younger sister Mlada to translate. Alejandro secretly had a thing for Mlada, but he never let on. He doubted Jake would have approved, and he wasn't a man you wanted to anger. Anyway, Mlada's devotion to her brother crowded out any interest she might have had in finding a partner of her own.

Alejandro figured either Nessa or Jake would shelter him. With luck, they might even have some news of Miguel's whereabouts. And when he found Miguel? That depended on the story. Who knew? Alejandro might even help him.

If he didn't kill him.

Physical labor was easy on most of the rocks floating in the Belt. Low gravity had its benefits. But as Ricard and Linh learned, profits drove everything here. Fueled by too little sleep and barely adequate food, slaves endured excessive work periods with no protection from hazards.

Stefan's muscular bulk towered over the thirty slaves in his charge. He snarled orders at the start of each shift and at the end barked at the sloppy work and inadequate haul. In between, he left supervision to a small gang of armed guards he called bulls. Punishments were mercifully few if only because the slaves had nowhere to run and nothing to do but work. And he had that black box, which he waved under their noses if anyone as much as hinted at slacking off or causing trouble. Ricard was certain it had nothing to do with nanobot control, but it proved effective. Everyone shrank before it.

The slaves worked laying track upon which a heavy extractor was maneuvered down the tunnels. The extractor fired finger-thin energy beams into the rock, boring holes into which larger surges were poured, causing the rock to rapidly heat and explode. The whole asteroid shuddered under the concussion as rock chunks pummeled the tunnel. You didn't want to be caught too close to the blast zone. Once, a rain of stone pelted one of the female slaves who had tarried too long behind the extractor. She lay on the rock ground, semi-conscious, for three hours while the work proceeded around her. When Stefan returned, he snarled at her clumsiness and shot her dead.

"Damn waste of labor!" he railed once the body had been removed. "Watch what the hell you're doing!"

Ricard never strayed from Linh's side and always rushed her well beyond the blast zone before the extractor sequence was initiated.

After explosions came the laborious process of loading fragmented rock into automated rail carts, which trundled back up the track with their cargo. The slaves were given no equipment. Loading was done manually, but in the low gravity they could heft even large boulders. It just took time and care. They spent most of their hours lifting and loading and grew quite sore by the end of the shift. Once the rock was removed, more track was laid, and the extractor pushed forward for another shot.

Food, such as it was, was given them in the pressurized, temperature-controlled tunnels where they worked. They slept there, too, in pitch dark, clad in their filthy rags. Some took advantage of the dark to pair up for sex. Ricard held Linh through the night so she felt safe, but they never went farther, even though small sounds of pleasure whispering through the cave sometimes aroused them.

Strangely, Linh's terrors receded as the days dragged on and the full weight of their circumstances settled on her. Ricard noticed but didn't remark on the change until she broached the subject herself after a work period that dragged on longer than most, sixteen hours by Ricard's reckoning.

"It's the breathing," she whispered as he held her in the dark.

"Breathing?"

"When you're lifting and hauling and dumping, you breathe more deliberately. I started paying attention. The focus, the awareness, I don't know. It calms me."

"Makes sense," Ricard said. "Breathing routines are used in some cognitive therapies."

"The next time Stefan shoves that black stick in our faces, I'm doing it. If it helps, I'll smack his eyes out of their sockets with a rock."

"That should help, too."

He wasn't joking, and she knew it, but she laughed quietly. "You can't help it, can you?"

"I suppose not."

"We're such a perfect match."

She felt his face turn toward her in the darkness.

"Are we?" he asked.

"You too serious, me never quite enough. Not when I'm myself, at least."

Ricard said nothing. She felt his breath on her cheek.

"I'm glad we left Mars together," she added. "I don't know what I would do without you."

What was going through his head? He gave her no indication. His breath felt warm on her skin as his arms kept firm hold on her, yet he said nothing. Maybe she shouldn't have spoken so?

Finally, his lips brushed her cheek in a gentle kiss. "When we get out of here," he began, but the thought seemed to vanish in the dark.

"Will we?"

"We will. Carrasco said he'd come back for us. I don't know why, but I believe him. Something about him is strangely like Dr. Hernandez."

"His face, for one thing," Linh agreed.

"And his manner. He's not entirely the mercenary. And Dr. Hernandez is a bit the mercenary. Does that make any sense?"

She laughed. "No. But when we get out of here. What then?"

"Marry me."

Linh rolled onto her side. Their foreheads touched. "Really?"

"Really."

Such an odd thing to say in such a horrid place, but it was exactly the moment Ricard would pick, wasn't it? She laughed again and kissed him on the lips.

"I assume that means yes," he said, as serious as ever.

"It does. But the consummation comes after the ceremony. No way are we doing it here."

She felt him smirk even though his voice remained grave. "Yes, ma'am."

A dust storm blew over the Tempe region, keeping Miguel inside the crater-rim base for six days. That gave him time to process samples, although his mind wasn't on the work. He expected nothing from these rocks, and they delivered it. No fossils, no useful minerals in useful quantities. The good stuff, from Nessa O'Clery's viewpoint, was farther south, in the Tharsis region, while what he sought was in Sinus Meridiani, soon to be home to a sprawling new colony.

Between processing and analysis sessions, Miguel studied the rover schematics and searched out weaknesses in the governors that kept them within Nessa's boundaries. Tampering, he discovered, would trigger a total systems shutdown. No way around it. He needed an alternative to sabotage. Once he realized that, the solution slapped him in the face: call for a ride. That would be simple. He had everything he needed to build a scanner and a transceiver. He could locate transmissions, raise a friendly settler, and arrange for rendezvous and rescue.

Okay, not entirely simple. Given the complexity of the Martian ionosphere, you couldn't be sure your signals would land where you wanted. Worse, Miguel might spend months trying to raise a sympathetic soul, only to find himself in contact with the likes of Carl Metzler and Jane Bonsell, who had handed him off to Nessa in the first place. But it was worth a shot. As the storm blew on, he built his device and packaged it to look like part of his survey equipment.

Finally, the winds exhausted themselves, and the airborne sand settled to ground. Miguel readied for another outing. Before leaving, he went to the medical section to visit Dr. Emil Sarkozy, the injured geologist who had paid a heavy price for his own escape attempt. When he came to Emil's room, he found it empty. The bed was stripped, the room sanitized, leaving no trace of its former occupant. Turning to leave, Miguel found Nessa leaning against the door jamb, arms crossed over her chest.

"He's alive, I hope?" Miguel asked.

"All better," Nessa said, "and wiser for the experience."

"I hoped to see him before I head out again."

"Sorry to disappoint you. He's gone to Tharsis. He'll be there for some time. Any luck in Tempe?"

Miguel shook his head.

"Pity, but not surprising. Emil told me this region was probably a waste of time." She motioned him to follow. They left the medical section and passed down the curving main corridor. "Jake says you know Carmen Rand."

Damn him.

"Socially or sexually?" Nessa asked.

He glanced at her. She was dead serious. "Yes."

Nessa walked on, ruminating. "I never met the woman, but I sense she and I have commonalities. Does she hate her husband?"

"No, but neither does she love him. Not in any normal sense. I suppose it's a kind of love. Theirs is a marriage of convenience. Her image is convenient to his image, and his wealth and power is convenient to her lifestyle."

"Didn't sleeping with you threaten her lifestyle?"

"We didn't broadcast the fact."

Nessa grinned and punched him in the arm. "I know, idiot. But Rand watches everything."

"She told me he didn't care."

"So why outlaw you?"

"We wanted the same piece of land."

Nessa shook her head. "Same piece of ass was fine, same piece of land wasn't. Men are weird." They came to Miguel's apartment. "Invite me in," she ordered.

He palmed the door open. "Please, come in."

"Thank you."

Inside, she settled on the couch and motioned him to sit beside her. "You're still thinking about escape."

No point in either confirming or denying it.

"You'll make for Sinus Meridiani, hoping to find more fossils before construction starts."

Likewise. What was she driving at?

Nessa got a faraway look as she absently tangled her fingers in her red curls. "You're too late. Word is, they broke ground this morning. I'd say I'm sorry, but I'm not. Now you have no reason to leave. Unless you're itching to see your rich lady friend again?"

The news hit him like a gut punch. He thought he had more time. "She'd be forced to turn me in. Neither of us want that."

"What if you could meet on neutral ground?"

Why would Nessa arrange that? "I wouldn't call this neutral ground."

"Nor would Carmen Rand. But would she visit you in a thieves' den anyway?"

The suggestion irked him. Nessa was playing on his presumed feelings for Carmen to get something. No, it more than irked him. He resented it. "What do you want, Nessa, to watch us get it on?"

She laughed. "You're cute when you're angry. I want certain people to stay away from certain places. Take Jake. He wants Andre Rand dead. Sooner or later, he'll defy me to make that happen, even if it means his own life. But I don't want Rand dead."

"Why not?"

"Because I don't want Jake dead."

Miguel supposed that made sense.

"Other thing is," Nessa continued, "too many scouts and trackers have disappeared out here. Eventually, someone will figure out there's gold in them thar hills. Rand would love to confiscate my Tharsis mines. If Carmen could keep him distracted, I'd bargain with her in a heartbeat."

He heard, but the point wasn't what caught his attention. "You found extractable gold?"

She gave him a disappointed look. "No."

"Then what?"

"You think I'd tell you?"

Of course not. Nessa had no illusions about Miguel's trustworthiness. But he wouldn't barter with Andre Rand, either. His life wasn't for sale, nor was Rand buying.

Once more sensing his thoughts, Nessa leaned sideways and rested her head on his shoulder. She rolled her eyes up and batted her eyelashes. Damn, she felt like Mona even though the resemblance was purely in attitude. Mona had been Egyptian, with dark hair and dark eyes and…

Miguel wanted to look away but couldn't.

Nessa's theatrics were in jest, but what she asked wasn't. "Would Carmen Rand manipulate her husband for you?"

"She'd manipulate him for her own sake. Probably not for mine. She gave me no more than occasional bits of information."

"That's not what I heard." Nessa winked and rose. "Don't run off, Miguel. We need each other, and frankly, you've nothing left but me."

Which wasn't quite true. He had his transceiver and friends in the wilderness. He could still escape. But to what end? If Meridiani was already a construction zone, his hope of obtaining more fossils dwindled by the hour. And he had to admit, seeing Carmen again would lighten his spirit.

But what would be the cost?

Chapter 12

A month ago, Alejandro touched down on Mars as an outlaw arriving illegally to commit an act of destruction. Now he came as an ordinary citizen—assuming the environmentalist hadn't lied—looking for an old friend. He passed through Lowell spaceport without raising alarms, so either Security's facial recognition scans didn't pick him out or they planned to nab him on the quiet. He booked a room in the low-rent district on Lowell's east side, set up rudimentary security, and waited for the midnight ambush. It never came. He wandered the colony, browsing shops, dining at mid-range restaurants, and touring the flashy environs of the new Casino Acidalia. He even played the randomizers long enough to lose several fistfuls of obols. He could afford it. Watching for pursuit, he saw nothing save a pickpocket having a successful day with her electronic skimmer in the casino.

So. The environmentalist had played fair. Mars no longer cared about him.

Now Alejandro could pursue his true objective: the region west of Lowell, where decades before a scattering of settlers had pushed beyond the colony's boundaries. Some scouted the terrain. Others prospected for minerals. A few built hydro stations to supplement the colony's main water supplies. They weren't rogues, just entrepreneurs with grand visions and little luck. None ever struck it rich, as far as Alejandro knew.

Jarek Zoric and his sister Mlada were among them. Jarek, who went by Jake, hunted metal-bearing clays. He spoke no English, so Mlada did his talking. "Aluminum," she told Alejandro when he asked what Jake was after, "and whatever else the colony will buy." When Jake located a modest titanium deposit, obsession blossomed. A mother lode, he was sure, slumbered below his feet. He never found it. The whole time Alejandro knew them, the Zorics scratched a living from the sterile Martian soil. To her credit, Mlada encouraged Jake to keep looking. Lowell Colony had never been her kind of place anyway. The wilderness suited her.

Thirteen years had changed the west end. Alejandro found the colony expanded far beyond the borders he knew. Corporate offices built in poor imitation of famed architect Yago Moncayo's naturalist style sprawled there now, and the low rise where Jake and Mlada had built their home stood empty a mere quarter kilometer beyond. Alejandro rented a rover and spent a day exploring the region. From the top of a crater rim, he spotted ruddy dust blowing high on the Martian winds. He lifted his televiewers and examined the land below, discovering a fenced mining operation crawling with automated machinery. Had Jake struck it rich, after all?

Alejandro returned to his dump of an apartment late in the day. At the kitchen table with a dinner of what appeared to be chicken and rice but probably wasn't, he activated his panel and researched Lowell's mining companies. Unlike the Belt, where mines proliferated like cockroaches, only three held licenses on Mars: Acidalia Industries, Polar Mining, and the newest entry, Zoric Minerals.

Well, hell, Jake, he thought. *You actually did it!*

The next morning, Alejandro travelled cross-colony to renew his acquaintance with the lucky bastard. Zoric Minerals occupied one of those new buildings on the west side, not the largest but certainly the fanciest, with a façade of mirror-sheen metal and translucent windows that gave the curious appearance of Martian sand.

Inside, everything was sunlight and electronics. The reception staff, life-size projections on a nearly invisible panel, felt almost real. A simulated black woman with a charming smile and beautiful voice asked Alejandro how she could help him. *Marry me*, he thought while searching for his voice. Fortunately, virtual people couldn't grow impatient.

"I'm here to see Jarek Zoric," he said.

The simulated woman ran her fingers over a simulated desk-top tablet. "I'm sorry, I can't locate anyone by that name."

"Jake Zoric, then."

She fiddled again with the imaginary device. "I'm sorry, sir. I can't locate that name, either."

He couldn't see Mlada as an executive, but he tried her name as well.

"No, sir, I'm sorry."

Virtual people couldn't lose patience, but Alejandro could. "Then who owns the damned company?"

"Zoric Minerals is publicly owned. The majority shareholder is CEO Andre Rand. He doesn't maintain an office here. Can I direct you to someone else?"

That made no sense. Jake wouldn't have sold out to Rand, not for the whole of Mars. "Forget it," he decided.

"Thank you, sir. Have a nice day."

"Go to hell. The wedding's off." Alejandro stalked out of the office, unsure what to do next. If Jake's house was gone and the company bearing his name didn't know he existed…

Damn. Maybe he didn't.

State dinner, Andre's message said. *Dress nice.*

A command, not a request. Attend, and dress *nice*.

He hadn't always talked to Carmen that way. Once, she'd been his confidant and ally, not a trained seal performing cute tricks to amuse his adoring subjects. Worse, *dress nice* was code of sorts, informing her that in the company of hugely important people, the Rands would dine on fare only Andre could afford while surrounded by videographers intent upon documenting his wife's cleavage. The circus atmosphere would distract everyone from the real purpose of the event, which no doubt involved bribery or other undue influence in a bid to secure some triviality Andre couldn't live without.

She hated those dinners, but she'd play her part as always. She'd dress nice, all right. She'd outshine the sun. The whole universe. Blinded by her daring and beauty, nobody would pay attention to Andre, not even whoever he was bribing. It would serve him right.

She picked a dress meant for Andre's eyes alone, a flame-red cascade of off-the-shoulder silk with a neckline that plunged to her navel and a short skirt with sides slit to her hips. She'd had it tailored for their anniversary two years back, but politics cancelled their intimate retreat, and in anger she refused to wear it thereafter. He'd never seen it. But if he insisted on putting her under surveillance and ordering her about like a dog, then he deserved to be upstaged and not a little embarrassed in public.

The dress performed its magic even before she arrived. In the rover Andre dispatched to retrieve her, she shed her envirosuit, after which the driver couldn't keep his eyes where they belonged. He wasn't bad looking himself. Carmen might have offered him a quick tumble had time permitted, but the schedule left none. Probably Andre meant to deprive the poor fellow.

News of her arrival preceded her. Andre enjoyed leaking that sort of intelligence to gain press coverage. She appeared at the mayoral residence amid a crowd of reporters and videographers and the mayor himself, done up in his most dashing flame-red suit. He matched her perfectly. How had he guessed? He extended a hand as she entered the reception room and the crowd gaped at her audacity. He smiled and kissed her cheek. She attacked his lips with impropriety while the videographers recorded every moment of it. To his credit, Andre maintained composure. Arm in arm, they moved further into the residence, followed by everyone with a press pass. Carmen took pleasure in imagining they were hoping the meeting would devolve into public debauchery. They always had been a gang of lechers.

Without losing a glimmer of smile, Andre whispered in her ear. "Why the whore act?"

"You said dress nice," she whispered back. "Isn't this nice?"

"Very. Got anything on under it?"

"Of course not."

"Walk slow. We don't want it falling off."

"They do." She tossed a happy smile over her shoulder to the cameras.

They came to the state dining room and its massive table set for twenty in crystal and bone china. Sunlight streamed through a great window behind the table. Heavy blue curtains framed the glass. Despite the light, faux candles on the table cast flickers from their holographic flames into the crystal. Servants stood about the edges of the room in white uniforms. Strangely, no guests were present. An unease swept over Carmen. Something was wrong.

Andre turned to face his entourage, gently rotating Carmen with him. The cameras played over her, capturing every exquisite inch of her body.

"I know you're excited to greet the first lady," he said. "And I guess you heard this is a momentous event with an open bar." He grinned. The reporters and videographers laughed. "But now that you have your vids…" He gave Carmen a salacious examination. "Damn nice vids." More laughter. Carmen, suddenly wishing she hadn't let her anger goad her, hid her embarrassment with a playful slap at his shoulder.

"We'll see you another time," he concluded. He stepped back, gently pulling his wife with him, and a pair of servants closed the double doors. A jumble of protests erupted beyond the doors, but the reporters knew the Rands wouldn't appear for an encore, not after that send-off, and a moment later silence fell as they withdrew.

Carmen eyed Andre. Somber, he waited for her to ask, so she did. "What happens now?"

"Now you meet someone truly important."

"Other than you?"

"Far more important than me." He touched her shoulder, nudged the hang of her dress. "I'm saying that for her benefit. Remember that. Everything I say from here on is for her benefit. Truth has nothing to do with it."

"As per usual."

Andre waved the servants off. All but one man left. That one stood by a side door, awaiting instructions. "Lights," Andre commanded. The servant circled the room, closing every curtain and extinguishing every candle but the one nearest the head of the table. Shadow cloaked everything. Carmen's eyes slowly adjusted, but she could see nothing beyond the fringe of dim candlelight. "Stand here," Andre said and maneuvered her to the chair nearest the light. He stood beside her at the head of the table. To the servant, he said, "Invite our guest in."

Soundlessly, the servant dissolved into darkness. A soft whisper of movement suggested the side door had opened and someone had come through. The door clicked shut behind the newcomer, and as Carmen squinted, she saw a shadow, a slight shape that felt oddly sinister for its lack of bulk.

The newcomer spoke.

"Why, Andre." The voice was as dark as the room, smooth, sultry. It might have been a woman's, but on the last syllable it sank into the baritone register. "She's the most beautiful creature I've ever seen."

"The most beautiful creature anyone has ever seen," Andre said with unexpected generosity.

"But then…" An oddly metallic laugh sounded.

"Nobody's ever seen you."

"Smooth, Andre. Perfect smooth. That's why you're the master of Mars." A chair dragged across the carpet, and the shadow merged with the far end of the table. "Your insight is unparalleled."

"In your presence, Celia, I'm nothing."

The air might have been sucked from Carmen's lungs. She grabbed the chair back for support. "Celia Fundichely?"

"Ah," Celia breathed. "The lovely lady has heard of me. I'm flattered. Forgive me, but I must ask. Are you wearing *anything* under that dress?"

Andre drew the chair out for Carmen, guided her into it, and sat in his place. "Shall we serve?"

"Oh yes, Andre," Celia replied, her voice spiraling upward into the soprano. "It's said you set the most generous table in the solar system, and I'm famished."

Andre reached out and tapped something. A bell rang with the tone of pure silver. In the dark, doors opened and servants swirled through the room. They left as quietly as they arrived, leaving behind the aromas of lobster and shrimp. Real lobster and shrimp. Andre had his own grow tanks buried beneath the mayoral residence to provide him with dishes nobody else on Mars could obtain.

Barely able to see, they ate in protracted silence. Their guest had no appetite for conversation, it seemed, and Carmen wanted only to hide. She'd heard disturbing things, horrifying things even, about Celia Fundichely. So long as she was far away in the Belt, Andre could take her money if he wanted. But to invite her here!

If invitation it had been.

Servants passed by twice more, once to remove plates and set out cheesecake with fresh strawberries, and again to remove those dishes and serve coffee. During the last pass, Carmen heard a surprised gasp from Celia's end of the table followed by a thud as though something heavy had been dropped. Before she could ask what had happened, Andre set a hand on her arm and whispered, "Say nothing."

"To business," Celia said, her voice now a broken alto. "My visit must puzzle your wife. Doubtless nobody ever made pilgrimage from the Belt merely to gaze on her beauty. Although…" The shadow sucked in air and the voice became feather light. "…she's well worth the cost of the trip."

Carmen felt she was being mocked, but Celia's ever-changing tone was impossible to judge. She must use a synthesizer to randomly modulate her voice. A disguise, like the darkness itself. But why?

"Carmen is uniquely perceptive," Andre said. He was full of praise tonight. "But I haven't yet spoken to her of this matter."

"I'm sure." The sound rumbled like thunder. "Enlighten her, Andre."

Andre set a gentle hand on Carmen's. She grabbed it as though tottering on the edge of a cliff.

"Celia isn't just rich," Andre said. "She's the richest person in the Belt. Maybe in the solar system."

"Earth is but a blue jewel in my crown," Celia said. She laughed lightly, like a little girl delighted by a hummingbird.

Andre continued, "Which makes her a target. It's also made her powerful enemies."

Carmen figured Celia's enemies were born of her methods rather than her wealth. People said she was ruthless, without scruple, not unlike Andre, not—come to think of it—too much unlike Carmen herself.

"Mars could be a safe haven for her," Andre finished.

A cold Martian wind blew through Carmen's soul. This planet was Andre's. He couldn't invite Celia in. She might be an ally now, but she wouldn't remain so. He couldn't cede one square meter of rust to her!

As though reading Carmen's mind, Celia spoke in soothing tones. "Oh, my beauty. Mars is such a big planet right now. It's so, so empty, and I ask so little. Utopia. That's all. Just Utopia. Utopia is far from here. Andre has no plans for it. I could be safe there. I would be in nobody's way, and nobody would ever find me."

Carmen squeezed Andre's hand so hard her bones might have fused with his. "But Andre!"

He squeezed back, and she realized he wanted her approval. He was desperate for it. Why did he care what she thought?

"You're giving her Utopia?" she asked.

"Selling."

"All of it?"

"It'll be fine," Andre assured her. "We've barely started on Mars. Once Schiaparelli Colony is on sound footing, we'll open Hellas to development. But think about it. A century will pass before Acidalia, Meridiani, and Hellas are built to capacity. By the time anyone even thinks about Utopia, we'll be gone. All three of us. Celia can live in secret the rest of her life. And just in case, I'll close it to development. I'll designate Utopia a research preserve."

A funny, unfunny thought leapt to mind. Carmen laughed bitterly. "Miguel wanted a research preserve."

"Ah," Celia purred. "Our dear Dr. Hernandez. Do you miss him, my beauty?"

How could she have known about that? Andre wouldn't tell her. Or would he?

Andre graciously returned to the subject to spare her the need to answer. "You will, of course, supply your own materials and equipment and pay all other development costs. We can't afford it."

"Of course, Andre, of course. I finance everything. All I require is your blessing and privacy. None must ever know of my presence."

"And conversely, your presence must in no way affect operations in the colonies or my other holdings."

"What I need, I shall bring. What I can't bring, I shall take from Utopia alone. Our paths will never cross."

Andre touched Carmen's shoulder. "Satisfied?"

Why did he care? He never sought her permission for anything, not even when he asked her advice.

Celia waited in a silence so deep, she might have ceased breathing.

"I accept your decision," Carmen told Andre.

The shadow shifted. "Carmen, beautiful Carmen. That isn't good enough. I won't come to Mars if you don't want me. I ask you to allow it, but I won't force myself on you." The voice dipped into a menacing base. "Nor will Andre."

A bit too quickly, Andre added, "It's your decision, Carmen."

But no, it wasn't. *Everything I say from here on is for her benefit*, he'd said. *Truth has nothing to do with it.* Aware of the danger, Andre was prepared to accept this incursion. He must have a reason. How could Carmen stand in his way?

His hand was still on her shoulder, pleading. She covered it with hers. "A century, you said."

"A century."

"Then I agree."

Andre exhaled in relief.

Celia's voice acquired a lilt. "Wonderful! I'm so very pleased. Thank you, Andre. And thank *you*, Carmen. I appreciate your generosity. I appreciate *you*. For such a long time, I've so wanted to meet you."

It had hardly been a meeting. Carmen had seen nothing of Celia, heard nothing of her true voice, learned nothing of her mind or motives.

In the dark, the shadow rose from the table and melted into the wall. The door opened and closed. Andre ran a hand through his hair and rang the bell again. A lone servant entered to turn up the lights and open the curtains. Carmen blinked into the brightness until her eyes adjusted.

At the far end of the table, another of the servants sprawled face down on the floor, a red stain spreading from the back of his neck over his white uniform. Carmen gasped.

Andre rose like an old man. He crossed the room, stood over the body, shook his head. "I told them," he said. "Don't get too close. Don't get close enough to see her." Returning to Carmen, he helped her from her chair. She couldn't take her eyes from the body, so he touched her cheek and gently turned her face to his. He gazed into her eyes for a moment before giving her risqué red dress a once-over. He looked sad.

"It's beautiful," he said. "But you should change before you go out in public."

Chapter 13

Flying sand engulfed their rover, dyeing the air the color of rust. Its tenuous fingernails scraped over the metal hull, hissing like a wraith probing for a way in. While the storm posed no danger to the vehicle, the Martian atmospheric pressure being so low, for hours sand whispered across the hull while inside Petrina and Martin Ulenga waited in anxious silence. Darkness fell, and still sand buffeted them. It blew through the night and into the diffuse glow of sunrise with no break in the storm.

They were six days out from Lowell, and nobody knew where they were.

"We shouldn't have come," Martin said. He huddled in the back of the rover, eyes closed, mind focused on his breathing. Images blew over him like the sand through the air, images of fire, destruction, bloodshed. He listened to his breath rise and fall while the violence slipped by and faded into the recesses of his brain.

In the front, Petrina fiddled absently with the panel. The storm blinded the craft's vids and veiled their solar panels. Comm dropped out every few seconds, rendering updates impossible. No weather data, no GPS data, no nothing. "Must be a big storm," she said.

The size of the storm didn't matter. "We weren't ready."

She glanced back, irritated. "We planned the route, stocked supplies, everything. Besides, we've been out with Dr. Hernandez enough."

"He forgot to teach us a few things. Like weather analysis."

"It'll let up soon."

Maybe, maybe not. Most storms remained localized, but some swallowed whole regions or, on rare occasions, all of Mars. Rather than argue, Martin dug out food for them, popped open the self-heating packets, and took one to Petrina. "Imitation omelets," he said. *"Bon appétit."*

They ate to the hiss of sand.

After tossing her container into the disposer, Petrina tapped absently on the unresponsive panel. "You think I'm overbearing."

Martin wasn't sure he should admit that.

"Come on, be honest."

"I guess. Sometimes."

"You guess."

"Maybe we shouldn't—"

"We should. We never talk, Martin. Not about important things. Let's be honest for once."

He laughed. "You're definitely doing it now."

She picked at her fingernails.

"Yeah, you can be a pain in the ass, but I'm used to it. I spent my whole life following your lead."

Petrina smiled a little. She tried the panel again, got the same results. No surprise, there. "I had to protect you. It was my job. I'm the oldest."

"Not by much."

"It counts."

Martin grinned and shook his head.

"When you took up with that girl a few years ago—what was her name?"

"Val," he said.

"Val, yeah. I realized someday it wouldn't be my job any-more. Someday, you'd have a wife to take care of you."

"You make me sound helpless."

She play-punched his shoulder. "You are."

"Yeah? What about you? Who keeps you out of trouble once I'm consumed with married life?"

Petrina stared at the sand blowing across the vid panel. It was nothing but a blur of rust.

"You never met anyone even moderately interesting?" he asked.

"Nope."

Maybe she didn't want to. Martin thought that sad.

She tried the panel one more time. "We may be stuck with each other. Who'd want us in this condition?"

He had no answer for that, hadn't even considered it. "Let's assume we'll get better," he said.

"Let's assume we find Dr. Hernandez, first. What do we do then?" Petrina slapped the panel and leaned back, eyes closed, breath slow and deliberate. "Will you kill him?"

"Why would I do that?"

"Why wouldn't you?"

If he couldn't contain his rage, he might. "Is that what you want?"

Petrina opened her eyes and scanned the compartment walls and ceiling as though seeing the sand streamers snaking over the hull. "I don't know. Should that frighten me?"

"Probably," Martin said, although he felt nothing, himself. Strange, that. If either of them had a thirst for revenge, it ought to be him. "But then, he probably deserves it."

The vid cleared for a moment. Petrina leaned forward to check it. Martin looked, too. A shape seemed to move in the distance, then it was gone, consumed by the storm.

"That's not what Dad taught us," she said.

Martin quoted the lesson: "'Everyone deserves a second chance. A dozen chances on Mars.' You know, I only just realized what he meant."

"Why Carmen Rand?" Petrina asked. "Of all the women on Mars, why her?"

Martin about asked why not. Ninety percent of men on Mars would screw Carmen Rand if the opportunity presented itself. But Petrina had a point. According to Martin's friend Samuel, Dr. Hernandez had been battling Mayor Rand for some time. Was jumping her part of the fight? A way of getting even? Or had he fallen for her?

"Maybe," he said, "we give Dr. Hernandez that second chance, after all. At least until we find out."

An alert beeped. The panel signaled someone requesting entrance. Petrina and Martin looked at each other.

"Who could be out there?" Martin asked.

"Someone must need help," Petrina said. Before Martin could stop her, she cycled the outer door open. Something thunked into the airlock, and once the chamber was pressurized, the inner door opened.

The newcomer clumped in wearing a dust-caked envirosuit. He removed the helmet, revealing a young man's face topped with a mop of blonde hair. He squinted at the Ulengas as though he'd discovered a new life form. "Who are you?" he demanded.

"Who are you?" Martin countered.

"What're you doing out here?"

Since the interloper hadn't answered, Martin didn't, either. Not exactly. "We got caught in the storm."

He set his hands to his hips and cocked his head.

"What?" Petrina asked. "People can't get caught in storms?"

"Yeah, but they don't go joyriding in them."

"We aren't joyriding," Martin said. "We're scientists. We're looking for a colleague."

"Oh. Hernandez."

Martin wondered how he'd known, but then how many scientists could be wandering the wilderness? And only one had been outlawed.

"What's your name?" Petrina asked.

Ignoring her, the other asked, "Why're you looking for him?"

The rover shuddered and rang like an empty shipping container colliding with a boulder. Martin grabbed a seat back to steady himself. "What was that?"

"You're being captured. I'm Zachary, by the way."

Petrina grabbed a seat, too, as the rover rocked and tilted nose up. "Captured! By who?"

"My friends," Zachary said, holding on to a seat of his own. He grinned. "This is gonna be fun."

Every muscle in Quan Linh's body ached. She'd spent the past sixteen hours loading rock into the haulers while Ricard Fulbert labored on the track ahead. This tunnel was longer and wider than the others they had worked, the equipment larger and more powerful, the crew and the haul bigger. Stefan, their overseer, now had fifty slaves at his command, organized to keep the extractor pushing toward the asteroid's core. Bone-shaking explosions erupted more frequently, catapulting chunks of rock to greater distances. They made rapid progress, but at a cost. Over the past week, two slaves had died and six had been severely injured. The injured got lucky, if luck it was. Stefan made the call to save them rather than euthanize them, figuring their cost of treatment was lower than the cost of replacement.

Linh and Ricard were reunited at the end of the shift and given six hours sleep time. They collapsed against a wall half a kilometer from the blast zone, enfolded in each other's arms, surrounded by their fellow slaves. In the distance, periodic explosions reverberated through the walls and floor. They didn't speak for a time, but neither could they sleep.

"He isn't coming back," Linh whispered. She felt no fear, no anger, not even regret. It was merely a fact. Alejandro Carrasco had abandoned them.

"Maybe not," Ricard agreed. "But he didn't give a timeframe."

"Can we escape on our own?"

"I don't see how. We don't even know where we are."

Linh rested her head on his shoulder. "Inside an asteroid."

"But not the same one. They moved us."

He had to be joking. How could they have been moved to a different asteroid without knowing?

"The composition of the rock is different," Ricard said.

"We work, eat, and sleep in the tunnels," Linh objected. "The only time we're not in the tunnels is when they herd us through the ship's showers or the med section to make sure we aren't too sick or weak to be profitable."

Ricard stroked her hair. "That's when they move us. While we're shipboard, they fly to the next rock on their list."

A funny image occurred to her. She laughed.

"What?"

"Can't you just see it? A gang of naked slaves erupting from the showers, overpowering the guards, and flying to freedom."

He didn't laugh. Not that she expected him to. He never quite got jokes. "Interesting idea," he murmured. "It might even work."

"I'm kidding, Ricard."

"I'm not. Let's give it some thought."

She closed her eyes. Suddenly, all she wanted to do was sleep for a hundred years. "No," she said through a yawn. "Let's not."

She shifted and fell asleep with her head on his chest.

Security stripped both Ulenga apartments down to the flooring. Agents removed, examined, dissected, analyzed, and recycled everything, then detailed procedures and findings along with ancillary interrogations in a three-volume report. A top analyst distilled the report to a single electronic document page and delivered it to Subcommander Leah Leaf's panel. She read it twice, once to get the gist and once to absorb the details. While she read, a minor dust storm hissed across the transparent roof. Light filtered by the ruddy particles dyed her compartment pale yellow.

The report said little. Petrina and Martin owned nothing unusual for grad students, had done nothing suspect aside from their visits to Dr. Gene Lloyd and Carmen Rand. They'd had no other contacts except one friend who had dinner with Martin but knew nothing of value. Lloyd told them about the nanobots, which may or may not have been significant. What the first lady told them was unknown since she was off-limits. Only two other fragments of information caught Leah's attention.

First, Martin and Petrina began writing with pen and paper after their visit to Lloyd. Nothing remained of their scribblings, but a blank sheet of paper bore marks suggesting it had backed a page on which they wrote. Varied pressure left haphazard impressions, most of which didn't suggest clear letters, but the analyst reported two words with eighty percent confidence: *nanobots* and *hack*.

Second, signals from the nanobots grew sporadic and finally fell silent when the twins dropped out of sight. Search and surveillance failed to locate them. Possibly they were jamming the signals, but Leah's people were good at finding lost things. More likely, the Ulengas moved out of range. That meant the wilderness, where Security had no reach. Had they been anyone else, Leah would have said good riddance. The wilderness consumed fugitives. If Mars didn't kill you, smugglers would. But the Ulengas were different. Petrina and Martin were Leah's only connection to Dr. Miguel Hernandez. Conclusion: he had vanished into the wilderness, too.

Leah swiped the report into storage and stood. Her panel fell dark. Legally, she had no options, particularly since Mayor Rand had just contracted with an outside security force to patrol the wilderness. But damn it, the Ulengas were hers. Hernandez was hers. She wasn't about to cede them to mercenaries. Her promotion would *not* blow away on the Martian wind.

She would hunt down and kill the trio herself.

From atop the rise, Nessa O'Clery scanned the dust cloud hanging on the horizon with her televiewers, both in visible light and infrared. The image, magnified sixty times, revealed little, just billows of dust. A microstorm? Debris kicked up by a rover? Whatever it was, it was headed their way.

She lowered the device. "No intel?" she asked.

Standing beside her in his bulky envirosuit, Jake grumbled something unintelligible, probably in his native language. She assumed it meant no. A larger storm to the east had jumbled their comm, leaving them with spotty info from Lowell.

"Alert security," she decided. "It may be another tracker."

"We kills three since Miguel arrives," Jake said. He held up three fingers as though Nessa didn't know how to count. "They doesn't learn."

"We'll fix it. He's introducing me to Carmen Rand."

Jake sputtered in surprise. Nothing much surprised him. Nessa wondered why this should. "When?" he asked.

"As soon as I convince him to do it."

He laughed. "Miguel is stubborn bastard. Maybe you don't convince him."

"Come on, Jake, you know I'm persuasive." She lifted the televiewers again. The cloud approached from the direction of Lowell colony at a steady pace, and now she could make out a dark spec leading it. A rover. "Definitely a tracker," she said. "Damn them."

"How does they know we are here?"

Good question. The only signals emanating from the crater-rim base were narrowly directed for comm with nearby rovers, yet three times—four, now—trackers had made right for them, neither smart enough nor stealthy enough to avoid the same fate time and again. Nessa figured they didn't know they were walking into an ambush, but they knew something was hiding in or near this crater.

"Let's get inside," she said. "They won't be here for a couple hours."

They trudged down the slope to their rover, and Jake drove them back to the base. Just before they arrived, he said, "Maybe I goes to see the first lady someday."

Nessa smirked at him. "Why, you want to bang her, too?"

"They says she is pretty, but nah."

"Jake."

"What?"

"You'll never get to Rand, not even through his wife."

Teeth clenched, he whipped around a small rock outcrop, nearly spilling the rover onto its side.

"Don't get mad at me," Nessa snapped. "You know I'm right. Get your revenge by sticking with me. We steal from Rand every damn day. Let that be good enough."

The hatred in his eyes said it wasn't. When they first met, she convinced him her way was better, but Rand's murderous betrayal had boiled within him so long that he could no longer deny his rage. He believed he could only be free with Rand dead at his feet.

"Stay away from the Rands, Jake. I mean it."

He said nothing. Reaching the crater, they ascended its wall and rolled down to its floor. Jake stopped near the north airlock to let her out. "Maybe I am persuasive, too," he said. "Maybe I convinces Miguel to takes me along."

There was no point in arguing, but Nessa wasn't letting Jake within fifty kilometers of Carmen Rand, even if she had to bind him and stash him in a crippled rover until the first lady went home. Miguel Hernandez wasn't getting his hands on her, either, neither metaphorically nor literally. If the meeting came, it would be just the women.

The unknown rover didn't make the crater. Not quite. It stopped half a kilometer out and sent a signal. Nessa's security team puzzled over their response for fifteen minutes before giving up.

Technically, they had but two choices: capture the vehicle or destroy it. Given the recent rash of trackers blundering in, destruction seemed safest, but whoever was driving knew something disturbing: Nessa's name.

Jake brought the news to her apartment along with his assessment. "We should kills him."

"After we interrogate him," she countered. "I want to know how he found out."

"It's a trap."

"Nobody's caught you yet, Jake."

"I don't likes it."

"Neither do I. That's why I want him interrogated."

Jake set his hands on his hips and shook his head. "I protects you. You listens to me this time."

And he called Miguel stubborn. "Transfer comm in here. Let's see what we can find out before we incinerate him."

"Waste of time," Jake muttered, but he sat beside her and used her panel to do her bidding. They had voice only. Neither the rover's driver nor Nessa transmitted imagery. "Talk," Jake commanded.

"I'll talk to Nessa," the interloper said. "Get her on comm."

Nessa set her hand on Jake's to signal him to silence. "Maybe she already is," she said.

"Nessa? Is that you?"

"What do you want with her?"

The interloper didn't reply.

"Better answer," Nessa said. "My lieutenant wanted you dead half an hour ago."

Jake grinned at her and mouthed, *Lieutenant?*

"I'm a friend of her father's."

Nessa should have cut the connection and told Jake to blast the fool. Her father didn't have friends, or if he did, they were all as dead as he. "What the hell's your name?" she demanded.

"Back then, it was Enrique Olvera."

Nessa rocked back on the couch. So did Jake. They looked at each other, looked at the panel, looked at each other. Nessa had no idea Jake had known Enrique, and from his expression, he didn't know she had, either. But how could Enrique still be alive? It had to be a trick.

"You must remember me, Nessa."

"Show yourself," she demanded.

Imagery activated, revealing a face lean and bearded, a face they both knew in younger form, a face—Nessa realized with a shock—strangely like Miguel Hernandez's.

"God," Nessa breathed. "Enrique! I thought you were dead. What are you doing here?"

"Searching for someone." Quickly, he added, "Not you. You know I wouldn't do anything to hurt you. But I think you might know where to look."

Nessa wanted to ask who, but that could wait. She needed to get him inside and hide his rover before anyone followed. She muted the comm and gave Jake instructions. "Scan the area before you bring him in. Make sure nobody's watching. We still have a few empty apartments on the south side. Settle him there. I'll be down shortly."

Jake lumbered out, a thoughtful look on his face. Before he passed through the door, she asked, "How did you know him?"

"He makes trouble," Jake replied without looking back. "I likes him, so I hides him once."

And now again, Nessa thought. She unmuted the comm. "We'll bring you in. Don't make my people nervous, Enrique. They get trigger-happy."

"I'll be easy on them," he promised. "And do me a favor. Call me Alejandro. Alejandro Carrasco. Enrique might still be on someone's hotlist."

"If you say so." She cut the connection and leaned back.

Enrique Olvera. He had been a friend, a good friend. Nessa would have died avenging her father had Enrique not redirected her wrath. Question was, who was he after? She believed he wouldn't hurt her, not intentionally, but if his goal was Miguel—and who else could it be?—somebody would sure get hurt.

For the moment, Carmen felt safer in Lowell than secluded in her home beyond the reach of politics and videographers. Since their meeting with Celia Fundichely four days before, terror had stalked her. It hid in the shadows of the mayor's residence, lurked in the halls of government offices, peered from shop windows along the transport tubes. She couldn't sleep, not even in Andre's protective embrace. He sensed her unease and lavished more attention and care on her than he had for years, but not even that comforted her. She breathed in menace with the air. They both knew its name, but neither spoke it, only of it, and then only when Carmen couldn't contain it any longer.

"You don't believe her," she said one night, entwined with him after a lovemaking that didn't still her fears.

"You've tortured yourself enough, Carmen. Let it go."

"I can't, not if I have to share the planet with her."

He sighed and tightened his hold on her.

"She's a thug. She killed a servant for no reason."

"She had a reason."

"A paranoid reason. At least when you kill somebody, you have good reason."

"And I thought you were squeamish."

"Liar."

"Guilty." He ran a finger along her cheekbone. "Yes, she's paranoid and unprincipled, and that makes her dangerous in the extreme. But that's why I couldn't say no."

He had a point. God knew what Celia would do had he refused her.

"Also," Andre said in a whisper as though he feared someone might be listening, "I learned something disconcerting."

"More than disconcerting than this?"

"Yes. I recently hired an off-world security consultant. The arrangement is getting out of hand."

"So fire them."

"Turns out, she owns them."

Carmen shivered. Andre was being drawn into a trap. Yet that made one thing more puzzling still. "Why did she want my approval?"

"Hell if I know. When she requested your presence, I had no idea she intended to ask your permission. All I know is, she wants Mars. I'll be damned if I hand it over to her, but this requires finesse."

Carmen rolled onto her back and stared at the darkened ceiling. Whatever Celia was up to, courtesy had nothing to do with it. Was she trying to forge a bond? Get Carmen on her side, use her against Andre? If so, she'd be disappointed. Bickering, infidelity, and separate residences aside, Carmen was devoted to Andre and Andre to her, whether anyone understood, whether they themselves fully understood. It wasn't love in the usual sense, but it was some manner of love. Reciprocal need bound them.

"Everyone's talking," Andre said. "You don't usually stay this long."

"You want me to go?"

"Of course not." He rolled on top of her, settled his cheek against hers. "I think you should stay indefinitely and drive the whole colony mad."

The darkness receded momentarily, and she laughed. "It would serve them right, wouldn't it?"

"It would."

"But Andre, what about her?"

"I'll take care of her."

"How?"

Andre lifted his head and ran his fingers through Carmen's hair. "Don't ask. Please."

He never said please. The word frightened her so, she had no desire to ask. "What should I do, then?"

"Spread your legs."

She pulled him down and kissed him.

"Make me," she said.

Chapter 14

They traveled two days, maybe three. Petrina wasn't sure. She and Martin remained manacled in the back of the undersized rover the whole way with only a silent driver for company. When they spoke to each other or tried to engage him, he growled, "Shuddup," without looking at them. Their own rover had been loaded onto a carrier. Petrina supposed it was following. From what she could see of the view panel, it wasn't leading. The sun's angle throughout the day told her they headed south.

They were fed little. When they arrived at their destination, Petrina and Martin were sore, hungry, and ready to punch someone. Martin kept his rages in check with his breathing exercises, but from his taught expression Petrina knew it had been a struggle. Probably it didn't much matter. Still manacled, he couldn't have hurt anyone but himself. A pair of thugs herded them out of the rover and through a cavern jammed with mottled, rust-red transports of all sizes, vehicles designed for invisibility against the Martian wilderness. Zachary was nowhere to be seen. Their driver and three other kindred brutes shoved the twins into an unfurnished room whose gray walls and floor were splattered with dark red. Locked in and alone, they remained bound.

Martin cringed at the stains. "Blood," he said. "They kill people in here."

"They won't kill us," Petrina assured him, knowing it an irrational hope. "We didn't do anything wrong."

"Depends on who they work for, doesn't it? If they're Mayor Rand's thugs…"

A door creaked open, admitting an Asian woman clothed in shimmering black. "They are mine," she said. "I do not share them."

Petrina puffed herself up, but the tremor in her voice belied her brave face. "Who are you?"

"I am Hitomi. Do not fear me."

Petrina denied the obvious. "Why would I?"

"I could kill you in the instant." From nowhere, a knife appeared in Hitomi's hand and touched Petrina's neck. "I would rather have your friendship."

Martin tottered on the edge of fury. "Leave her alone! I'll rip your damn—"

Suddenly the knife was against Martin's neck. "Will you?"

Anger melting into fear, he held his breath.

"We didn't do anything," Petrina pleaded.

Hitomi lowered the knife and stepped back. So smooth was the movement, she might not have been touching the floor. "You seek Dr. Miguel Hernandez."

How could she have known that? Carmen Rand wouldn't have told anyone. Or would she?

"I also seek him," Hitomi added.

Martin yanked at his shackles. He succeeded only in hurting his wrists. "Why?"

Petrina slipped back into her defiant face while forcing her breathing into a steady rhythm. She had to keep a clear head. "We won't lead him into a trap."

"I offer you and your brother a gift, Petrina. How unfortunate if you refuse it."

"You just want the bounty," Martin said.

"I am not Andre Rand's puppet." She extended her hand palm up, holding between her thumb and index finger a small black disc. Like the knife, it appeared from nowhere. Petrina suspected invisible pockets in her black clothing. Hitomi tapped the disc. The shackles released and clattered to the floor. "He is mine. I will protect you from him. In return, you will help me recruit Dr. Hernandez."

Martin kicked the shackles away. Petrina rubbed her sore wrists. "What do you mean, recruit?"

"I have need of him."

"Go to hell," Martin snapped.

Hitomi's expression changed not at all. "An unfortunate attitude. Mars is inhospitable."

Seeing the glint of rage in her brother's eyes, Petrina set a hand to his shoulder. "We've survived so far."

Hitomi didn't reply at once. Petrina guessed from the slight narrowing of her eyes that she wasn't used to contradiction. Her quiet threats must prove effective on most victims. The Ulengas presented her with a puzzle requiring a different approach.

"I mean Dr. Hernandez no harm," Hitomi said. "I offer him an opportunity."

Petrina's touch had sufficiently calmed Martin that he could focus on his breathing. He barely registered Hitomi's words. Petrina heard but didn't trust them. "Like what?"

"He seeks life. I will lead him to it."

"Where?" When Hitomi declined to answer, Petrina added, "Beyond Mayor Rand's reach?" She wondered how Hitomi could know where to find evidence of life, why she wouldn't have claimed it herself, if she did know.

Hitomi placed a surprisingly gentle hand on Petrina's shoulder. "Yes." She motioned the students to follow and led them from the blood-stained room down a dim corridor to a great rock chamber filled with smells of food and the murmur of low conversation. A few dozen people sat in black chairs around black tables eating and talking in the low light.

"Take nourishment," Hitomi said. "You will soon be with Dr. Hernandez."

"You mean we're the bait," Martin said.

"I mean what I say." She activated a panel embedded in the table and ordered food and drink for them. "We shall talk again soon."

The Ulengas watched her melt into the dimness.

"We're the bait," Martin repeated.

Petrina nodded. "Where do you think she means? Someplace beyond Rand's reach?"

"It's a lie. She's working for Rand."

"I don't know, Martin. Look at all these people. Places like this aren't supposed to exist in the wilderness. I don't think Rand knows they're here."

Martin rubbed his temples. "He must. He just keeps it secret."

Petrina doubted it. What would be the point? Rand claimed all of Mars for himself. He wouldn't hide a successful development from his videographer thralls.

"Either way," Martin continued, "we can't lead her to Dr. Hernandez."

She agreed with that much, anyway. "I wish Ricard was here," she said. "He'd know what to do."

"Ricard and Linh are lucky they got out. We should have gone with them."

The food arrived, but they had little appetite.

Alejandro Carrasco, formerly Enrique Olvera, raised his glass in a toast. "To your father," he said and tossed back the drink. Nessa and Jake downed theirs in unison, and Alejandro poured another round. "And if I may…" He raised an eyebrow at Jake, who waved him on. "To Mlada."

They drank again, and Jake took a turn pouring refills. He downed his without a toast.

"I'm sorry," Alejandro said. "I wish I'd been there. We'd have taken out the bastards together."

Jake shook his head. "Rand gives nobody chances. Nobody sees him coming. You has no way to defend."

"That's just smart," Alejandro said. "But what he did to you and Mlada…" He set his glass down and stared at it. Images of what Jake had told him burned in his head. The explosion that destroyed their homestead with Mlada in it. The charge that Jake killed his own sister to secure sole ownership of the ore deposits they had discovered. Rand's seizure of their property. Having disposed of the competition, he twisted the knife by branding the new mining company with Jake and Mlada's last name. "Evil," Alejandro finished.

Nessa put down her glass, too. "We don't honor the dead through suicide. You taught me that, Alejandro. I've tried to teach Jake." She eyed him. Jake refused to look at her.

That was their problem, not Alejandro's. "I'm not here for Rand," he said. "I'm looking for that outlaw scientist. I assume you heard of him."

"Miguel Hernandez," Nessa acknowledged. "Yeah, he's been in the news."

"Any idea where he's hiding?"

"If he's smart, he left Mars."

"He's smart," Alejandro said. "But not very bright sometimes. How'd he get in trouble?"

"Blew up a hydro station, they say."

"Why would he do that?"

Nessa shrugged. "Why does anyone do anything? Maybe he got bored with lecturing. What do you want with him?"

She'd grown sly in the years since Alejandro last saw her. She knew more than she admitted and hoped to tease additional intel from him, but he didn't care to play games, not with her. Their relationship had always been one of trust. He decided to rely on that. "Don't let it out of this room," he said.

Jake set a finger to his lips.

Nessa laughed. "I can't imagine you harboring dark secrets involving rouge scientists, but you have my word."

"Miguel Hernandez is my big brother."

She put a hand to her forehead. "Damn, no wonder you look alike. How the hell did that happen?"

"Blame our parents," Alejandro said. "Miguel's brilliant, like our mother. I'm a troublemaker, like our father was in his youth, except I never outgrew it. Miguel and I have a schizoid relationship. I nearly killed him once. That's why I ran off to the Belt."

"You tries to kills your own brother?" Jake asked.

"I was a hothead, and he was a control freak."

Nessa went for the bottle and poured herself another. "And since you're both outlaws now, you figure it's a great time for a family reunion."

"No, Nessa. I made him an outlaw. *I* destroyed that hydro station. It just was a job. I didn't get why they picked me until they circulated that bad vid of my face to pin it on Miguel."

"Ah." Nessa sipped her drink. "You *are* after Andre Rand."

"No. Rand may be involved, but something else is going on. Something bigger than him."

"Because?"

Because Rand's grasp didn't extend into the Belt. Because that environmentalist wasn't Rand's style. Because Rand wouldn't have bothered with no-account students. "Because I say so," he replied. "Come on, Nessa. All I want is Miguel's location. Once I have it, I'm gone. I didn't see you, you didn't see me. Fair enough?"

"Except for one thing," she said.

"That being?"

"He works for me. And honestly? I don't want to lose him."

Miguel had nudged Jake over the course of two more research outings until the big man's resistance cracked. "You gets me to Carmen Rand," he offered, "and I no more tags along." It wasn't the active assistance Miguel had in mind, but it at least afforded him escape opportunity. He agreed. Only then did Jake add a condition.

"I sees her alone. You takes me there, but you stays out of it."

Miguel almost refused. Jake's target was Andre Rand, and who knew what he'd do to Carmen to get to Andre. But the meeting might not happen, not if Miguel made his escape first. "Agreed," he said, "but don't hurt Carmen."

Jake laughed. "Why? You loves her?"

That was an unfair question, largely because Miguel couldn't deny it. He'd used Carmen and she'd used him, yet underneath their consensual treachery something more lurked. At least it did in his heart. Hers might be another matter. Regardless, he couldn't speak of that to anyone, particularly Jake. "Because whatever her husband did, she wasn't involved."

"You thinks I can't be clever? Hurting her will gets me killed. I can be clever."

That didn't comfort Miguel, but it would have to do. They sealed the deal with a handshake, and thereafter Jake stopped tagging along when Miguel surfed the desert.

Today, Miguel pushed south, keeping to the eastern edge of Tempe Terra, the limit of the rover's permitted range. He sampled soils while his transceiver probed the radio spectrum. Weak signals crisscrossed the wilderness. By triangulation, he located twelve distinct sources, the strongest being leakage from Lowell Colony. The rest would be settlers, smugglers, maybe trackers reporting in.

Miguel hadn't expected so much activity. Too many potential targets, and the wrong choice could prove fatal. Yet his only chance of escape lay in raising a friend or sympathetic stranger. A rotten gamble, this: roll the dice and trust to luck or resign himself to life as Nessa's servant.

At the end of the eleventh day of his trek, Miguel stopped on a cratered plain and watched the sun sink below the horizon. Darkness erased the land. He got his fossil-bearing rock out of storage and examined it. Odd that so much trouble had come of this nondescript chunk of Mars.

Radio chatter dropped off with the light, leaving only signals from Lowell and one other location. The latter emanated from the heart of Lunae Planum, where the Tharsis highlands gave way to the northern lowland plains. He had crossed the fringe of this region years before and met no settlers. They may have been there, hiding, but he suspected this signal revealed a newcomer. Like most transmissions, it was encoded. The broadcaster might be friend or foe.

Very well. Roll the dice. He sent a directed distress signal and settled back to wait.

For fifteen minutes, he received no acknowledgement. He resent the signal, waited another fifteen minutes, tried again. And again. At length, an unencrypted answer arrived.

"What's your location?"

Miguel relayed his coordinates.

"Who are you?"

A logical if dangerous question. "Paul Westerfeld," he replied. "I'm a geologist for a small mining company." In the silence, Miguel hoped they didn't have access to Lowell databases to check the claim.

"What company?"

He pulled a name out of the metaphorical hat. "Utopia Industries."

"Never heard of them."

"We're new and not very big." Miguel hoped they would take that without question. He wasn't sure he could improvise details. Logically, a company named for the Utopia lowlands should be operating there, not here, but nobody would be mining such a remote location.

"How long until you're dead?"

That was indelicate, but he played along. "Less than twenty hours."

"We'll see what we can do. Don't go anywhere for the next twenty. After that, do whatever you want." The connection expired without fanfare.

Since he wasn't low on oxygen, Miguel laughed. Not that his situation was a laughing matter. When they came, they could be anyone: settlers, smugglers, mercenaries, slavers. In the Belt, a smuggler once told him, mining companies routinely grabbed conscripts wherever they could, and the authorities were too weak to stop them. He hoped he hadn't set a trap for himself.

He picked up his fossil-bearing rock and examined it again, turning it this way and that, running his fingers over the bumps and ridges, examining the pits where samples had been scraped for processing. It looked like any other Martian stone. Only the embedded microfossils, invisible to the eye, made it priceless.

Miguel set it aside and closed his eyes.

Maybe he should forget it, throw the rock out, let it disintegrate at leisure over a few thousand years. He had plenty of life left in him. He could go anywhere. The outer solar system, where he'd sent his students. Back to Earth. He could find Mona and Sef again. Sef would be a young man by now, and Mona would have found someone else. Still, it would do him good to see them. Would they feel the same?

No. He was dead to them. Sef wouldn't even know him. Nobody ever returned to Earth, anyway, with good reason. Mars changed you, and rarely for the better.

He stashed the rock away, closed his eyes, and tried not to think about it.

Nineteen hours and fifty-seven minutes later, a blonde-headed kid named Zachary showed up and cheerfully informed Miguel he was being captured.

A slave revolt wouldn't work. Ricard had mentally run a dozen simulations and come up empty. If he and Linh were to escape, they'd need stealth. Fortunately, the cretins who herded the mining crew through their days had grown sloppy—or always had been. They didn't believe escape was possible, so they didn't guard against it. True, the overseers and their bulls packed weapons in their dark blue coveralls, and yes, and the slaves primarily lived and worked in the confines of the tunnels, from which there could be no escape. But every so often they were herded into the ship's ramshackle sanitation and medical facilities, where long years of decay had exposed unwatched hidey holes. Ricard catalogued them all and stashed the map in his memory. Soon, he had an idea.

Linh, although skeptical, let him coach her on his plan. They drilled at the start of every sleep period, whispering it to each other step by step. The single-file march through the showers. The semi-organized clustering of dripping bodies in the UV room. The jumbled egress through a dim passage into the dressing room. The ventilation shaft with its loose grille. Of the four catches meant to secure the corners, three were broken. They could quickly swing the grille aside, duck in, and pull it back into place. Ricard doubted anyone would raise the alarm, since at that point in the process, the slaves were focused on the light up ahead.

The next bit was an educated guess, but Ricard was eighty-five percent certain—based on comings and goings he'd witnessed as they were herded through the facility—that the crew's showers were on the other side of the bulkhead. He hoped they were accessible from the shaft. If so, they could pilfer clothing and assume the role of someone, anyone, other than slaves until they could find a way back to civilization.

Once they internalized the plan, they physically walked through the first part three times on successive shower days, each time pulling aside the grille just enough to assure themselves they could get through. Nobody paid attention to this prodding. Their fellow slaves might have been cattle following a well-worn path. But entering the shaft would be the easy part. They couldn't practice the bad gamble that followed, a gamble more likely to end in death than freedom. Ricard knew it, and his pseudo-optimism didn't fool Linh. Yet she'd chance it for him, not because she believed they could succeed but because she needed him by her side. She had control of her terrors now, which made bearable those work shifts when the overseers separated them, but she'd rather die than lose him.

As ready as possible, they waited for escape day to come, and then they were in line, stripping off their filthy, ragged clothing, tossing it into the incinerator bins, shuffling with the naked hoard single file through the lukewarm streams of water, taking their places in the UV room and covering their eyes during disinfection, moving then in a disorganized herd toward the dressing room where piles of gray clothing waited. When they came to the shaft, Ricard eased out the loose grille while Linh ducked behind it, then he did a quick fade into the darkness and silently pulled the grille back. He waited, breath held, listening for an alarm, but the mass of bodies filed by, soundless save the shuffling of feet. And then even that faded.

In the lead, Linh crept down the dark shaft toward a spot of light, where she found another grille on the left. She leaned forward as though looking around a corner and peered through the holes, hoping not to be seen.

"You're right," she said. "Showers, dressing room. Blue coveralls like the bulls wear. The lights are dimmed. Nobody's here." She carefully tested the grille. It didn't budge. "Damn. No way in."

"Let me try," Ricard said. She moved ahead to give him access, but he couldn't budge the grille, either. "Maybe I can free it," he said. He stuck a finger through at the corner and felt around.

"How?" Linh chided. "The only equipment you have is what you were born with."

Ricard supposed that was a joke.

"Come on," she said. "That was funny, under the circumstances."

He found what felt to be a catch and pushed at it from one side, then the other. "What circumstances?"

"We're stark naked."

"Is that funny?" He tried again, and the catch clicked. The corner of the grille shifted half a centimeter out. "Ah. There. Now the other side."

"Of course, it is. Now, anyway. I was mortified the first time they marched us through the showers, but you get used to it fast."

The other catch clicked, then the one at the bottom. Leaving the fourth engaged, Ricard swung the grille to the side. "Why were you mortified?"

"Forget it. Let's get dressed and get out of here."

They slipped into the room, and Ricard replaced the grille. Linh grabbed a coverall that looked his size and tossed it to him, then got one for herself. They hadn't even stuffed their legs in when the lights came up and boots clomped across the floor and a female intruder, as startled as they were, gaped at them. "Really, guys?" she asked. "In here?"

Chapter 15

How the hell had Miguel gotten *there?*

Lunae Planum lay well beyond the programmed limits of Nessa's rovers. Nessa grilled Jake on it until, sick of her badgering, he grabbed and shook her, which she allowed for all of two seconds before extricating herself and throwing him against the wall. Alejandro wasn't sure how she'd managed that. It happened so fast he barely saw her move. She might be strong for her size, but no way was she *that* strong.

Jake settled into a sulk while Nessa muttered curses to herself. She had called the men to her apartment upon receiving word that Miguel's rover had moved into the northern lowlands. While disabled. That made no sense, yet there it was. She replayed the telemetry on her huge wall panel. Other than the panel, which was excessive by most standards, her rooms looked much like any other in the facility, if with a better view. Her window looked out on an undulating plain pockmarked by craters. Although powerful, she remained practical and refused to surround herself with luxury. Alejandro approved.

"How is he doing that?" she demanded for the third time.

"You're forgetting two things," Alejandro said. "Miguel is damn smart and really damn stubborn. He obviously figured a way to beat the rover's governors."

"He beats nothing," Jake snarled. "He can never beats nothing. He cheats!"

"Cheating works like beating, so long as you aren't caught."

"Those systems," Nessa insisted, "are unhackable. It's physically impossible to disable them without disabling the entire rover."

Alejandro figured that was hubris talking. Every system had its weaknesses. But suppose she was right. What would Miguel do? If he thought like Alejandro, which he largely did, he'd swap out for an unhobbled rover. Which didn't explain how a dead one could move that far unless it was…

…taken in tow. Right.

"What's in Lunae Planum?" Alejandro asked.

Nessa looked out the window at the desert. "Nothing. It's too remote from Lowell to be useful to smugglers and not rich enough for mining operations."

"Settlers?"

She approached the panel and, with a series of hand motions, flipped through various data displays from the rover. Mobility disabled. Comm disabled. Life support disabled. The only thing functioning was the tracking beacon.

Jake dropped into a chair and thumped his fists on the cushioned arms. "There are settlers once," he said. "A family. Man, woman, two kids. They are all killed."

Alejandro waited while Jake drew a long breath.

"I finds them. I don't likes to remember."

"An accident?" Alejandro asked.

Jake looked away, mouth set in a fierce line.

"It was brutal," Nessa finished for him. "Word got around. No settlers dared go there after."

Jake must have seen Mlada's fate mirrored in that family's. "How long ago was this?"

"A year or so," Nessa said.

Assuming Nessa's assessment of the area was correct, Andre Rand would have no interest in Lunae Planum. But maybe his agents discovered unexpected wealth there. Or someone else appropriated it for purposes unknown. Whatever the case, Miguel didn't end up there by choice.

Alejandro joined Nessa at the panel. She pointedly ignored him, which told him she knew what he was about to say. He didn't bother saying it.

"It's too dangerous," she told him.

"Not for me." She had no authority over him unless she wanted to take him prisoner. Given their history, she would only do so if threatened.

"How do I know you'll bring him back?"

"Where else would I take him?"

Nessa returned to the window. The red of the sands reflected in her face and hair. "The Belt. He's your brother."

"I'm not rescuing him, Nessa. I'm not even sure I like him. I just want information. Once I have it, he'll be safest with you."

She thought about that. "Jake should go with you."

Jake rose, ready to leave.

"I'd rather do this alone," Alejandro said.

Nessa said nothing, so Jake took command. "I goes with you, or you doesn't goes at all."

"C'mon, Jake. This is between Miguel and me."

"Then I stuffs my fingers in my ears when you talk."

Damn stubborn, he was. Just like the rest of them. Somebody had to bend or they'd none of them see Miguel again. "Fine," Alejandro said. "But it won't end well."

Jake grinned. "I makes sure it ends good."

Alejandro didn't find that reassuring.

Linh could all but feel the monitor's bony fingers grope her flesh. A battered desk with a balky tablet that flitted madly through a rainbow of colors separated her from the creep, but she knew what lecherous thoughts played in his mind. Randall was his name, disciplining the crew his job. His breath shallowed as his eyes drank her up. Randall had read the report on how Linh and Ricard had been caught in the shower room and couldn't stop thinking about having a turn with her himself.

"We were just changing," Ricard said, all business, all honest. "Nothing happened." They stood at near attention before the desk, side-by-side, awaiting Randall's verdict. If they were lucky, he might fire them and tell them to get the hell off the asteroid. Linh didn't know how serious the charge was, but in their circumstance, being kicked out would be a lucky break.

"Uh-huh. Together. Outside scheduled time for either men or women. C'mon, be honest. Everyone knows Cassie's a lazy bitch. We only have her 'cause the boss won't pop for a cleaning bot. You figured you'd be alone. If she hadn't finally decided to drag a mop about the place, you'd of been hard docked half a minute later."

Clearly, truth wasn't going to work. Linh decided they might as well play along. "Can't blame us, can you?" She winked at Randall, who swallowed and licked his lips. "The risk's half the fun."

"Yeah, well, the boss don't like disruptions. Word gets around you two were screwing in the showers, next thing you know, everyone's doing it." He gave Linh an excessively long examination. "Hell, even me. Tell you what. I'll look the other way for a quickie here on my desk."

Ricard's jaw clenched. Linh put a hand on his arm. "Better not. Like you said. The boss wouldn't like it."

Randall fiddled with the panel, then pounded on it. "I can't get this damn thing to show me your names. Nothing works around here. Look, maybe…" He licked his lips again. "No, you're right. Too dangerous. A week from now, my quarters." Raising an eyebrow at Ricard, he added, "Nothin' personal, just a business deal. Fair's fair."

"No," Ricard said before Linh could reply. "It wouldn't be appropriate. We're engaged."

Rising, Randall sneered at him, but Ricard was taller and stronger, so it failed to rattle him. "I could make life bad for you," Randall said. "Real bad."

"So fire us."

"How long you been here? Nobody gets fired. Anyone misbehaves, they get thrown in the mines with the slaves."

Panic engulfed Linh. Her grip on Ricard's arm tightened as she silently initiated her breathing exercises to fight it off.

The threat didn't faze Ricard. If anything, it amused him, which was odd because so little ever did. "Go ahead," he said.

"Sure, then I can take her whenever I want."

"Hey," Linh said. The men looked at her as though they'd forgotten she was there. "It's all right. Let us go, and you can have me." She hoped she knew what she was doing. If she miscalculated, things would turn ugly on several levels. "We'll just wait a couple weeks, like you said."

"I said one week," Randall snapped. "And don't think I'll forget after two. I won't."

"I'm willing," she said. "But two weeks, just to be safe. And to give this guy time to come to terms with it." She gave Ricard a light punch on the arm. He was as close to seething as she'd ever known him.

Randall pouted. "What's to come to terms with?"

"He's possessive."

Huffing, Randall dropped into his chair and slapped at the panel. "Damn thing never works," he grumbled. "Fine. Two weeks. But if you don't show, I'll come for you. And I won't be gentle."

"I'll show," Linh promised.

"Get back to work."

Linh steered Ricard out of the cramped office, down a narrow, rusted corridor, and on to the armory, where they picked up weapons and gear based on what they'd seen the bulls toting. "That was stupid," Ricard said. "It doesn't matter if he throws us back with the slaves. We know how to escape."

"I don't want to do that again. It's too risky."

"You don't want him jumping you, either."

"Not going to happen," she insisted. "We have two weeks to get off this rock. Once we're gone, we're gone. The Belt's a big place, and we'll be all the way to Ganymede, right?"

Ricard hooked a transceiver on his belt. "I should have broken his neck."

"You're a scientist." She raised herself on her toes and kissed his lips. "Not a killer."

"For him," Ricard said evenly, "I'd make an exception."

The last time Miguel tangled with a woman, he found a knife kissing his throat. Only his pride had been injured that time, but he wasn't sure his luck would hold now. This woman had the spring of a cheetah, the calm of a soaring falcon, and a blade of such dark beauty, it ought to have been in a museum.

"Obsidian, isn't it?" he asked, feigning calm while the point hovered centimeters from his left eye. The floor and walls of the room in which he was shackled were speckled with dark red. Blood. Pirates called such places killing holds. Prisoners who went in came out dead.

"You have a good eye," the woman said with an ironic smile.

"Which I'd like to keep. Obsidian is brittle. You don't want to break a beautiful specimen just to blind me, do you?" *Keep her talking*, he told himself. *Keep her talking*. So far, there'd been only threatened violence. Bound, he'd had no chance to fight, and the woman had no fear of him. The men had left upon depositing him here, and she entered alone. She and that mesmerizing knife.

"So you are knowledgeable. I had doubts." The blade vanished into the woman's black clothing. Another took its place in her hand, this one dark metal, possibly a pseudo-alloy of titanium and synthetics. He'd used excavation tools made from similar materials.

"I assume there's a reward," Miguel said. "Whatever it is, I'm worth more to you alive."

"There is a reward," she said. The knife vanished. "We have no interest."

"Who's we?" Miguel wouldn't put it past Andre Rand to stage a public execution.

"I am Hitomi. I am the eyes and ears, the claws and teeth of the true mistress of Mars."

Great. Psychos. The planet was overrun with them. Rand could hardly be called sane anymore, and Miguel was none too sure about Jake and even Nessa O'Clery. Now this woman. But it was safest to play along. Keep her talking. "And who's that?"

Hitomi answered with her ironic smile.

"A woman, at any rate. What does she want with me?"

"Every great one requires operatives. You have skills crucial to the administration of this planet."

"Rand doesn't think so. He views me as an obstruction."

"Andre Rand," Hitomi said, "is a fool. He ceded control of Mars without realizing it."

The enemy of my enemy is my friend, he thought. "Then why am I bound?"

Hitomi showed him a small, black device. When she tapped it, his shackles fell and thunked on the floor.

Miguel rubbed his sore wrists. "Thank you. What happens next?"

"What you seek will be found in Utopia. You will go there."

He almost laughed. He'd claimed to work for the fictious Utopia Industries, but as a destination, Utopia would be a disaster. He'd long since rejected it as a research site. Besides, Hitomi wouldn't be interested in the search for life. Why did she want him there?

She seemed to read his thoughts. "We are building facilities. You will be the administrator. Much remains to be done. You will develop hydro stations and mines, improve the spaceport, and install necessary defensive emplacements."

An exobiologist for a facilities manager? "Doesn't the true mistress of Mars have people for that?"

"She has you."

"What if I refuse?"

"That would be unfortunate, Dr. Hernandez, for your students as well as for you."

"My students?"

Hitomi inclined her head.

"They're long gone. I sent them away."

She produced the obsidian knife again and gazed on it with evident affection. "You did. I found them. They are now my guests." She ran a finger along the flat of the blade.

For a moment he was on Earth watching Mona walk out the door, Sef cradled in her arms, refusing to look back or even say goodbye. He had no defense; everything had been his fault. Was history repeating itself? He'd tried to spare his students, his surrogate children, but once again those he cared for were trapped in the web he had woven. He'd done everything right this time, followed the rules—at least where the science was concerned—and still the world fell apart. He should have foreseen this, should have sent the students off Mars long before. Once more he had no defense, only a plea.

"Don't hurt them. Please. They have nothing to do with it."

"You are sharp in some matters, Dr. Hernandez," Hitomi said, "but dull in others." She put away the blade and gave him a look of mock pity. "Had you listened, you would have understood. Your students have everything to do with it."

Chapter 16

"Watch my eyes." In constant motion, Salvador bobbed left and right, back and forward, gloves raised before him, jabbing at his sparring partner without connecting.

Miguel tried to anticipate his movements and dodge or block the attack. "Your eyes aren't doing the punching," he said. That earned him a knock in the shoulder, a blow he didn't see coming.

"Your opponent's eyes show what he's thinking."

Miguel threw a punch. Salvador blocked it and scored with a right hook. Staggering back, Miguel resumed a defensive stance. "How? If I'm looking at your eyes and you're looking at mine—"

"Don't argue. Just do it."

Fifteen minutes more, and Miguel had had enough. He'd only landed one good hit and taken more punishment than his ego could stand. They left the mat and undid their gloves. "Good thing you're a scientist," Salvador said. "You'd never make it on the streets."

"I never wanted to. I'm only doing this for you."

"Oh, thank you, big brother. Or is it surrogate father?"

"Don't start," Miguel snapped. "My face isn't on the GBI reward vids."

Salvador clapped Miguel on the back a bit too hard. "I'm a folk hero. Let's hit the showers, then you can buy me dinner to show your gratitude for the lesson."

Miguel didn't need lessons. He might not be much of a boxer, but neither were those muggers he'd encountered two months back. He fended them off well enough, even if they cracked one of his ribs. Salvador, though, had made a career of tangling with thugs, not to mention trained security guards. Since their parents' death in a shuttle malfunction seven years ago, the younger brother had advanced from petty theft to grand larceny and now sabotage. The latter put him in the Global Bureau of Investigation's sights. Salvador only avoided prison thanks to his reckless embrace of a popular insurrection in western Australia. As much as the government longed to bury him, a lot of ordinary folk talked of erecting statues in his honor.

But the tide was turning against them both, and Miguel couldn't make Salvador understand. Worse, Miguel would soon be on his way to Mars, leaving his brother with no hand, steady or otherwise, to guide him.

That subject, never far from the surface, arose again over a steak dinner at a modestly priced restaurant. "You know why I took you to the gym," Salvador said.

"To beat me up."

"Besides that."

"No clue."

Salvador lowered his voice. "Mars is rough. It's not like Earth. You gotta be ready for anything."

"Earth isn't exactly paradise. Violent crime is up six percent this year alone, five without you."

"It's not about numbers, Miguel. It's about staying alive."

Miguel sawed off a chunk of meat and twirled it on his fork. "I didn't know you cared."

"You never gave me a chance."

"I tried. You flew way off trajectory."

"Can't you just be my brother? You're not Father."

All their conversations crashed in this same barren field. "No," Miguel admitted. "But I do try to be what he wanted me to be."

"Uh-huh. First you screw up your career, then you tuck your tail between your legs. Mona—"

"Don't go there," Miguel warned, pointing a fork at his brother.

Salvador leaned back. "Truth hurts, huh?"

"I begged her to come with me. I never wanted…" Miguel set down his utensils and folded his hands in his lap to stop the shaking

But Salvador wasn't done with him. "When you dig your grave, you always dig a few others. They don't send just anyone to Mars. How'd you get that ticket?"

"We weren't talking about me. We were talking about you."

Salvador dropped his fork on his plate. The clank drew attention from nearby diners. "You've crossed into my world whether you admit it or not. I know how it works. Either you qualify, or you pay under the table. You don't qualify, and you don't have the cash for a bribe. So who'd you fuck? Would you have banged her extra hard to buy Mona and Sef passage?"

Miguel about shoved the table into Salvador, but neither of them dared get into a brawl. He had to keep a low profile until he was away from Earth, and his brother had to avoid prison.

"You can run from Earth, but you can't run from yourself," Salvador said. "Or from Mars. Mars devours people. You'll lie, cheat, steal, and screw your way through life, or you'll end up dead. Watch their eyes, Miguel. Always watch their eyes." He turned his attention to his meal.

That eye thing again. Miguel couldn't even see Salvador's now. "What about you? You're wanted by the whole world. Where will you end up?"

Salvador shrugged. "Wherever I'm needed," he said.

Lying on a hard bunk in a bare, gray room, Miguel stared at the gray ceiling, remembering. Salvador soon fled to Mars, too, bearing the name Enrique Olvera, where he predictably sank into a new life of crime and landed on Lowell Security's hotlist. After one final bout with Miguel, this one real and nearly fatal, Salvador vanished into the Belt, an outlaw with an attempted murder charge dangling over his head.

Is that where you're needed? Miguel wondered. *A would-be Cain, banished to a cold rock in the silent dark?*

Salvador didn't fit anybody's image of a prophet, yet he'd been right about Mars. No matter how judiciously Miguel played by the rules, he found himself on the wrong side of Andre Rand time and again. He learned to watch his opponents' eyes and countered them at every turn, yet here he was, outlawed, hunted, twice captured—thrice, if he counted Carl Metzler's betrayal—and locked in a little gray room. By Hitomi's decree, he was bound for Utopia to manage development of a new colony. While that made zero sense, he couldn't refuse. She had his students. Their safety depended on his cooperation. Her eyes had betrayed no falsehood.

Salvador had been right about Miguel, too. To survive, to avoid oblivion, he fought by whatever means necessary. What was Carmen Rand but a weapon against her husband? With a bit of chicanery, he'd slipped from Nessa O'Clery's allegedly unescapable trap. Now, swept up in Hitomi's talons, he needed a knife to pry them open, and he didn't care whose blood he spilled, so long as it wasn't his students'.

The door creaked open, and Zachary slipped in, his mop of blonde hair in disarray, his lanky form as relaxed as ever. "Time to go," he said.

Miguel noted the firearm hanging on his belt and looked him in the eyes. Zachary was all but laughing, begging Miguel to attack. Either he was a quick draw, or there were guards nearby.

"Utopia?" Miguel asked.

"Yep."

"That's a long ride."

"Not on a sub-orbital."

Miguel rose. "You have one?"

"We got everything. We're well-funded."

Which meant someone rich stood behind Hitomi. "Andre Rand must love you."

Zachary laughed. "He hates us as much as we hate him."

That supported Hitomi's claim that Rand was her plaything. Either she was stealing from him, or her cash hailed from another port. Probably the latter. Earth had long since lost interest in Mars, so not from there. A few wealthy financiers bankrolled development in the Belt and beyond. Had one of them found something of value on Mars?

Zachary motioned toward the door. Miguel passed through ahead of him. As he thought, a pair of burly security guards waited outside. They escorted him to a rover, where all four suited up. A ten-minute drive across the rust soil brought them to a small space-port where two ships were docked, a needle-shaped interplanetary cruiser and a winged suborbital capsule not much bigger than the rover. They marched Miguel across the sand-coated tarmac and into the little craft. In the passenger compartment, Miguel found two familiar faces.

"Petrina! Martin!" He rushed the Ulengas and embraced them. "Are you okay?"

"We're fine, Professor," Petrina said, although she seemed less than enthused at the reunion.

Martin grimaced and looked away. "We didn't think we'd ever find you," he said.

Miguel released them and stepped back. "Find me? You were supposed to leave."

"You were in trouble," Petrina said.

Damn them. He should have put them on the ship himself. Miguel sank into the seat beside Petrina. An awkward silence settled over them. Whatever had happened, it must have been bad.

"What happens now?" Petrina finally asked.

"We're going to Utopia. Someone's building facilities there. I've been told that's where I'll find what I want."

Martin frowned. "Why would anyone think that? Nobody's even done a mineral survey of Utopia."

"I don't know." Miguel lowered his voice so the guards wouldn't overhear. "Whoever's behind this has money, and it's not Andre Rand. Someone wants to steal Mars from him."

"Professor," Petrina said, leaning toward him. She sounded like an angry mother about to scold a delinquent child. Martin looked about to punch something.

"What's wrong?" Miguel asked.

"Everything."

The engines roared to life, affording them acoustic cover.

"Tell me," Miguel said.

Petrina told him. Without mercy.

Once the shadows receded from her mind, Carmen left Lowell Colony for her home in the cliff. Promising Andre she would return soon, inviting him to visit for the first time since she moved outside the colony, she boarded her rover in the predawn dusk out of sight of the hoard of videographers.

The long ride through the desert gave her too much time to think. Her fear of Celia Fundichely had sublimated, leaving questions. Why did Celia want Carmen's blessing? How did she learn of Carmen's affair with Miguel? And most important, why did she want Utopia? Not as a hiding place, certainly. Andre called Celia paranoid, but even she had to know there was no place to hide on Mars. Her whereabouts would be discovered, sooner rather than later. Utopia must offer something she wanted.

Carmen moved into the forward seat beside the driver, a handsome if timid young man. He gave her a nervous smile before focusing on the sand that stretched to the horizon. He was new to this detail, but he must have heard rumors.

She smiled at him. "I need comm."

"Yes, ma'am." He tapped a button and a comm panel activated before her.

She looked up Dr. Gene Lloyd, Miguel's friend and colleague, one of her few academic contacts. Although he was ignorant of Carmen's dalliance with Miguel, Gene had met the first lady at a few ceremonial events. He would remember her.

When Gene's image appeared, he looked older than she recalled and not a little spooked. "I'm honored, ma'am," he said. "To what do I owe the pleasure?"

"I trust you're well, Dr. Lloyd? You look troubled."

He didn't respond. He didn't even smile.

"Don't worry," she said. "This is a private connection."

"You're certain?"

"Andre won't abide anyone eavesdropping on me."

"Except himself."

"Not even him. You've no cause for worry."

Gene didn't look mollified. "Sorry. I have a history with Security."

That surprised her. She couldn't imagine Gene ever getting into trouble. "Nothing I care about. I'm a bad girl, myself."

He looked down, embarrassed. "How can I help you, ma'am?"

"What do we know about Utopia?"

If the question surprised him, he didn't show it. "Not much. No on-site research has been conducted. There's no point. It's too far away to provide resources to Lowell. Why do you ask?"

"My lust for revenge." She gave him a conspiratorial wink. "Andre and I were playing a little game the other day, picking places for future generations to build colonies. I suggested Utopia. He laughed at me. I want to prove him wrong, make him apologize."

Gene didn't buy it. She could tell.

"What?" she asked.

He stuck to her question. "On Earth," he said, "humans live in the most inhospitable environments. We always find ways to survive. Given enough time, Mars will be the same. We don't know much about Utopia now, but yes, someday people will colonize it."

"That's a brilliant argument. I'm going to use it. But it would be even better if, say, we could mine gold there." She laughed.

He didn't. "Ma'am."

"Yes?"

"You're sure this is secure?"

"Absolutely." It wasn't strictly. Andre could tap in if he wanted, but he wouldn't. Not right now. Thanks to Celia Fundichely, he was more protective of Carmen than usual.

Gene nodded without conviction. "A pair of Miguel Hernandez's students visited me. Martin and Petrina Ulenga. Do you know them?"

Those two had been busy. "I do. What about them?"

"They hacked into my records. At least, I think they did. Someone accessed files I haven't touched in a long time."

"What sort of files?"

"Everything I had. They seemed particularly interested in medical files."

"Why would they care about those?"

He waved off her question. "The point is, if they broke into my files, they could have broken into Miguel's."

Undoubtedly. It probably would have been even easier, given nobody would be around to notice. "What would they find?"

He looked away in embarrassment. "I'm sorry ma'am, but it was obvious to me, even if no one else noticed. He mentioned you a few times. When he talked about you…" He shrugged.

"Ah." She tried to keep her expression serious, but she couldn't quite manage it. She liked Petrina and Martin's initiative. "So that's how they knew."

Gene gaped at her. "They told you?"

"Oh, more than that. They thought I knew where Miguel went. They tried to twist my arm."

"I hope this doesn't cause any…" He shook his head.

"It won't."

"Meaning no offense, but your husband can be cruel."

Of course, he could. It came with the territory. "Not to me," she said. "My affair with Miguel is over, and it was never anything to do with you. All I hoped from you is information about Utopia. If there's nothing to tell…" She shrugged.

"This is more than a game, isn't it?"

Denials would only raise suspicions, so she told the truth, or at least part of it. "Andre's thinking about declaring Utopia a research preserve. There must be something special about it."

That intrigued Gene. He tapped on his panel and read the display. "Nothing I can find. I seem to recall Miguel considered it a potential collection site long ago, but he eliminated it."

Carmen didn't imagine Celia Fundichely had an interest in fossils. "Oh, well," she said. "I guess we'll find out in due course. I appreciate your time."

During the conversation, the driver had kept his eyes forward, but once Carmen terminated the connection, he glanced at her. "You and Dr. Hernandez?" he asked. His voice nearly squeaked.

Carmen leaned back and winked at him. "I get bored easily," she said. "And I'm about to ask for something that will lead to days of boredom."

He swallowed and neither looked at her nor inquired.

"Take me to Utopia," she said.

"Ma'am?"

"Utopia. Can you do it?"

"I…" he shook his head. "It's too far. We'd need a lot of supplies. And if anything went wrong, we'd be dead before a rescue party could reach us."

"You'd enjoy dying with me."

He gaped at her and nearly ran them into the rim of a small crater.

"Can you do it?" she repeated once he had the vehicle back under control.

He shook his head, then nodded, then tapped on the panel and got a course plot. He studied it for a moment. "I guess," he said. "With enough supplies."

"Put 'em on my tab," she said.

When she commandeered the stealth rover, Subcommander Leah Leaf knew her career, if not her life, was over if this didn't work. Andre Rand would see to that. Security only had three of these vehicles. No one less than a subcommander could authorize their use. Heavily armed and camouflaged, invisible to radar, equipped with tracking systems, they'd been built to locate and disrupt illegal mining operations. They seldom found use. Security had their hands full keeping order in and around Lowell Colony, so the Martian wilderness remained lawless, or would until the mayor's outside consultants ramped up operations. Although she had the rank, Leah lacked a valid reason to commandeer the rover.

Yet here she was, skirting the northern fringe of Lunae Planum, trying to make sense of the electronic environment. Dozens of distinct signals crisscrossed the land where none should. The tracking systems had been monitoring since she left the vicinity of Lowell. The farther out she got, the more signals appeared. Triangulating as the rover moved, the computer generated a map pinpointing their origins. Some were fixed, others on the move. Some were sporadic, others nearly steady. Most signals were directed, while some skipped off the fickle Martian ionosphere, making their sources impossible to locate.

One of the strongest, steadiest sources lie to the south, in the heart of Lunae Planum. The vid cameras hadn't picked up anything yet, but some manner of installation was nearby. She meant to find it. With luck, the residents would have word of Dr. Miguel Hernandez and his students. If not, she at least could provide valuable intelligence for Mayor Rand. Nobody suspected the wilderness harbored so much activity. He'd want to know as much as possible about it. If she didn't find Hernandez, that intel could save her skin.

She waited until nightfall, then eased the rover forward through the dark with the help of ultra-low-light vids. Zeroing in on the transmission point, she advanced at a crawl over the course of four and a half hours. A quarter kilometer out from the source, she began to circle it, recording a full-spectrum map of the area. An hour later, she had the results on the rover's panel: a cleared area with a scattering of low buildings and several spacecraft, some orbital, some suborbital.

Somebody had built a primitive spaceport.

Leah had disrupted smuggling operations before. They tended toward small and temporary. Whenever Security found them, smugglers ran with everything in tow. A firefight was the last thing they wanted. People, equipment, and merchandise held too much value. Therefore, these weren't smugglers. A facility on this scale could only be Mayor Rand's outside security force. They must have built it well before they cut the deal. He'd be furious. For now, best not to cross orbits with them. She positioned spy vids around the perimeter and retreated eastward, following another signal, this one weaker and sporadic.

Later in the day, the spy vids caught a suborbital launching from the spaceport on a trajectory for Utopia.

Why the hell go there? Leah wondered.

Before she could speculate, her rover came under attack.

The suborbital landed in southeast Utopia, where the cone of Elysium Mons rose in the distance. A barely adequate stretch of rock had been cleared for landings and takeoffs. Alongside, a lone building jutted from a scarp on the northern edge of a scalloped depression, three levels tall with dark windows along the façade. Dr. Miguel Hernandez and Martin and Petrina Ulenga were escorted in envirosuits across the scraped rock and given a room each on the first level. Once the retreating footfalls faded to nothing, Miguel tried to open the door, but it refused to budge. He wasn't entirely cut off, though. He'd been provided a panel and found that his students had accounts on the facility network. They could at least talk, but not likely in private. Someone would be monitoring. They kept conversation to a minimum.

He poked around the network for a time. He had access to little and learned less. Petrina and Martin told him far more on the way out: their capture and torture, the severe aftereffects, Dr. Lloyd's reluctant help, the nanobots, their meeting with Carmen. They were all but drowning in the dust of Mars, for which they—Petrina particularly—blamed him.

He accepted responsibility. All they'd suffered and whatever was still to come rested upon his shoulders. He could almost get on board with serving Andre Rand's shadowy nemesis but for one thing: his students were Hitomi's gun to his head. He could sacrifice most things for the right price, but not them. He had to free them from her snare, and for that, he needed more information. Might as well go to the source. Activating his panel, he sent a message addressed to Petrina but saying, "We need to talk, Hitomi."

A vid connection opened all but instantly. Hitomi's serene face gazed at him from the panel. "Very well, Dr. Hernandez. Talk."

"If I'm to work for you," he said, "I need to know the parameters."

"You will be provided the necessary parameters at the appropriate time."

"We may not agree on what counts as necessary."

The corners of her mouth lifted.

"Who am I working for?"

"Consider me your manager."

"That's not an answer."

"It suffices."

Given that she'd gone to some trouble get him here, Miguel doubted she'd off him merely for being obnoxious, so he powered forward. "It doesn't. Who's in charge? What do they want with me? What do they want with Petrina and Martin? I won't be party to—"

"Be still, Dr. Hernandez. In due course, your questions will be answered."

"You'll find me stubbornly uncooperative until then."

Hitomi answered with another subtle smile.

"You don't need them as a threat. If you're upfront with me—"

"You have considerable capacity for treachery," Hitomi said. "You and Carmen Rand were well matched. But you would neither betray nor abandon your protégés. Fail to cooperate, and you will watch while they suffer far worse than Andre Rand meted out."

Damn her! Backed into a corner again, Miguel made one last

effort. "At least give me something. Who are we working for?"

"You accept the position?"

"I have no choice."

Hitomi inclined her head, a gesture as profound as a full-on bow. "I am gratified."

"Wonderful," he said. "Now that you have my cooperation, let the Ulengas go."

"No, Dr. Hernandez. It would be folly to trust you. Moreover, they have other uses."

"Like what?

"That will be revealed in time."

"This 'true mistress of Mars,'" Miguel pressed. "Who is she?"

"An enigma, Dr. Hernandez. A mystery known to all but fathomed by none."

The connection broke. Miguel stared at the now-blank panel, dumbfounded as the pieces fell into place. Rich. From the Belt. Well-known yet enigmatic.

Good God.

Celia Fundichely wanted Mars.

Chapter 17

The bulls—Quan Linh and Ricard Fulbert among them—herded the slaves into the cargo hold before making their way to the rec deck, or wrecked deck as most of them called it (with good reason). Most of the hologames were on the fritz. The space billiards globes were all cracked and missing balls. And the vid library offered nothing newer than ten years old. Mostly, the bulls talked and slept in decrepit chairs surrounded by stained gray walls. A few were gambling on the rolls of lightly magnetized icosahedral dice in a metal tray. Ship's acceleration was currently Mars-normal, but the extra stick made it harder to cheat by bumping the table.

Linh found space billiards fascinating despite the damaged units. In a meter-radius crystal globe, a collection of colored metallic balls floated in a magnetized vacuum that simulated zero gravity, occasionally colliding with each other and the rim of the globe. When she touched the crystal, small electric charges zapped any ball within a few centimeters, altering its trajectory and spin. The object was to knock as many balls as possible into a chute at the bottom, where they were collected and scored. Linh understood the physics, but nudging them just right proved delightfully challenging.

Ricard Fulbert thought it maddening. He understood the theory as well as Linh but didn't have her finesse. In the first five games, she outscored him twelve percent, and his current score was worse. "Damn it," he muttered as he sent a blue ball skittering off in the wrong direction. "I hit that too late."

Linh manipulated a green ball, which careened into a red ball, which knocked a yellow ball toward the chute. It missed by five centimeters. "Don't force it," she told him. "Just kiss it."

"I'm not putting my lips on this thing. God knows when it was last cleaned."

She laughed. "You're always so literal."

Moving around the globe to stand beside her, Ricard tried another shot, this one coming a bit closer to the mark. "I overheard some talk," he whispered. "We're taking on supplies at a station today. Some of our esteemed colleagues are planning to jump ship." He nodded toward a huddle of three bulls talking in the corner. "They hope to sign on a freighter."

"Is that allowed?"

"They're at the end of their contracts. They can re-up or walk."

"We didn't sign on in the first place," Linh said. "If they find out…" She took a straightforward shot and knocked a purple ball down the chute.

"They won't," Ricard said. "Slaves can't escape. Nobody's looking for us. So long as Randall doesn't catch on, we'll be fine."

Linh shuddered, remembering the monitor's leer, her false promise to come to him, his threat to be rough should she fail to show. But Ricard wouldn't let her come to harm. She didn't need to see him fight to know he had the advantage of size and a fierce determination to protect her.

Putting Randall from her mind, she asked, "Think we can find a ship to Ganymede?"

"Depends. We may have to make some transfers. The problem is money, but I have an idea for that." He glanced at the gamblers. After another failed shot, he threw up his hands. "I give up. You're clearly the winner again."

"Six in a row," she chided. "Care to make it seven?"

"Absolutely not."

They found a pair of unoccupied chairs that weren't disintegrating and sat apart from the others. Linh leaned her head back and closed her eyes. Images flitted through her mind, a collage of everything they'd suffered since leaving Mars. Her torture at the hands of Lowell Security seemed so far off, she could almost believe it hadn't happened.

"Did we make a mistake?" she asked.

"Mistake?"

"Maybe we should've stayed with Petrina and Martin." She opened her eyes and studied Ricard's face. He seemed as composed as ever.

"I doubt they've had it any easier."

"But we would have been together."

Ricard shifted toward her and put his arm around her shoulders. "We can't undo what's done. We're here. Our objective is Ganymede. That's where Dr. Hernandez wanted us."

She knew, but she missed working with the others, missed the night around the faux fire, missed the haunting landscape of Mars. The Belt had been a nightmare and Ganymede remained a ghost she couldn't quite see. Mars was home. She wept for it while Ricard held her and the ship slipped through the darkness.

"Speaking of which," Ricard said once she had calmed. Rising, he approached the gamblers and watched until they invited him to play. When he made a show of being broke, they each floated him a small loan. Linh hoped he was better at dice than billiards. Ninety minutes later, he rose, paid back his debts, and returned to her side.

"How'd it go?" she asked.

"Passable," he said with no sign of emotion.

"How passable?"

He shrugged and said with a straight face, "I wonder if they have a casino where we're going."

It must have gone better than passable. "I hope not. You'll probably lose it all again."

Hours later they docked, and the crew debarked on a station bearing a designator too long for its size. Unofficially, according to the guy working the food counter where they ate, the place was called Morana. He wore an electronic nametag pinned to his grimy white hat. It read, "Yevhen."

"Where does Morana orbit?" Ricard asked as Yevhen slid them plates of a reconstituted amalgam of stuff they didn't want to think about.

"In space. What matters it? You're in the Belt. However you got here, you'll live and die here and never know where you are."

"We're going to Ganymede."

Yevhen eyed Ricard with skepticism before giving Linh a more upbeat review. "Why? You do something bad?"

"No. We're—"

Linh nudged Ricard. It wouldn't be smart to advertise their identities.

"We're sick of herding slaves," he said. "We want some gravity under our feet."

"Yeah, but Ganymede?" Yevhen asked. "That ice ball? You should pick a decent station. If you have money, leastwise."

"We don't," Linh said.

"Me, neither. That's why I'm here."

Linh and Ricard took a table in the back, not that it gave them much cover. There were only ten tables in the place, three of them taken. Still, the inadequate lighting hid them, and they ate in silence, not much caring that the food tasted like sulfur stuffed with salt. They were about finished when a fellow crew member shuffled in, ordered, and took a seat near the front. Linh tapped Ricard and pointed.

Randall.

"Damn it," Ricard mumbled

Linh slid down and covered her face with her hand.

Through the night, explosions tore into sand and rock, and fire engulfed the stealth rover. Subcommander Leah Leaf gave as good as she got, possibly better, returning blast for blast. The armor held up against whatever they hurled at her. Unfortunately, she only vaguely knew where the enemy hid and had no idea who she was fighting. As the sun burst over the horizon, her vid panels revealed a jagged expanse of red littered with blast craters, metal fragments, and bodies—a dozen bodies in ruptured envirosuits thrown about the landscape, their blood mingled with the sand.

And one other thing.

Atop a rise, the barrel of a massive gun pointed square at her. Smoke belched from the muzzle, and her rover flipped as a roar ravaged her ears. Moments or hours later—she couldn't be sure—hands grabbed her, and she was hauled half-conscious from the rover and dragged across the face of Mars to a great rock cliff. Then darkness, sounds of metal and muted voices, and her helmet was removed. She sucked in cold, recycled air.

Somebody kicked her in the ribs.

Leah lay face down on a stone floor, dust filling her mouth. She turned her head and spat it out. A pair of black boots stepped before her face.

"Who are you?" The voice was male, sharp, that of someone used to running interrogations.

She tried to look up, but one of the boots settled on top of her head.

"Don't. Tell me your name."

"Carla," she said. "Carla Livingstone."

"Where from?"

What kind of question was that? There was only one place on Mars to be from. Or was there? She remembered the previous night, before the attack, the sea of signals, the spaceport. "Lunae Planum," she said.

"Damn it," another voice growled. "I told you not to mess with those people."

"How was I to know? That rover screamed Lowell Security."

"Then you should have left it."

"Shut up. Let me handle this."

"I'm telling Mudiwa."

"Yeah, you do that."

The boot returned, this time shoving at Leah's shoulder, forcing her onto her back. She looked into the dark eyes of a skeletal man with jet skin. He seemed too young to project such authority. "Carla Livingstone," he said. "What are you doing here?"

Flat on her back, Leah met his eyes. "Prospecting," she said.

"For what, sand?"

She figured that didn't need a response. Her tormentor did. He kicked her again. "Keep that up," she warned, "and I'll rip that leg off."

He drew his weapon, a nasty-looking silver number, and pointed it at her face. "You think?"

He was good at threats, anyway. Leah wondered if he was as good at follow-through. "It may be the last thing I do," she affirmed, "but yeah."

"Big talker. Sit up. You look like a whore, lying there with your legs open." He stepped back, keeping the weapon trained on her face.

She hadn't realized she was in that position. Pushing up, she sat cross-legged on the floor and tried to stare down her captor. He wore a dark green jumpsuit that might have been a uniform. They were in the middle of a small rock chamber, rounded at the corners, with passageways on two sides. She didn't like her chances of escape. One passageway probably led out, but the odds of getting it right weren't great. "What do you want?" she asked.

"Revenge. You killed a lot of our people."

"What do you expect? You fired first."

"We expected you to run away."

She supposed that made sense. Not many rovers blundering into an ambush would have the armor and armaments to withstand it. "So you were wrong."

"You were looking for a fight. A rover equipped like that..." He shook his head. "You weren't joyriding."

"I like being prepared," Leah told him. "You never know who you're going to run into out here."

A woman appeared in the passageway to her left. "Ain't that the truth," she said. Another step, and the light revealed her to be as black as Leah's captor. She wore the same manner of dark green jumpsuit but with a white bandana tied about her head. Leah thought they had met once, long ago, but she couldn't quite place the face. It was older now, worn by hardship. Those dark eyes were harder than any she had ever seen, yet humor lurked behind them.

The woman waved the man off. He holstered his weapon and stood back without relaxing his guard. "I'm Mudiwa," she said. "I'm the boss. And you are?"

"Carla Livingstone," Leah said. "From Lunae Planum."

Mudiwa wagged a finger. "Na, na, na. You're Leah Leaf, from Lowell Colony. You tortured me nine years ago."

"Wasn't me," Leah objected, although it could have been. She'd been a senior interrogator then. "I never heard of anyone named Mudiwa."

"Oh, I changed my name, baby. And you're a big, big girl now, soon to be commander of Schiaparelli Security. Putting people through hell really worked out for you, didn't it?"

"I don't know you," Leah repeated. "I'm from Lunae Planum."

Mudiwa squatted in front of her and stared into her eyes. "Question is, what the hell you doing out here?" Her eyes widened in mock surprised. "Oh, oh, oh! I know!" She looked over her shoulder. "Oh, Jimmy, I know what she wants! She wants that scientist, that Hernandez fellow. Of course!" She stood and laughed at Leah. "Oh, baby, you're in for a big surprise. He's gone. Poof!" She spread her fingers. "Like a ghost. Not that I have any use for him, but I do listen. I do hear things. Trackers vanish when they go after him. Also like ghosts. Mars eats them alive."

Theatrics and wild stories about her missing trackers didn't interest Leah. Only one thing did, so she dropped the pretense. "Mayor Rand will pay to get me back. Name your price."

"See, Jimmy? She is so Leah Leaf from Lowell. No, Leah. Rand can't pay my price. You tortured me. Those nasty little nanobots are still in my body. But I've made peace with them. I've been saving them for the day I could share them with you. And sweetie, that day has come."

Not if she could help it. She got to her feet, keeping her eyes on Mudiwa's. "You've been hiding in this rock for nine years, waiting for me to blunder by?"

Mudiwa waggled her hand. "Mmmm. Doing odd jobs. A little smuggling, a little mercenary work. I finally landed a big, big contract. Huge. Hugest ever. I'll be set for life. You blundering by was a bonus, Leah. Oh, I'm going to enjoy this."

Leah laughed at her. "You're mad. What big contracts ever come to Mars?"

"You don't know? I thought you of all people had to know."

"I know about Schiaparelli, but that's hardly something you'd be involved with."

"In a roundabout way, I am," Mudiwa said. "Celia Fundichely is bankrolling Schiaparelli, and I'm here for Celia." She made a gun with her fingers and play-shot Leah in the forehead.

Which made no sense. No way would Celia Fundichely set foot on Mars. She hid in the shadows of the Belt. People said nobody ever saw her, not even her closest advisors.

"Now come." Mudiwa motioned Jimmy over. He trained the gun on Leah again while Mudiwa indicated the passageway from which she had entered. "This way. You and I are going to play."

Alejandro tracked Miguel's rover to here, a small spaceport inexplicably sited in Lunae Planum where nobody was supposed to be. Jake hadn't contributed much to the mission so far, but when they found the spaceport, anger consumed him. "This is where the settlers are killed," he growled. "I tears it down with my bare hands."

"Not now, Jake," Alejandro cautioned. "An operation like that will be heavy on security."

He monitored for a time. The spaceport sent few signals, and the only movement was the launch of a suborbital capsule. Alejandro pulled up a projected trajectory on the rover's panel. The capsule was making for Utopia, a strange destination given that nothing was there. Then again, nothing was supposed to be here, either. He had two options: search this place for Miguel, or assume he was on that ship. He asked Jake for an opinion but got only a grunt in reply.

"I say we follow," Alejandro suggested.

"Why?" Jake asked.

"Miguel needs to hide. Utopia would be one great hiding place." He fiddled with the scanners. "There's another suborbital at the far end of the field. I can pilot, assuming they don't have remote overrides. If Miguel's not in Utopia, we come back here." He transferred the departed ship's trajectory to his personal panel.

Jake rose. "And I kills anyone who gets in the way."

Alejandro preferred not to be conspicuous, but if Jake meant it, there would be no stopping him. Clearly, he saw a connection between this facility and the murdered settlers, who in turn reminded him of Mlada. The settlers had died about a year ago, according to Nessa O'Clery. They must have been taken out to make way for construction and maybe as a warning to others to keep their distance.

"We'll walk in," Alejandro decided. "Less chance of being spotted. Small arms. If anyone asks, we're maintenance."

They left the rover behind a cluster of boulders seven tenths of a kilometer from their target and made their way across the broken ground to the tarmac, veering north to put the ship between themselves and the spaceport buildings. The tack worked. Nobody rushed to stop them, at any rate. In under ten minutes, they made the ship's boarding hatch and passed through the airlock. The passenger cabin sat empty and darkened. Alejandro removed his helmet and listened. No sound from the crew compartment. Waving for Jake to follow, he moved forward.

They had just reached the flight controls when from behind someone called, "Hey!"

Alejandro turned, but Jake had already delivered a savage uppercut to the intruder's jaw, which sent the man flying in the weak gravity. He crashed against the rear bulkhead with Jake already on him, hands about his neck, crushing his throat. A moment later, Jake stuffed the body into the airlock.

"Not here," Alejandro warned. "Jettison him once we're in flight."

"Fine," Jake said. He lumbered into the crew compartment and dropped into the co-pilot seat. "You say you can flies this thing."

Taking the pilot chair, Alejandro nodded. He uploaded the trajectory from his panel to the capsule's system and set for takeoff. Minutes later, they were airborne, and minutes after that, a familiar voice intruded over a suddenly open comm channel.

"Hello, Alejandro. You surprise me. Why are you not in a comfortable bed on Vegas station, surrounded by expensive women?"

He gaped at the panel.

Jake eyed him suspiciously. "Who's that?"

"The environmentalist," he said.

"Who?"

"My boss."

"Alejandro does not know my name, Jake," the woman said, her voice silk. "Where are you taking my ship, Alejandro?"

How they hell had she known who Jake was? "I'm—looking for someone."

"Your brother, perhaps?"

Again, how had she known? Somehow, she knew everything. No wonder Alejandro could never outmaneuver her.

"You will find him in Utopia," she assured him. "And you have my blessing. But I require one thing."

"Just one?"

"When you are done, bring my ship back."

Her ship? What was going on? "Understood," he said.

"Who," Jake insisted, "are you?"

"I am Hitomi," the environmentalist replied. "We shall soon meet."

The comm channel went dead.

"Nice lady," Jake said.

Alejandro grimaced. "Not really. She's twisty."

Jake grinned. "Like us?"

"Not at all. We're as straight as it gets."

The ship reached apogee and began its descent toward Utopia. Jake sauntered to the airlock to dump the body.

Chapter 18

Sleek as a panther, grinning like she'd won a jackpot, Mudiwa displayed a hypo of clear liquid. Sunlight streaming through a crystal-covered crack in the rock overhead sparkled in the substance. "My, my, it's such a beauty, isn't it?" she said. "You'll never guess how I got it."

Subcommander Leah didn't know what it was, much less how Mudiwa acquired it. Stripped naked, she was strapped to a smooth rock table through which seeped the Martian cold. It chilled her flesh. The man Mudiwa called Jimmy stood by the wall, eyeing Leah with contempt or lust or both.

"A doctor in the Belt was experimenting with these babies. Putting them into people, pulling them out of people. After you got done with me, I stowed away on a freighter. They caught me and threw me into a mine on a slave gang. This doctor found out you'd shot me full of nanobots. Really turned him on. He bought me and gave me a starring role in his experiments."

Mudiwa lowered the hypo and play-punched Leah in the shoulder. "God, did that scramble my brains. Later, he told me he'd extracted half the bastards and put them in a vial. I don't know why. Some technical gibberish. Then he went at me again, to see how effective half the load could be. Care to know?"

"Not really," Leah said. She tugged at the restraints, but they had no weakness, offered no way out.

"Baby, let me tell you. It hit a new high in psycho. My doctor friend was astounded, but not half as astounded as when I stabbed him through the heart with his own scalpel." She laughed again. "And now, thanks to him, I have these. Or should I say, you have them."

None too gently, she injected the fluid into Leah's side. Leah grimaced but refused to make a sound.

"Now," Mudiwa said. "We'll give them a few minutes, then we'll chat with them." She held up a black box like those Lowell Security used in interrogations. "It'll be fun. For me. Hell for you, I should think."

Leah figured she could handle it. If Mudiwa could, if Hernandez's students could, she certainly could. Meanwhile, she could do some work. "You have a vendetta against Celia Fundichely, too?"

"No, girl, that's just a job. A sweet job, though. Two, in fact. Celia's coming to Utopia. When she does, I get to do what I do best."

"Kill her," Leah suggested.

"Oh, yeah." Mudiwa made a gun with her fingers and play-shot Leah between the eyes. "Then I get a new life. I become Celia Fundichely. Isn't that great? I'll be the richest bitch in the cosmos!" She spread her arms and twirled.

"A trained bitch on a short leash."

"I'm fine with that."

"Yeah? Who's holding it?"

Mudiwa waggled a finger. "Ah, ah, ah. That's a secret."

Leah switched gears. "What if you kill the wrong woman? Nobody knows what Celia Fundichely looks like."

"That's the best part. They say she looks like me!"

Leah couldn't help it. She laughed. "And you believed them?"

Mudiwa laughed with her. "For that kind of money, you're damn right I believed. Don't be jealous. I'm sharing the wealth. You get some of my torture bots. And when we're all done, Jimmy gets you. He's been such a patient boy." She turned and winked at Jimmy, who grinned back.

"Scramble my brains if you want," Leah warned, "but if he so much as drools on me, you're both dead."

Mudiwa waggled the black box at Leah. "Ooo, big talk from someone so immobilized." She tapped the device.

A supernova exploded in Leah's head. Spinning through its heat and brilliance, she tumbled in space until she dove headlong into another sun that seared her retinas and set her body aflame. She could smell her own flesh vaporize as the blaze fragmented into a garish spectrum while a dragon roared in her ears. Oxygen was ripped from her lungs, then she plummeted into a frozen ocean. Encased in ice, frigid water filling her throat, she tried to scream, and the sound was like all the symphonies ever composed battling to be heard. Something caught her in a tight embrace and turned her agony to a pleasure so intense there was no difference. Eyes shut tight, she saw the universe pulse with radiation. Wave after wave of pleasure-pain crashed upon her until her lover and tormentor released her and a great emptiness filled her. She groped for something, anything, to hold to. She found something, though she knew not what. Her fingers sank into it and tore it to shreds while a scream echoed through her, a scream not formed in her own throat.

At the end of eternity, the nightmare dissolved into darkness and silence. Her limbs quivered. Her hands were covered in warm, sticky fluid. Vision returned like a curtain rising on a darkened stage. The lights came up, revealing but one actor.

Leah herself.

She crouched naked on the stone floor, gasping as the world reformed around her. What she saw made as little sense as the hallucinations: she was hunched over Jimmy's twisted body, his throat ripped open, her hands bathed in his blood.

"What the hell," she muttered. She clawed her way to her feet, leaned on the stone table, shook with cold, confusion, fear. She was alone with the corpse. The other woman, Mudiwa. Where was she? Had she even been there?

Yes, she had. The black box lie smashed on the table. Leah picked at the fragments as though she might reassemble it. Shredded remains of the restraints encircled her wrists and ankles. She sat on the table, tugged them off, and used them to clean the blood from her hands.

Where were her clothes? She hopped down and located them in a haphazard pile in the corner along with her envirosuit. Only her helmet was missing. She gathered everything up and returned to the table to dress. Her side felt sore. She probed her abused flesh, trying to think, trying to remember. There had been talk. A medical procedure. An injection.

Nanobots.

Hell, Mudiwa must have activated them at one hundred percent. Nobody did that, not unless the subject was slated for death. Only Leah hadn't died, maybe because she only received a partial load of nanobots. Mudiwa had said something about that, something about experiments. Whatever the reason, Leah turned berserker, tore free of the restraints, and killed Jimmy with her bare hands. Either Mudiwa had fled, or she had left Leah in Jimmy's charge before the torture climaxed.

Something struck her as funny, and she laughed before realizing what it was: Jimmy got to play with her after all, just not the way he wanted.

Where had Mudiwa gone? Leah remembered something. A fragment of conversation. A single word: Utopia. Mudiwa must have gone to Utopia.

Leah finished dressing and began to explore the cave.

They almost got out unnoticed. Randall ate at the table near the front, his back to Quan Linh and Ricard Fulbert, showing no interest in his surroundings. When done, he made for the door, leaving a tableful of trash for someone else to clean up. Pausing by the exit, he turned as though he'd forgotten something and saw them. Now he was looming over them, hands on hips, eyes ablaze. "You're jumping ship," he accused. "You're trying to cheat me."

"No," Linh objected. "We were coming back. We just needed to get out for a while."

"Liar. You're coming with me. Now." He grabbed for her wrist, but she jerked her hand away as a wave of panic washed over her.

Ricard put an arm about her and drew her to his side. "Breathe," he whispered. To Randall, he said, "Leave her alone."

"I covered for you, damn it, and she promised me sex. That was the bargain."

Ricard rose. Ten centimeters taller than Randall, he looked down on his adversary. "Leave."

Linh hugged herself and took a few deep breaths. She couldn't let the men fight. Not here. If someone called security, she and Ricard would be dumped back into the mines. But how to get rid of Randall? She could think of only one feint. It required him to be dumber than he probably was, but it was all she had. "Wait," she said. "It's okay. I'll do it. But not on the ship. I can't stand that junkpile. Find us a room."

Randall grimaced. "I'm not paying for a room."

"We'll pay. Just find us a place. I'll wait here while you look."

"Linh," Ricard said. "No."

Why did he always take things so literally? Why couldn't he see what she was doing? "It's okay," she repeated. "Go on, find us a room."

"Like hell," Randall said. "You're coming with me."

Linh shuddered. He wasn't that stupid after all.

Ricard stood his ground. "We aren't doing this."

"You're too possessive," Randall said. "I'll give her back."

Putting a hand on Ricard's arm, Linh rose. "It's okay."

He did a double take and finally got it. "Fine. But I'm coming with you. To make sure he does give you back."

Randall smirked and led them to a dim section of the station where temporary quarters were available for cheap rent. He waited while Ricard operated the automated rental kiosk and used some of his gambling winnings to secure a room. A palm print was required to program the door. Randall pushed Ricard aside and slapped his hand on the reader. "So you can't interrupt," he said.

Once they located the room, Randall palmed the door open and pushed Linh through. Inside, the place was a dump. The walls were scarred and the furniture barely holding together. Linh wondered if she could break off a chair arm and use it as a weapon.

Before Randall could close the door, Ricard pushed through. He took up position against the wall, arms crossed over his chest, a murderous glint in his eyes.

"Decided to watch?" Randall asked.

"Making sure you don't get rough."

"I get to. I warned her." He turned on Linh. "But maybe you like it rough. Is that it?"

Linh backed away and fell onto a couch at the side of the room. It creaked when she landed on it. Randall moved in, a hungry wolf stalking its prey. Panic swept through her again. Eyes shut, she turned away and wrapped her arms about herself as though that would render her invisible.

Randall never touched her. Instead, Linh heard a grunt, a crash, a yelp of pain, a terrible crack, and then a stillness that frightened her more than the noise. Shaking, she peeked and caught a glimpse of Ricard standing tall, fists at his side, looking down.

Catching her movement out of the corner of his eye, he said, "Don't look."

She squeezed her eyes shut and whimpered. Then Ricard's arms were around her. He lifted her to her feet and warned again, "Don't look." He led her like a blind woman out the door and down the corridor. She felt rather than saw growing light, and finally opened her eyes. They were in the transport center. A ragged scratch ran down the left side of Ricard's face. A smear of blood tainted his right hand. She gaped at him.

"It's nothing," he said. "Look, here's the port schedule." Leading her to a panel listing ship arrivals and departures, he scanned the entries. A modest flow of people passed them by, boots clomping on the metallic floor while in the distance machinery rumbled. "No passenger ships anytime soon, but this freighter debarks in twenty minutes. Maybe we can sign on."

Linh felt disoriented. Mustering her breathing rhythm, she clung to his arm and stared at the ship data. "It's not going to Ganymede."

"None of them are."

"It's going to Mars."

"It doesn't matter. We need to leave."

"Why?"

He pulled her close, kissed her hair, whispered in her ear. "You know why."

Randall was dead. Ricard had killed him. Murdered him. She felt like throwing up.

"Come on," Ricard said and led her to the freighter's docking bay.

The Utopia facility, Miguel discovered, was bigger than it looked. Built into a scarp, its entrance accessed the lowest of three levels. The first consisted of apartments, but having been locked in his, Miguel had no idea how many units, let alone if any were occupied. He got an introduction to the second level that morning when Hitomi messaged instructions to come to room 215. As soon as he received them, his apartment door spontaneously opened.

Arriving at his destination, he came into a modest conference room with a pristine white table surrounded by matching chairs, some still in film wrappings. Someone was seated on the far side of the table, eyeing him. Someone not Hitomi.

Miguel gaped. "Jake!"

Jake flashed his maniacal grin. "You doesn't expects me, does you, Doctor?"

"Not at all. What're you doing here?"

"I brings you someone. He wants to talk to you." Jake rose and lumbered to a door in the back. He swiped it open and vanished into the dimness beyond.

Miguel figured it would be Nessa. Had Hitomi captured her, too? But another surprise awaited. When his visitor entered, Miguel almost thought he was looking in a mirror. "Salvador?"

His brother spread his arms and took a bow. "In person."

"Why are you here? They'll kill you if they catch you."

"So we're in the same boat. Speaking of which, the name's Alejandro Carrasco. Memorize it fast."

Miguel didn't care what the name was. His brother had returned, which was cause for both joy and dread. He often wondered what had become of Salvador, but little went well when they were on the same planet. "If you say so. You still shouldn't be here."

"Somebody had to find out what the hell you got yourself into." Alejandro grabbed an unwrapped chair and dropped into it. He motioned Miguel to do likewise.

Clearly there would be neither hugs nor handshakes, only business. Miguel sat.

"You met Hitomi," Alejandro said.

"She told you?"

"She did."

It figured. Whatever Hitomi was after, she was drawing together everyone close to Miguel. He didn't like the implications.

"That little dust devil at the hydro station was her doing," Alejandro continued. "She hired me to blow it up and used my face to frame you."

"Damn it, Salvador—"

"Alejandro."

"That's low even for you."

Alejandro's jaw tightened.

"Maybe you should've killed me when you had the chance," Miguel added. "Saved everyone the trouble."

"Shut up for once. I didn't know. It was just a job. I only realized after."

Yeah, that would be Salvador, Alejandro, whatever the hell, taking odd jobs blowing up critical infrastructure without thinking about the consequences. Destruction had leeched into his genes. "Great, now we both know. What happens next?"

"Tell me what's going on. Somebody went nuclear to ensure Andre Rand marked you for death. Who and why?"

Excellent questions. Until Hitomi showed up, Miguel assumed it was all Andre. But if she had framed him, why swoop in and rescue him now? "I wish I knew," he said. "I thought it was the scientific gold I struck in Sinus Meridiani."

"Which gets you into the history vids. Go on."

Simplistic, if not entirely false. Miguel figured it best not to argue. "I'd already been working the area when Rand announced plans for a colony there. I tried everything to save the site for research, but he plays dirty."

"What a surprise, but grains in a sandstorm. Why outlaw you? Why go after the kids?"

"They aren't kids."

"Whatever. Why torture them?"

"Maybe to find me. I tried to get them out. I told them to leave Mars."

"Which two of them did, for all the good it did them."

Miguel's gut knotted. "What do you mean?"

"Hitomi had me intercept them on Itokawa Station and sell them to a cut-rate mining outfit."

"Damn you, Salvador!"

"Keep calling me that, and I'll ram a chair down your throat. I had no choice. Hitomi knew they were coming. But don't worry, they'll keep until I pick them up."

Miguel ran a hand through his hair. Everything had fallen apart at Hitomi's command, yet she wasn't calling the shots. Her "mistress" was. This was Celia Fundichely's operation, which could mean only one thing: Andre Rand was being set up for a fall, and they were all components in her trap.

"Why are you here, Sal—Alejandro?"

"I'm done being used." Alejandro looked to the ceiling. "Hear that, Hitomi? I'm done!" To Miguel, he said, "Somebody owes me answers. All this started with you, so tell me: what did you do to tick off Andre Rand?"

Miguel figured Alejandro shouldn't have to ask. Everyone knew Rand's *modus operandi*. "Step in his path and he'll run you over. I learned to dodge and refused to back down. That was enough."

"Dodging that man is a trick," Alejandro said. "How'd you manage it?"

His secret was out anyway. Hitomi knew. Martin and Petrina knew. Andre Rand likely knew. Alejandro might as well know, too. "I slept with his wife."

"Whoa, you banged Carmen Rand? You've outdone yourself, big brother. She's one hot lady."

"Smart, too. She fed me intel when it suited her, but mostly she gave up nothing but herself."

"So she knew your game."

"Like I knew hers. Like Hitomi knows yours."

Alejandro stood. "Hitomi's all but omniscient. She knew you and Rand would get into a firefight. She knew you'd be forced into the wilderness. She kept an eye on the kids. She knew my every move before I made it. I wonder if me showing up here really surprised her.

Probably not. Damn, that woman is good." He addressed the ceiling again. "If I didn't hate you so much, I'd marry you."

"Why's Jake here?" Miguel asked.

"Must be your popularity with the ladies. Carmen Rand wants you, Hitomi wants you, Nessa O'Clery wants you. Jake's here to make sure Nessa gets you. Although…" He looked more than usually thoughtful for a moment. "I doubt he'll convince Hitomi to turn you over."

Alejandro left him with that thought. Miguel mulled over the information until Hitomi's voice sounded overhead. "Please return to your room, Dr. Hernandez."

He considered finding out what would happen if he refused, but likely it wouldn't be pleasant, so he complied.

Nobody took note of Leah wandering the smuggler's den. Mudiwa's operation sprawled through caves natural and human-excavated, a maze of storage areas, transport bays, life support and comm facilities, and living quarters. The equipment was dated, some disintegrating. A small army of techs tinkered with broken stuff while grunts shuffled contraband between a makeshift spaceport and the distribution docks. Leah wouldn't have trusted even a prisoner's life to any of the rovers in this fleet, but the smugglers showed no qualms placing theirs on the line. Each hour, one or two vehicles trundled into the Martian wilderness loaded with cargo bound for settlers and unscrupulous dealers in Lowell Colony. How many drivers would perish out there? Leah wouldn't have given them better than even odds, yet an empty inbound arrived for every laden outbound departing. Somehow, the rovers held together.

Regardless of the risk, she needed transport. Projecting authority, she questioned techs about the status of various rovers. She must have looked and sounded official because nobody raised an eyebrow. She soon found a vehicle that checked out save a minor glitch in the solar collectors. "I'll have that fixed within the hour," the female tech assured her. Leah requisitioned it and warned her not to release it to anyone else. The tech didn't question the order.

Leah then prowled until she found the supply depot and ordered a mountain of provisions delivered to her rover. Again, her orders were obeyed. She hoped the ruse would hold. Sooner or later, somebody would stumble on Jimmy's body, but thus far it remained undiscovered. That, or it was being handled quietly. The latter prospect made her departure urgent.

Once supplies were loaded and the rover certified for travel, she struck into the wilderness and made for Utopia, and none too soon. Within minutes, she picked up comm chatter regarding a murder and confused back-and-forth seeking Mudiwa's whereabouts. Apparently, the boss had vanished without leaving word of her destination or purpose. Tense, Leah watched for pursuit, but it never materialized.

An hour into the journey, she relaxed. She might yet die in the wilderness, but she could deal with that. The frozen, all but airless landscape was at least a natural force. Unlike Mudiwa, it harbored no malice, broke no laws, deserved no punishment. Mudiwa and her ilk had earned what they got. Leah felt nothing in meting out justice, neither anger nor pleasure, satisfaction nor superiority. But this was different. Having borne the full weight of Mudiwa's hatred, lust for revenge now swallowed her whole. She could envision Mudiwa's broken body lying before her, its blood watering the dead land. No, more than envision. She saw it as surely as she saw the red soil. A tide of blood gushed from the rocks before her eyes. The regolith became an undulating red sea over which the rover sailed like an ocean vessel, cresting red swells whipped to a froth by the wind. She smelled the iron, tasted it on her lips. Red spray washed the deck, clung to her clothing, coated her hands. She bathed in it. Her skin acquired the hue of Mars. She looked at her blood-soaked hands and laughed with delight.

The vision faded. The sun had set. The rover sat silent on a darkened plain, conserving battery power for life support to carry her through the deep Martian night. Leah was sucking on a wound on her left thumb without knowing how she'd acquired it. The blood in her mouth was her own. Wracked by a chill, she checked the environmental readings. Internal temperature: twenty Celsius, just as it should be.

What had happened, what had she done while the vision carried her off? Was this a side effect of the torture? She'd heard of such things but never paid them much mind. Nobody cared what happened to criminals. Now that it was personal, she felt an unusual pang of fear and chased it off by reflecting that this affliction, whatever it was, might serve her purpose. She'd killed Jimmy in a blind rage. Maybe she could do it again. Maybe when she caught up with Mudiwa, she would sink into lethal frenzy and rend her enemy's flesh.

She smiled in the dark.

And then what?

Then the payoff. A grateful Celia Fundichely would shower her with gold, enough to buy the whole of Mars. Leah wouldn't need Andre Rand anymore, wouldn't have to kowtow to him. She'd make a rug of his skin.

Damn, was this going to be fun!

"Dr. Lloyd. Welcome back. How are you? How are your wife and daughter?"

The polished wood doors whispered shut behind Andre Rand. He stood tall and confident, his smile brilliant. The light seemed to follow him as he moved into the conference room. Or was it an art gallery? It could have been, with Martian landscapes on the wall, abstract sculptures on the tables and sideboards, and now Andre—a living sculpture—occupying pride of place wherever he moved.

"We're fine," Gene said, folding his hands on the dark tabletop to hide their shaking. Had the question been a greeting or a threat?

"I watched Kara all but steal the gold at the quadrathlon last week. You must be very proud. I hear she's landed a security post in the Belt. Field agent, right? Ready to give the bad guys hell?" Rand slipped with the grace of a dancer into a chair opposite Gene, then his shoulders drooped as though a vulture had landed on them. "Listen, I need your help."

"Whatever I can do," Lloyd promised. He'd already betrayed Miguel, his friend and colleague. What more of any consequence could Andre ask?

"I need an assassin."

Gene leaned back. "What?"

"An assassin. Someone young, strong, and determined."

He might as well have asked Gene to create a more impressive moon for Mars. Why wasn't Andre grilling him on his talk with

Carmen or his meeting with Martin and Petrina Ulenga? "That's outside my field, sir."

Andre cocked his head.

Gene swallowed. "You must have...you must know..."

"I do," Andre acknowledged. He rose and shook off the vulture. His usual self again, he wandered to the wall, examined a painting of the view from the summit of Olympus Mons, studied a half-meter tall abstract iron sculpture. He picked up the sculpture, turned it this way and that as though appraising its value. "This particular impediment requires careful handling. I need someone not connected to me." Glancing over his shoulder, he smiled a less friendly smile at Gene.

"But I don't know anyone...suitable."

"Give it a few minutes' thought, Dr. Lloyd."

What was there to think about? The request made no sense, but worse, it frightened him. Gene couldn't be drawn into murder, especially not one Andre Rand himself feared. "You want someone expendable," he said, voice quavering.

"If it comes to that." Andre approached, holding the sculpture like a club. "And I need them now."

"But I don't know anyone!"

With a sigh, the mayor passed behind Gene, set a hand to his shoulder, bent down, whispered in his ear. "Kara, don't you think?"

Horrified, Gene tried to stand, but Andre pushed him down.

"Young." Andre said. "Strong. Determined. Moves like a falcon. Soon to disappear into the Belt. She's perfect."

"She's not a killer!"

"Not yet," Andre agreed. He struck Gene in the side of the head with the sculpture. The scientist spilled to the floor, consciousness seeping away in a flow of blood.

Andre dropped the object on the floor next to his face. "But we'll make her one," he said. "Traitor."

Chapter 19

Hard work had grown easier since their time in the mines. Ricard Fulbert and Quan Linh signed on the Mars-bound freighter just in time. The captain, snarling about the lack of honest workers, had given several of his crew the boot shortly before debarkation. That sent the suddenly short-handed chief mate into a towering rage. The stevedores, too, were in a tizzy since the fracas slowed loading and made everything more chaotic. But with Ricard and Linh on duty, stowing and final inventory proceeded apace and wrapped up with three minutes to spare. The ship debarked on time. The captain authorized a round of drinks for everyone but the pilot, then authorized a second round for himself.

In space with high acceleration providing uncomfortable gravity, the ship settled into a routine of idle chatter and boredom. On the third day of the flight, the captain sent for the newcomers. When they entered his quarters, they didn't even know his name much less protocol for approaching him. It turned out there was no protocol. A greying, balding fellow, he sat in a metal chair with his feet up on a metal desk and a flask of red liquid in his hand. He took a swallow and waved them in.

The place wasn't much to look at. As gray as the captain, his quarters contained only the desk, a worktable, and three chairs on runners to keep them in place during maneuvers. A doorway in the back led to the captain's bunk. On a small panel secured to the wall above the desk, a raven-haired woman danced atop a bed while slowly undressing. The captain dropped his feet to the floor and swiped his hand over the desktop. The panel went blank.

"Don't suppose the young lady needs to see that," he growled, but not in anger. That was just his voice. He grinned and waved them in. "Sit, sit. Don't know what kind of ship you're used to, but we're not regimented here. So long as the work gets done, that's all I care about. And by God, you got it done. I'm grateful. You wouldn't believe the slackers I've had lately. Here." From the bottom desk drawer, he took two glasses and poured the red fluid into them. He set them on the table for Linh and Ricard, then thunked the bottle down and leaned on the table with folded arms. "Won't ask if you're happy. Nobody's happy on a freighter. But I pay good and we make some great ports. Not like that last one. Morana's a dump."

Ricard sampled the drink and nodded to Linh that it was acceptable. While she tried it—it tasted like chili-lime with a serious kick—he asked, "Then why go there?"

"A job's a job," the captain said. He thrust out his hand to Ricard. "Parker Ryan, by the way." Ricard shook his hand and introduced Linh and himself. "Yeah, Morana's a dump," Parker continued, "but it's got more terbium than any asteroid currently mined. Whatever the hell terbium is."

Linh about choked when Ricard explained, "It's a rare earth element. It's used in solid state components, high intensity lighting, high-energy lasers, and—" She nudged him. He gave her a confused look but stopped the recitation.

Parker raised an eyebrow. "Impressive for a couple of grunts. Where you from?"

"Mars, originally," Linh said. "We got lost out here."

"That's the usual story. Got lost myself, looking for my fortune. Ended up with this." He gestured at his metal cocoon. "Not that she's a bad ship, but she ain't a cruise liner." He poured another round and downed his with alarming speed. "Mars, huh? You leave by choice or necessity?"

Ricard about answered, but Linh shook her head at him.

Parker grinned. "More'n half the people I hire have…what's the old term? Checkered pasts. Long as you work, it's all the same to me. But why the hell'd you pick a ship bound for Mars? Last place you'd want to go, I'd think."

This time, Ricard looked at Linh before attempting an answer. She agreed; it might be best if she piloted. "It was the first ship leaving," she said before realizing she'd blown it, too.

"Trouble's following you," Parker said. "That's fine, long as it didn't board with you."

"It didn't." Linh was as sure of that as she could be, although she wondered if she and Ricard weren't themselves the trouble.

"Good. If it shows up on Mars, though, you're on your own. I can't get involved."

"We wouldn't expect you to," Linh assured him.

"Even better. More?" He held out the bottle.

Linh and Ricard both declined. They'd barely started on their second rounds.

"If you don't get caught or killed, you're welcome to stay on. Next port of call is hush-hush, but they got some great facilities. Grub, gambling, and girls like you wouldn't believe."

Linh laughed. "Ricard will appreciate the food. He's a gourmet. And I've taken a liking to space billiards, if they have that."

"They do. Hate it myself, but whatever shoots you into orbit. Are you two…" He waggled his fingers between them.

"Yep. Engaged, in fact."

"Then he doesn't need the girls. Congratulations! But look at this, I'm serving you this stuff. Don't have anything better, I'm afraid."

"It's not that bad," Ricard said and lifted his glass in an unspoken toast to the captain. They all clinked glasses and drank.

"If a couple plans to marry, they shouldn't wait. That's my philosophy. I'll be happy to perform the ceremony. Never done it before. It'd be a real pleasure. Well, you don't have to answer right away. Talk it over and let me know."

He dismissed them, and Linh practically skipped down the corridor. Ricard, though, was lost in thought until she tugged at his arm and asked what was wrong.

"Why would Mars import terbium?" he asked. "Lowell doesn't have the technical capacity to use it. It buys prefabbed components from factories in the Belt."

"Maybe somebody's expanding," Linh suggested. "Forget it. We've got more important things to think about."

"Like what?"

She grabbed him and kissed him. He responded, but it wasn't clear if it refreshed his memory.

It hadn't been Carmen Rand's most memorable fling. Her driver Matteo Keller spent days focused on driving and nights struggling to muster sufficient confidence to make love to the first lady of Mars. All through their encounters, he quivered as though Andre might spring from behind a rock and storm the rover, intent upon their deaths. Worse, Carmen couldn't keep her mind on Matteo. She wondered constantly: why Utopia, why her? And she had no answers.

On the last night of the journey, they gave up. She didn't invite him to lie with her, and he made no move to seduce her. But neither did they sleep. She listened to his breathing, to him flopping from side to side, until he slipped into the pilot's seat and stared at the stars splashed overhead, his shadow outlined by faint illumination from the controls.

She went to his side, sat next to him, watched the universe with him.

"I'm sorry," he said.

"Don't be. Neither of us is at our best."

"I'm a rotten liar. If anyone asks…"

She waited for him to continue, but he never did.

"I must be legendary," she said. "I deserve the rep, but rest assured, it's my policy to neither confirm nor deny."

Matteo shifted in the dark. "I'm not judging you. I'm way below your level."

"Level, hell. We're both just people. What do you want, Matteo?"

"Ma'am?"

"What do you want from Mars?"

He didn't answer. Maybe he couldn't.

"Look at yourself," she said. "Your whole life is ferrying people who don't even see you to places you could never get into. You're the rust on the surface of a dead planet. But that's not what you want. I know it isn't. It sure wouldn't be what I wanted."

"What else is there?"

Carmen leaned over and whispered in his ear. Whispers had power, and he needed some. "Everything. This whole damn planet's waiting for someone like you to do something with it."

He leaned away as though she was toxic. "That's great for guys with money."

"How much do you need?"

Matteo had no idea. He'd never thought that far, she was sure.

"You're elite now," Carmen purred. The sound drew him back, and her lips brushed his ear as she spoke. "You've slept with Carmen Rand. Rumor is, she's generous to her lovers."

"Like Dr. Hernandez? What'd you give him?"

Settling back in her chair, she resumed conversational volume. "Just what he needed. A push out the door. What do you need? If it's not too ridiculous, you'll have it."

A long silence ensued. Carmen felt sorry for him. She knew what it was like to believe your desires beyond reach, but she couldn't imagine not knowing what you wanted to begin with.

Matteo's shadow rose. He stood beside her, a statue in the dark, staring into space. On the horizon, a brilliant star shone accompanied by a fainter secondary below. Earth and Luna.

"Ah," Carmen said.

"It's too ridiculous. Nobody goes home."

"I can get you there."

He dropped into the seat. "What I want isn't there anymore."

Making an educated guess, Carmen asked, "What happened to her?"

"Suborbital crash. No survivors."

And I, she lamented, *was your first since then. What rotten luck.* "I'm sorry," she said, for both tragedies.

Dawn touched the eastern sky, brightening rapidly as the sun lit the thin atmosphere.

"I don't need anything from you," Matteo said. "But I appreciate what you tried to give me."

Carmen could now see his face in the morning glow. He looked serene but oddly distant. "Likewise," she said.

Leaning forward, he danced his fingers over the controls, and the rover churned to life. "Let's go see about Utopia." He flashed her an embarrassed smile. "Maybe we'll both find something we want there."

Captain Parker Ryan's idea of a wedding was, in his own words, "Get registered and get to bed." He wasn't kidding. He placed Ricard and Linh before him in a cramped conference room with two witnesses pulled from the crew, a young female navigator-in-training and a bearish mechanic. He asked the happy couple if they married of their own free will, and once they affirmed it, he pronounced them joined. He collected everyone's fingerprints and retinal scans to authenticate the electronic documents and promised to transmit them post haste to the relevant authorities.

Part one done. On to part two.

Privacy being in short supply, Parker gave his chief mate's quarters to Ricard and Linh for their honeymoon suite. Linh was grateful but figured they'd be on the mate's list when they arrived in port and the heavy work began. In the meantime, they enjoyed four days of wedded bliss behind a locked door, oblivious to anything else happening on board. Only once did they wonder what was happening. Late on the third day, acceleration all but cut out for a time, leaving them in near weightlessness.

At the end of their four days, with Mars glowing large and orange on the viewports, Parker called them to his cabin. They found him not as before with his feet up on his desk and a drink in his hand but standing nearly at attention, hands quivering at his sides. Linh felt terror creep up her spine and slipped into her breathing routine to counter it. Once she fought down the sensation, she asked, "What's wrong?"

"Nothing," Parker said in a half-whisper. "Just…just don't try to see her." He squeezed by Linh and slapped the touchplate on the bulkhead to close the door behind him.

Before Linh and Ricard could think what to say, the lights slowly dimmed, and the blackness of space consumed their surroundings. Linh slid closer to Ricard. He put an arm about her shoulders.

"Don't be afraid," an oddly metallic voice said. "But do stay where you are. I would hate for you to die so soon after your wedding."

Linh gripped Ricard's hand. "Who's there?" she whimpered.

"Let us ask, rather…" The voice slid upward and became as soft as a breeze. "…who are you?"

If Ricard was unnerved, he didn't let on. "Exobiologists," he said. His grip on Linh remained steady.

"Ah yes, students of the great Miguel Hernandez." The voice descended into the bass range and rumbled in laughter. "Oh, children, you deserve better. You especially, Quan Linh. You deserve to be me."

Linh trembled, barely able to focus on her breathing. "Who are you?"

"Me?" The voice twittered like a small child. "I'm Celia Fundichely."

Linh's legs nearly gave out. Ricard held her up, still unfazed. "Why would Celia Fundichely be on a freighter?" He might have been asking the time.

"Inquisitive, aren't we? Yes, that goes with being a scientist." The voice changed constantly, rising, falling, wavering between young and old, male and female. "Shall I tell you? Of course. That's why I'm here. But no questions, Ricard. Not if you wish to live."

Linh was too scared to speak. She felt no fear in Ricard, but neither did he question the command.

Celia laughed. "You learn so fast! I knew you would. That's why I chose you. Ah, ah, no questions."

Ricard shifted, the first sign he wasn't at ease, and pulled Linh tight against him. She felt their bodies might fuse.

"With wealth and power," Celia said, "comes risk. My enemies are legion. So I've decided to hide in the one place nobody would think to look."

"The Martian wilderness," Ricard said.

"You married a brilliant young man, Linh. Yes. I'm building a refuge there, far from the reach of my enemies."

"A well-defended refuge. That's why you need terbium."

Linh tugged at Ricard's sleeve and whispered, "Please, don't say anything."

Celia laughed again. "Don't worry, Linh, he's doing well, drawing the right conclusions without asking a single question. Correct, Ricard. My plans call for defensive lasers of a very specific design. You'll build them—and other devices and facilities—in situ. They'll ensure no unauthorized landings within a thousand kilometers of my compound. But other threats must be mitigated, threats against which lasers are useless. That's why I want Linh."

"You can't have her," Ricard said, his tone matter of fact. He made no threat.

"Of course, I can. I get whatever I want. But don't be afraid. I wouldn't break up such a beautiful relationship. I'm taking you both."

Linh didn't understand. Of what use could they be to someone like Celia Fundichely? How did she hear of them, how did she know where to find them? They'd traveled such a random trajectory: enslavement, ship after ship, escape after escape, even—she shuddered—murder. How had Celia tracked them and cornered them here?

"What do you want with us?" Linh all but whispered.

"Mmmm, how fortunate I didn't tell *you* not to ask questions." Celia's voice acquired a lilt, then just as quickly lost it in favor of a drawl. "You, Linh, shall become me. My double. My decoy."

Linh sucked in a breath and squinted into the darkness. It couldn't be. "I look like you?"

Celia laughed a strange, wheezing laugh. "Not much, no."

"Then how can I—"

"Enough questions, Linh. Henceforth, you are Celia Fundichely, which isn't a bad thing to be."

Ignoring her injunction, Ricard hazarded a question of his own. "Then who am I?"

Celia paused long enough to make Linh nervous, but when she spoke, her synthesized, ever-changing voice rang with humor, not anger. "You know the one awkward aspect of being Celia Fundichely? Her lovers don't wake up come morning. As my surrogate's lover, you can be the exception. And her bodyguard. And my technology chief. You're qualified for all three roles."

The lights slowly came up. Ricard and Linh stood alone in the captain's cabin. Celia might have dissolved into smoke. Linh longed to peek into the back room but dreaded what she would find. Before she could move, Ricard turned her about and steered her toward the cabin door.

"Come on," he said. "We've been dismissed."

This days-long confinement was worse than being stuck in a hospital bed with wires and tubes crawling over and through his body. Knowing it futile but needing something to do, Miguel took up his panel and probed the network once more, hoping to learn something, anything about the Utopia facility. He was stunned to find he now had admin access. Everything was laid bare before him: schematics, shipping and receiving logs, financial records, personnel records, geologic surveys...

Geologic surveys?

Curiosity piqued, he dove into the reports. A massive mineralogical survey had been conducted over a year ago in Utopia, shortly before ground had been broken for the facility. The survey results were underwhelming, as he expected, but the focus was odd. The researchers had an inordinate interest in bastnäsite, monazite, and other rare-earth-bearing minerals. The notes made matters clear: they were looking for sources of terbium.

Why terbium? Miguel wondered. With only a handful of uses for the element, a scattering of asteroids adequately supplemented the supply from Earth. Celia Fundichely must already have her hands on the stuff. But then Miguel recalled Nessa O'Clery's offhand comment about a find in Tharsis. Not gold, she said, something else, something she refused to reveal. Had she found what Celia wanted? Did Celia know?

Speculation was pointless. He set aside minerology and ran through files on the facility's layout and construction, pausing again when he stumbled upon another unexpected find. Celia didn't have one secret base on Mars but two: Utopia and Lunae Planum, constructed simultaneously. This wasn't a new foray. Mars had been under assault for over a year without anyone's knowledge. If Miguel had any doubt left about Andre Rand's involvement, that killed it. Andre never would have allowed this incursion.

What a puzzle! Why had they given Miguel access to such damning information? Did they expect him to take command, to navigate Celia's conquest of the planet, to wrest control of Mars from Andre?

Damn, that was a tempting thought. They probably did expect it.

But that wasn't his agenda. Not yet. Miguel's first concern was getting Petrina and Martin off Mars, his second rescuing Ricard and Linh from the hell into which Alejandro had dumped them. Alejandro said he planned to get them out. Maybe Miguel could get him to conduct all four students to the safety of a research colony beyond the Belt, where they could put this nightmare behind them. Only once they were away could he consider what he wanted for himself.

They would need transport. The network reported all orbital capsules departed and no rovers on base save a pair with serious environmental control issues. If a bluff, it was an effective one. Nobody would risk stealing those. A shipment from the Belt was due later today. Maybe Alejandro could sign himself and the students on for the return trip. He checked the facility map and found Alejandro and Jake had been assigned rooms at the north end of the first level. Hitomi might have put him in charge, but she was doubtless monitoring communications, so instead of messaging his brother, Miguel went for a walk.

Passing down the metallic corridor, he checked each door. They were all unlocked. All opened on pristine, unfurnished apartments. None harbored Petrina or Martin. When he came to the north end, he heard Jake and Alejandro arguing in the next to last apartment. Best to wait, then. Those two could do serious damage individually. Together, they could be an apocalypse.

Miguel returned to the airlock at the centerline of the building. The cool air smelled vaguely of rust, as though Mars had tried to slip in through the seals. Next to the airlock, a lifter gave access to the second and third levels. Miguel found he could get to the second, but it refused passage to the third without an access code he didn't know. Exploring the second level, he found it silent save his own footfalls. Here, offices and conference rooms stood open, awaiting the arrival of a tenant. Most were absent furnishings, and his students were nowhere to be found. In one long, narrow room, a smoky window afforded a view of the wilderness beyond. Miguel looked out over the rocky red landscape. It reminded him of Acidalia Planitia: a jumble of boulders dotted with craters, and everywhere the corroded sand that distinguished Mars.

In the southwest, a thin plume of dust rose on a light wind. The cloud approached, neither swirling nor altering course. It wasn't a storm in the making. Someone must be coming. He watched and waited, wondering who it could be, wondering if Alejandro could commandeer their rover. Probably. That sort of thing was Alejandro's forte. Now he just needed to find the Ulenga twins. They must be on the third floor, which meant Miguel needed that lifter code. Maybe it was on the network somewhere. Being the administrator, he ought to have access to it.

He watched the plume grow and felt a pang of regret. With Meridiani lost, his future looked as barren as the Utopia plain. Even if he got his students to safety, what would become of him? Hitomi said he'd find what he was looking for here, but she couldn't have meant microfossils. Nobody, having found such priceless remnants, would hand them to another. What had she meant?

The dust plume grew near, preceded by a glint of metal. A rover.

Miguel stared into the dust.

Someone was coming.

Chapter 20

At midday, they topped a rise and discovered a broken, orange-brown land, an abstract painting flecked with white frost peeking from the shadows. Its raw beauty stole Carmen's breath. In the distance, a ruddy scarp framed the northern edge of the scene. At the cliff's base where nothing but rock should have been, a gray block building had been constructed, its center marked by an airlock, a long, smoky window on the second level, and dots of windows on the third. A smooth circle in the center of the depression suggested a landing pad, although it was so crude Carmen imagined it had been cleared with hand brooms. She laughed at the thought of workers in envirosuits trying in vain to sweep away blowing sand.

Beside her at the rover's controls, Matteo Keller gaped at the building. "What the hell?" he murmured.

Celia Fundichely must have constructed this before asking permission. Andre would be furious when he found out, but what could he do? Celia was a shadow, a wraith wielding blades of fear and unparalleled wealth. Maybe she planned to snatch Mars from Andre. The thought would have chilled Carmen had Celia not begged permission to come. Outright conquest wasn't her goal. What variant of space billiards was she playing?

"What do we do?" Matteo asked.

"Say hello," Carmen replied. She waved him on.

Poor Matteo had gotten more from this trip than he'd expected. He'd gone from Carmen's driver to her awkward lover to—though he didn't know it yet—her protector. Oblivious of the danger, he guided the rover down the rise and wove among the scattered boulders toward the facility. Peril must wait there, but curiosity overrode Carmen's fear. Was Celia here? How did Carmen figure in her plans? This was no hiding place. Contrasting with the scarp, the building would be visible to surveillance satellites. A decoy, then, meant to be found?

They trundled across the landing pad and halted before the airlock. Matteo pointed out tracks leading to the far end of the building. "They must store and service their rovers down there," he said. "Should we check it out?"

"Let's knock on the front door," Carmen suggested. They suited up, secured the rover, and walked a dusty ten meters. Matteo led, watching everything at once: the airlock, the windows, the sheer cliff towering overhead. They reached the airlock without incident, and Matteo examined the controls. "Not secured," he said. "Anyone can walk in." He punched a button, and the hatch slid open.

Carmen followed, uneasy. This didn't seem like Celia. Maybe someone else had built the place? Not smugglers, certainly. It was too far from their customers in Lowell Colony.

Matteo pressurized the airlock and opened the inner door. Stretching out an arm, he stopped Carmen from passing through and took a furtive peek up and down the corridor. Satisfied, he motioned her in. They peeled off their red-dusted envirosuits and stashed them in a bank of lockers between the airlock and a lifter.

"Now what?" he asked.

"Let's explore," Carmen said. "Fun, huh?"

"Not really."

She didn't think so, either.

They prowled the corridor, opened doors, checked the empty apartments behind them. They gave up before reaching the end. "Why's nobody here?" Matteo wondered. "Maybe they're all on another level?"

"Let's find out," Carmen said.

They took the lifter to the second level, where they discovered more empty rooms. These suggested a nest of future offices, but only one was furnished, harboring a conference table surrounded by chairs, most cocooned in plastic.

"No tenants," Carmen said. "Shall we try the top level?"

"You won't get there," a familiar voice intruded from the corridor. Startled, Carmen and Matteo turned to find Miguel Hernandez puzzling over them. "It needs an access code," he added, "which I don't know yet."

Carmen gaped. "Why are *you* here?"

Miguel's smile warmed her as always. She wanted to run to him, embrace him, loose herself in him, but she knew better. Whatever feelings swam below the surface, they'd never been honest lovers. Besides, Matteo was there, fists half-raised in anticipation of attack. She couldn't betray his loyalty.

"I'm in charge of the place," Miguel said. "Or so I've been told. You?"

Carmen didn't know if he meant it or was joking. "Broadening my horizons."

His eyes roamed her. She could feel his distrust as clearly as his desire. Or was it her own? Who knew? Their relationship had been a symphony of dissonance from the start. She never should have given herself to him, and he shouldn't have forced her to push him out the door.

Matteo stepped to Carmen's side. Carmen hooked her arm through his to keep him from rash action. *This will either be fun or horrifying*, she thought.

Miguel raised an eyebrow. "Who's this?"

"A friend. Matteo, this is Miguel Hernandez. You've heard of him?"

"Yeah," Matteo said. "His face was all over the news vids."

Miguel met Matteo's stone gaze. "I don't suppose Carmen mentioned my innocence."

"It never came up," Carmen told him. To Matteo, she said, "But he's right. Ironic that he's been outlawed for the one thing he didn't do." She released Matteo and sat on the conference table, legs crossed and swaying to a tune not even she heard. "What's this managerial gig you've landed?"

Miguel and Matteo both watched those legs swing. "I didn't land it," Miguel said. "It was forced on me."

"Ah. You're working for Celia Fundichely."

Matteo gaped at Carmen. "*She's* here?"

Carmen touched a finger to her lips to silence him. The enormity of the danger must finally have registered. He groped for a plastic-shrouded chair and dropped into it, not bothering to unwrap it.

If Miguel thought Carmen's protector pathetic, he didn't let on. "Someone else."

Carmen laughed. "God, Miguel, I've slept with you enough to know when you're lying. Oh, don't worry, Matteo knows about us."

"What, you did an interview on the subject?"

She blew him a kiss. "What does Celia want with you?"

"Why do you think she's involved?"

"Why wouldn't I?"

Miguel gave her another once-over, either admiring her or calculating her role in this. Or both. "You're the first to mention her name," he said.

"But you guessed. Fair enough. So, what happens next?"

Miguel approached Carmen. He almost reached for her, but Matteo's presence stopped him. He looked at the other man for a moment. "Who is he, anyway?"

Carmen shrugged. "Maybe you should ask him. He knows how to talk."

Matteo stood. "I'm the lady's driver."

Carmen could all but feel Miguel's thoughts churning, but it wasn't rivalry. Not only. He wanted something. Very well. Since they were both operating in the dark, maybe a bit of openness wouldn't hurt. She slipped from the table and leaned into Matteo, who put a protective arm about her. "What's your theory, Miguel?" she asked. "What's Celia up to?"

Miguel winced and turned away. Carmen hadn't expected that. Was he jealous? Did he feel something real for her, after all? "At a wild guess," he said, "she's stealing a planet."

"She asked Andre's permission to come."

"And he allowed it?"

"What else could he do? She's Celia Fundichely. And he needs her. She's financing Schiaparelli Colony development."

"Damn it. She told me..." He looked at the ceiling in a vain effort to hide the slip. "Her minion told me I'd find what I want here."

"Fossils?"

"I assumed so, but probably not."

"What do you want, besides that? And me?" She meant it as a jab, but maybe Celia intended them to reunite. That was a nasty thought.

Risking Matteo's anger, Miguel caressed her cheek. "Carmen, I need your help."

Matteo looked ready to punch him. Carmen leaned into Miguel's hand and gave him a coy smile before shaking her head.

"Please."

She brushed him away. "You've already had too much of me."

"It's not for me. They're holding my students."

"Petrina and Martin?"

"You know them?"

Of course, she did. She'd tried to warn them off, the fools. "Slightly. Where are they?"

"On level three, I think. I need to dig up the access code. Once we find them, they'll need your rover to escape."

"Escape!" Carmen laughed. "Escape from Celia Fundichely?"

"Yes."

Challenging Celia wasn't on Carmen's to-do list. Not yet. First, she needed to know what the woman was up to. She felt sorry for the Ulengas, but it was their own fault. Until she understood the situation, Miguel and his students would have to fend for themselves.

"Please," he whispered.

Matteo frowned and looked at Carmen. Whatever he saw, it motivated him. He stepped between her and Miguel, raised his chin, and said, "Go to hell."

Miguel met Matteo's eyes.

And punched him in the gut.

Shortly after the freighter entered Mars orbit, Captain Parker Ryan summoned Linh and Ricard to the cramped observation deck. The orange disk of Mars filled the viewport, streaked with black and gray, smudged by a dust storm tracking across the southern hemisphere. Fearing another encounter with Celia Fundichely, Linh had flown into a panic. Ricard held her and whispered her into her breathing rhythm. By the time they reached the observation deck, she had regained outward calm although her insides still churned like a star on the brink of supernova.

Parker had a glass in hand. Two more sat by a bottle on a battered table. He downed what remained of his drink, poured a round for himself and his guests, and downed half of that before speaking. "She's gone," he said. "We docked with a luxury ship once we were in orbit, and she left."

Linh collapsed against Ricard. "Thank God," she muttered.

"The Almighty wasn't involved. She left instructions." Parker handed a black data card to Ricard.

Ricard turned it between his fingers. "What kind of instructions?"

"The kind that get me killed if I peek. That's all I know."

"Did she mention how we access it?"

The captain finished his drink and poured himself another. "We land, dump our cargo, and beat it. Without you. That..." He pointed at the data card. "...will auto-connect to the facility network down there. I don't envy you. It's a remote location."

"How remote?" Linh asked.

"Utopia Planitia."

Linh didn't see how that could be. There was nothing in Utopia.

Ricard, though, looked thoughtful. "The perfect place for her to operate," he said. "It's off everyone's map. Lowell, smugglers, everyone. And water is plentiful."

"But why?" Linh asked. "Celia Fundichely operates in the Belt, not on Mars."

"I expect you'll find out," Parker said. "Myself, I don't want to know. I'm not involved."

"You aren't," Ricard agreed. "And neither are we. We'll work another voyage or two."

Parker stared into the liquid in his glass and swirled it. "Where you running to?

"Ganymede."

With a snort, the captain snatched up the bottle and refilled Linh and Ricard's glasses. "Figures. But she'll find you there as easily as anywhere."

"We'll take our chances," Ricard said.

"What's there for you?"

Parker had been good to them. Linh didn't think he'd betray them. He might even help them. So she told the truth, at least in basic. "We're scientists. Exobiologists. Our mentor wanted us to take our research to Ganymede. We've had a little trouble getting there."

"More than a little," Ricard added. Linh expected him to crack a smile, but no. He was as serious as ever.

Parker nodded. "Trouble's never far in the Belt. Only the rich and the ruthless make it there. Best to be both, like..." He scowled and refused to speak the name. "Like her."

Linh sipped her drink. "What about you?"

"What, I don't look rich?"

She laughed. "Not so much, no."

"Got my own ship, don't I?" He waved an arm about.

"Such as it is, yeah." She grinned at him. "What about ruthless?"

"Don't think I'm not just because I like you. I'm not having my ship blown up on account of you two. Once we land, I'm throwing you out." He gulped down the rest of his drink. "Damn shame. I could use hard workers like you."

Linh took the data card from Ricard and studied it. Celia Fundichely said Linh would become her double and Ricard would be Linh's bodyguard, among other things. Her life would be in danger the moment she set foot on Mars. She dropped the card on the table and looked at Parker with a growing sense of dread.

The captain thunked his glass down on the table and wiped his mouth on his sleeve.

Ricard put an arm about Linh. "Point taken," he said. He scooped up the data card. "No hard feelings. Let's go, Linh. Captain Ryan's done all he can."

She held her silence until they were in the crew quarters, then she descended into hysterics, and not even Ricard could pull her out.

Petrina was cracking up. An hour had passed, maybe two, since Hitomi shut the door and left her on her own with no light, no sound, no sensation of any kind save the hard floor beneath her. She didn't know if her eyes were open or shut, if her ears were stopped. Nothing bound Petrina save fear, but that was enough to keep her still.

Why was she here? Had Hitomi left her to die? And where was Martin, what was happening to Martin, what were they doing to her brother? It was the torture session without the explosion of confused sensation, with only the darkness and her own thoughts to torment her.

Purple sparkles began to wink in the distance. They crackled with energy, brightened, grew louder, edged closer and closer and closer until they engulfed her. Purple detonated all about her. She covered her eyes to keep them out, but they came from within, growing louder and brighter, splitting her ears and searing her retinas. A barrage of shock waves pummeled her. She curled into a ball to protect herself.

Sometime later, quiet settled in and a new light grew, white light this time, and her surroundings emerged. She was balled up on the gray floor of a small gray room. Footfalls approached, tapping out a steady rhythm until they halted centimeters from her face.

Petrina half uncurled and opened her aching eyes. Hitomi stood over her, thin and severe. "Up," she commanded.

Shivering, Petrina pulled herself to her feet.

"You must not fear darkness," Hitomi said. "You must be one with it. It is your cloak."

She didn't understand, couldn't speak, though maybe her eyes conveyed her confusion.

Hitomi sank to the floor, her legs crossing as she dropped. Petrina thought of vids she'd seen of trees losing their leaves in autumn on Earth. When Hitomi motioned to her, she sat, too, although with much less grace.

Hitomi looked into Petrina's eyes. She had a deep, disconcerting gaze. "When first I met *her*," she said, "she was but a shadow in the dark. She has remained ever so. Yet I have been gifted one glimpse of her. In that moment, I understood. She does not hide in darkness; she *is* darkness. You must become darkness, too, Petrina. It is your destiny."

"I don't understand." Petrina's voice sounded small and distant to her own ears.

"You will. Until then, take darkness as your friend."

"But—"

Hitomi put up a hand to silence her. "Your friend. Your protector. Without it, you will soon be dead."

Hitomi's words might have been the pop of the purple sparks, random, without meaning. "What's happening to me?" Petrina whispered.

"You are transcending yourself. You are becoming the image of her. You are becoming her shield. It is an honor, Petrina."

"Where's Martin?"

"Do not fear. You will be together soon. He is your shield, as you are hers."

Riddles, riddles, riddles! What did the woman mean? Who was this other, this *she*?

"Again," Hitomi said. "Lights off."

Darkness engulfed them. "No," Petrina whimpered, "No, no, no!"

"Be still," Hitomi whispered in the blackness. "Focus. Breathe. You have done it before."

"How do you know about that?"

"Nothing happens without her knowledge. Be still. Focus. Breathe."

Petrina breathed. Gradually, the blackness shed its terror.

Chapter 21

Twenty kilometers beyond the edge of Lowell Colony, in the bottom of a pink gash on the face of Mars, an irregular cluster of six black buildings had been erected. Boulders the size of small houses littered the channel while deep shadows hid its fringes. It had a dangerous feel, this jagged, unpredictable land laden with monsters waiting to spring from the dark.

Lieutenant Conrad Egger's ten-person team of security officers watched from a distance atop the canyon wall south of the facility. They'd seen little human activity, but each day a few heavy vehicles, likely automated, crept in after sunset and crawled away before dawn, threading the jumbled obstacle course. IR and UV signatures revealed nothing definitive, but Egger knew what this was. He'd seen its like before. An unregistered mine, stealing minerals for export.

From within his assault rover, he and his team watched the latest departure. Trundling south, a small convoy passed their position and disappeared around a bend. Egger turned to the junior member of his team. "What's your plan, Officer Leaf?"

Leah Leaf's blood was a cocktail of excitement and fear. At nineteen years of age, this was her first field assignment. Why would Egger hand her the lead? A test, she supposed.

She eyed the vids. "No sign of defenses."

The Lieutenant's face might have been carved from stone. He gave up nothing.

"The operation is probably automated," she continued, "so few potential defenders. The channel offers natural cover for approach. The large building will be the main operation, the smaller ones storage sheds and barracks. They move at night, coming and going to the south. We could move in from the north after dawn when they aren't active, come on them unawares, and clear the smaller buildings before taking out the large one."

"Could?" Lieutenant Egger asked. "Or will?"

Leah kept her body tall though her spirit flagged. "Will."

He nodded permission if not approval. The other team members exchanged anxious glances but dared not object. Leah couldn't blame them for doubting her. A neophyte had been given command. She might lead them into disaster.

She knew it as well as they, but she refused to show fear. She ordered the driver to relocate north. In the pitch night, he maneuvered off the ridge, guided by radar. Once out of sight of the illegal mine, he activated the floodlights and crawled onward. The sun had flared over the horizon by the time they returned to the ridge and picked their way down to the canyon floor. The descent took nearly an hour. Moving south again, they wound through the stream of boulders and played tag with the shadows.

When just one house-sized boulder separated them from their target, Leah ordered a halt and considered her options. The rover afforded fast approach but would be too visible a target. Should it be seriously damaged, they'd have no means of escape. While a ground assault would be slower, a natural camouflage of red dust would quickly coat their envirosuits. Even so, both plans were fraught with uncertainty. A difficult calculus, and Lieutenant Egger awaited her call.

"We attack on foot," she decided. "No sudden moves. Advance single file on the closest building, straight and slow.

Capture it as quietly as possible. I'll call subsequent targets as we go. Remember: slow, deliberate, quiet." The team showed no enthusiasm, so to boost morale, she added, "It should be easy."

They didn't believe her.

Neither did she.

They suited up and moved out, weapons at the ready, Leah second in the line, Lieutenant Egger bringing up the rear. Rounding the boulder, they found the first structure a hundred meters off, its solid black walls glowing like polished onyx, revealing no sign of an entrance. Damn it, the doors must be on the opposite side, facing the other buildings. Why hadn't she thought of that?

Nothing could be done about it now. They had to move in, find the entrance, and capture the building. They slow-shuffled through the sand, keeping their line straight to present the smallest possible target. Rust coated their envirosuits, rendering them all but invisible in the ascending sun.

When they were twenty meters from the building, red laser light flared from its apex and swept the land. It crossed the lead officer's chest before falling dark.

"Damn it," the officer said over his shoulder. "Motion activated scanner. They made us."

"Halt," Leah ordered the column. "Don't even breathe."

Nothing happened for a long minute. Had they escaped detection? What should she do? If she pressed on, they might walk into an ambush, but to turn back was to admit failure. She felt Lieutenant Egger's impatient gaze on her back.

The laser rekindled and struck the lead officer's chest. He turned panicked eyes on Leah.

"Down!" she cried. "Roll!" They hit the dirt and rolled off their line, some left, some right, as an intense blue beam seared the thin air, struck ground, fused sand into glass. The team scattered, crawling further from the line of attack. The assault laser sliced through the heart of their original position. Sand melted and bubbled wherever it touched. It swept the line time and again, broadening its path but unaware that its quarry had escaped.

Leah scrambled to her feet. "Retreat! This way!" Stooped over, she loped off at an angle to their original course. The team followed and made the safety of a modest boulder. Out of sight of the buildings and their defenses, they collapsed against the rock, panting. She allowed them only a minute to catch their breaths. "To the rover," she said, "before they dispatch a response team."

They reached the rover and escaped. No sign of pursuit materialized. The driver exited the canyon with more speed than he'd entered, bouncing recklessly up the pitched wall and down the other side. Below the ridge once more, Leah's first command ended as Lieutenant Egger, hands on hips, fixed his stone gaze on her. "Lessons learned," he demanded.

Only that she wasn't fit to command. She'd nearly killed everyone.

"Nothing?"

Nothing at all. Where had she gone wrong? Based on what she knew at the time, the plan seemed sound enough. Who could have known a smuggling operation would have defenses of that grade? Scanners, maybe, but assault lasers? If she wasn't omniscient, neither was anyone else, Lieutenant Egger included.

But he awaited an answer.

She kept it simple. "I can't know everything."

"And therefore?"

"Don't rush in. Observe. Test. Learn as much as possible."

Lieutenant Egger nodded.

"But when is it enough?" she asked. "There will always be unknowns."

"Damn straight," he said. "That's what backup plans are for. And you didn't have one, did you?"

A different situation confronted Subcommander Leah Leaf now. The unknowns were legion and impenetrable, the facts few. Celia Fundichely, it seemed, had already claimed Utopia. At least, she had built something here. Mudiwa planned to kill her and take her place. The region's rocks and craters afforded no advantage, no hidden approach to the blocky facility stretched along the base of the distant scarp. The facility's uninspired form offered no data, only questions. Worst of all, Leah couldn't be sure Mudiwa was here. The long-range vid revealed a solitary rover parked before the facility airlock, but it had the sleek look of a colony transport, not the heavy rovers she'd seen in Mudiwa's den of thieves. So someone else was here, too. She watched for comings and goings over the course of hours but saw no sign of movement.

Leah had come with no plans, neither primary nor backup, only a thirst for revenge, a monster lurking in her skull, and a notion that Celia Fundichely might reward her. Lieutenant Egger would have called this mission a dud asteroid, the security equivalent of those unjustified hopes that consumed luckless prospectors in the Belt. She knew better, yet here she was, wanting only to disembowel Mudiwa and claim a prize.

What was the plan, then? A fast, straight approach was the only option. Mudiwa would be inside the facility if present at all, and the only visible entrance was that airlock. Go in armed, in search and destroy mode, and trust that when the time came the berserker slumbering within her would wake and make short work of her adversary.

God, was that a stupid idea, but she had no other, much less a backup plan, so she set course for the facility, trailing an orange cloud of dust. She hadn't made a quarter of the distance when a blazing star ignited in the sky and fell to a gentle touchdown in the primitive landing zone. When the dust settled, an aging freighter sat on the plain, surrounded by a swarm of vehicles and envirosuited workers unloading cargo, which they transported to the far end of the facility.

Leah brought her rover to a halt and watched on the tele-photo vids. There was another entrance down there. A new idea blossomed, no more mature than her original plan but stealthier. So long as it worked.

She changed course for the freighter, determined to insinuate herself into the crew and help deliver the goods.

Two hours. That's all Captain Parker Ryan gave the crew. Two hours to unload, stow the shipment in the storage bunker at the far end of the facility, and return. Anyone not on board by then would be left behind. He gave Ricard Fulbert and Quan Linh a raised eyebrow as he issued these orders. He needn't have worried. Ricard had given his word.

The work commenced. Ricard and Linh donned envirosuits and set foot on Mars once more. For Linh, it was a strange home-coming here in the wastes of Utopia far from Lowell. The distant building had a cold, alien feel, and the freighter they had briefly called home was now off-limits. They were cut off from everything they knew and at the mercy of whoever operated the facility. Panic touched her with cold fingers.

Ricard took her arm. "Breathe," he said.

How had he known? But of course, he would. He was part of her now. She slipped into her calming rhythm, and the world righted itself.

Parker came bearing terbium, other raw materials, and crates packed with who knew what. None bore any markings. All were massive, requiring heavy transports to get them from ship to building. A handful of the crew retrieved the necessary equipment from the storage bunker. No stevedores in sight, they grumbled upon return. Why did they always have to do everything themselves? Parker told them to unload or take a one-way hike into the wilderness.

Seven round trips later, the work was done. While the crew stowed the last load, Ricard and Linh faded into the shadows and secreted themselves among the goods. The grumbling workers failed to notice they were two bodies short when they sealed and repressurized the bunker. For half an hour the students hid, expecting someone to come looking for them, until the walls shook with the thrust of the ship's engines. When the rumble faded, they removed their helmets and began searching for the facility entrance. They came upon it at the back of the bunker behind a rack of nonperishable food supplies.

To their shock, they weren't alone. A woman stood before the door, helmet in hand, about to palm the controls. Catching sight of Ricard and Linh, she froze and eyed them like a cat sizing up its prey. Linh gripped Ricard's arm.

"What the hell?" the woman demanded. "You!"

Ricard cocked his head. "You know us?"

"I know your faces." She approached, wary. "Are Hernandez and the Ulengas here, too?"

Linh clung to Ricard and shivered. The woman had to be Lowell Security. Who else would recognize them and connect them with Martin, Petrina, and Dr. Hernandez? And yet, why would a Lowell agent be here? She hadn't been after them; their appearance had surprised her.

"Not that we know of," Ricard said. "We're here by accident."

"Not by accident," a new voice intruded. Through the now-open door stepped an Asian woman arrayed in black, as stark and beautiful as the night sky. "All transpires according to design. You could not help but return to Mars. As for you, Subcommander Leaf, it was inevitable that you'd follow your nemesis."

Subcommander Leaf. Linh had heard that name, a name whispered in fear, never spoken openly. Leah Leaf was Andre Rand's trigger finger.

"Mudiwa," Leah all but spat. "You used her to set me up."

"To invite you," the woman corrected.

"Who signs the invitations around here? You? Hernandez?"

With a sly smile, the woman stepped aside and motioned them through the door. None moved. "I, too, am but a servant," she said. When they still refused her invitation, she added, "Do not fear. I offer answers. How unfortunate if you choose ignorance."

Unflappable as ever, Ricard put his arm about Linh's shoulders. "Answers would be appreciated. Let's start with you. Who are you?"

"I am Hitomi. Come, all of you, and discover the shape of your futures."

Hitomi slipped through the door before anyone could object. Leah motioned Ricard and Linh forward. At first, Linh couldn't move. Ricard wrapped his arm about her shoulders and whispered,

"Hitomi must be Celia's underling. She won't hurt us." His confidence would have to suffice; she had none of her own. She passed through the door with him, and Leah brought up the rear.

They entered a cavernous space three stories high. The walls glowed, bathing the room in light, yet the place was as empty as the Martian desert. No equipment, no people, nothing. Leah stared at the distant ceiling, fists planted on hips. Though Ricard seemed uninterested, Linh knew he wasn't. He'd already memorized the size and shape of the room and wondered at its emptiness, too. That emptiness swallowed Linh. Its brightness engulfed her like the night. She floated in a void that drew the warmth from her body and sucked the air from her lungs.

"Do not fear," Hitomi said. Her voice sounded distant, as though she spoke from far overhead. "You each have a role to play."

"In what?" Leah demanded.

"The conquest of Mars."

"I thought that was Andre Rand's prerogative."

"As does he. But no, Subcommander. It is the prerogative of she who built this place."

"Celia Fundichely," Ricard said. "Where is she now?"

The light failed of a sudden, and in the darkness a pitch shadow darker than dark advanced toward them. When it spoke, its voice rang metallic without inflection. "My darling Ricard," it said. "How wonderful to see you again."

A great joke, she had said. *Yes, a great joke to play on your friends.* Petrina Ulenga didn't know what that meant until this moment. Ricard and Linh stood inexplicably before her, not in the Belt, not on Ganymede, not where they were supposed to be. What had gone wrong? Still, she was overjoyed to see them, and oh how she wished she could run to them, embrace them, laugh and cry with them. Only she couldn't. She had no freedom of movement in this dead black envirosuit. Unlike anything she had ever worn, the impossibly thin suit hugged her body and controlled her, bending her limbs to its will. The helmet felt like a liquid poured over her head, covering her face with a transparency that painted the world in infrared signatures of red, yellow, green, and blue.

Nor could she speak to them. The voice projected by the envirosuit wasn't hers. Her words were confined by the helmet, and no matter how she cried out, "It's me, Ricard, it's me Linh, it's Petrina, it's *me!*" they couldn't hear. The suit spoke for her in a tenor that spiraled upward into the soprano: "My darling Ricard. How wonderful to see you again. And your beautiful wife, too. Oh, and my precious Leah! You've been of special interest to me for a long, long time, Leah dear." The synthesizer laughed like a little girl then rumbled in the bass register. "I'm so pleased you've all joined my team."

For a moment, none of them answered. Linh trembled in fear. Then Leah spoke the most unexpected of words: "You're in danger."

Another laugh issued from the suit. "Am I, now? From whom?"

"A thug named Mudiwa. She intends to kill you and take your place."

The voice turned silken. "My place is not easily taken."

"She's lethal," Leah insisted. "And she looks like you."

Petrina wondered what she looked like to Leah, Ricard, and Linh. *You are become shadow in the darkness*, Hitomi had told her. Hitomi, too, had become shadow, huddled now along the far wall, a speck of heat against a heating system port.

The voice squealed in delight before crackling with static. "Then I'm fortunate to have you. All of you. Petrina and Martin, Linh and Ricard, Leah and, yes, even Mudiwa."

Ricard squeezed Linh's hands in his but kept his silence. It seemed to Petrina he had been party to this conversation before.

"You have Petrina and Martin?" Linh asked, her voice bordering on terror.

The lights came up like the sunrise on Earth. The transparency switched from infrared to visible, then the entire head covering seemed to melt away, revealing Petrina's face, as baffled as anyone's.

"Petrina!" Linh gasped. She shook off Ricard's grasp and ran to embrace her friend. "What are you doing here? What are you...*doing*?"

Petrina clung to her. "Me? You're supposed to be on Ganymede!"

"Long story." Linh stepped back and inspected Petrina's black suit. "Damn, that looks good on you. But what's going on?"

"I'm Celia Fundichely's body double."

Ricard joined them. "You, too?"

Petrina had no idea what he meant.

"She told us Linh was to be her body double," he explained.

Leah advanced on the students, fists balled. "Where's your brother?" she demanded of Petrina.

Petrina only knew Leah Leaf by reputation. Standing in the woman's presence now, she didn't know whether to fear or hate her. Leah may well have ordered the students' torture. Petrina still didn't know where they'd taken Martin, but she wouldn't have told Leah even if she knew. Not that she had to. From somewhere in the suit, a voice emanated, starting high and gradually sinking to a low rumble.

"Martin is safe enough. You all are, so long as you obey me. I am generous to those who are loyal. For the disloyal, swift death awaits. But you've all proven yourselves capable of loyalty, haven't you? From this day forward, be loyal to me, and you shall want for nothing."

The voice fell silent, and no amount of questioning would wake it. Hitomi materialized from the edge of the great room and came into their midst. She gave Petrina a smile of approval, as though to say, "Well done!" Passing them by, she called over her shoulder: "Come. We have but begun."

Chapter 22

Mudiwa's orders were simple: don't think, just do. She'd been given a lifter code, a grenade of undisclosed design, and a plan, to wit: (1) get to the coordinates and infiltrate the building; (2) use the code to access the third floor; (3) lob the grenade two meters into the last room on the south end; (4) get out. Done. From then on, her employers would run the Fundichely empire while she played the mysterious figurehead.

Who could pass up such an opportunity?

In hindsight, it was too easy. She arrived to find the isolated Utopia base crawling with people, including Leah Leaf. How had that bitch survived? Mudiwa began to suspect the job wasn't what she'd been told. Departing from the plan, she reconnoitered the first floor and watched unseen while a shadowy figure addressed a group in a cavernous workroom. From the talk, Mudiwa assumed the shadow was Celia and nearly chucked the explosive at her, but something felt wrong. It was a damn good thing she hesitated. Moments later, the shadow proved a decoy.

Hell. She'd nearly wasted her only charge. How many other decoys lurked behind the facility's closed doors? Best to follow orders, after all, and hope for the best. Mudiwa ducked out, found the lifter, and punched in the access code. On the third level, she slipped down the dead silent corridor to the southernmost room. It stood open, revealing nothing but darkness. Grenade in hand, she pressed the arming button, drew a long, slow breath, and stepped into the doorway.

She might have passed through an airlock into the cosmic void. In the darkness, a shadow deeper still moved, as though someone paced back and forth, back and forth, waiting for the world to end.

So it would. For them.

Mudiwa tossed the grenade. As it clattered on the floor, a glint of brilliant white teeth flashed in the face of the pacing shadow.

Dread froze Mudiwa's limbs, stranding her in the kill zone.

"Ah, Mudiwa. I so hoped you'd come." The voice swirled like the distant lapping of waves on a sandy shore. It could be but one person. Yet…why was she smiling?

"You…" Mudiwa's voice caught in her throat. This was wrong. Frighteningly wrong. "You expected me?"

"I couldn't be sure. You were the one thing I had to leave to chance. But I had faith."

The grenade was a fake. Mudiwa had been set up. Robbed of her prize, she found herself unable to move, unable to think. Standing on the brink of death, she had no plea, no defiance, no wish, no regret.

"Come in," Celia Fundichely said. "You're safe here."

As though compelled, Mudiwa took one hesitant step into the room. The door slid shut behind her, and she sank in the terrifying black. The dark sucked the breath from her lungs.

"Relax, Mudiwa. Relax. We were born to the darkness, you and I. Watch."

A faint glimmer sprinkled down from above. The dark receded imperceptibly, giving Mudiwa's eyes time to adjust. Floor and walls and ceiling materialized about her, and the shadow took on substance. Once the light grew bright enough, she found herself face to face with…

With…

Herself.

It wasn't a mirror. While Mudiwa stood as still as stone, Celia spread her arms as though gathering in the universe.

"I do look like you," Mudiwa whispered. "I look exactly like you!"

Celia laughed.

"How can that be?"

"Because," Celia breathed, "you dear, dear lady, you are my identical twin."

It might have been a passenger shuttle bound for a casino instead of Alejandro Carrasco's quarters. Alejandro brought the whole gang here after wading into Miguel and Matteo Keller's slugfest and breaking it up with fair prejudice. Now they were packed in, occupying all available seating in the cramped common room: Alejandro and Jake (both irritable), Miguel and Matteo (both a bit bruised and bloodied), and Carmen (amused or aloof or both). Miguel and Matteo eyed each other with hostile intent. Jake sneered warnings at them. Carmen ignored everyone. Alejandro wished they'd get the hell out.

Succumbing to Jake's implied threats, Miguel released Matteo from scrutiny and turned to his brother. "We've all been manipulated, not just you."

An understatement to end all understatements, but Alejandro didn't comment. Miguel's science smarts never left much gray matter for common thought.

Nodding to Matteo, Miguel added, "All but you. You're here by accident."

Matteo half rose until he caught Jake's look and sank back.

"Don't let Miguel rile you," Carmen warned. "He perfected his technique on my husband, for all the good it did him."

"Your husband," Miguel snapped, "drove me into the wilderness like a criminal."

"You are a criminal. So's your brother. So's Jake. Matteo and I are the only innocent ones here."

"Right. You, who betrayed Andre a dozen times."

"More than that, dear, but only sexually, which doesn't register on his balance sheet."

"God!" Alejandro roared. "Enough! Yeah, Hitomi's been knocking us around like balls in a game of space billiards. But why? What's she up to?"

"Not Hitomi," Carmen said. "Celia Fundichely. And no point asking why. She's the darkest enigma in the solar system."

Matteo shifted in his seat. "It's all about power."

"What does a driver know about that?" Miguel asked.

Jake lumbered up to Miguel and stabbed a finger into his shoulder. The force knocked Miguel back in his seat. "Little guys knows more of power than anyone. We gets squashed by it all the time." He turned on Carmen. "I wants to talk about that. I wants your husband to know what he does to my sister. What he does to me."

Carmen's eyebrows lifted.

Alejandro figured she could guess. She knew her husband's capacity for cruelty. "I get Celia using Andre Rand," he said. "But the rest of us? What are we? A couple of troublemakers, a scientist and his students, a temptress, a nobody driver. What good are we to her?"

Carmen arched her eyebrows in amusement. "Temptress? I'm just bored."

"Whatever. Why the hell does Celia need you?"

Miguel rose and wandered to the door. He stared at it absently as though not quite sure why it was there. When he turned back, revelation illuminated his features. "We're all ways of getting at Andre." He tapped himself on the chest. "Political thorn." He pointed at Alejandro. "Crime." Then Jake. "Revenge." Finally, Carmen. "The one person he cares for."

"What about Matteo?" Carmen asked.

Miguel's voice acquired a bit of sympathy. "He could steal you from Andre."

"I'm not stealing her," Matteo objected.

"You may be the only one who could. You love her for her own sake. Tell me that doesn't mean something, Carmen."

Carmen didn't tell him anything. Matteo blushed.

Alejandro didn't see any point in psychoanalyzing the driver. "You're saying we're pawns in a game to oust Andre Rand. So, what do we do about it? I'm not flying to Rand's rescue, but I'm sick of playing the pawn."

"Celia's a bigger threat than Andre," Miguel said. "As much as I hate to say it, we may have to rescue him, at least for now."

"I wants Rand dead," Jake said. He eyed Carmen as though sizing up her potential as a murder weapon.

"Forget it," Carmen told him. "I won't betray Andre."

Jake sneered at her.

Matteo interposed himself between Jake and Carmen. "Leave her alone." He couldn't hope to take Jake, but he showed no fear.

"Shut up, all of you," Alejandro snapped. "Miguel's right. Rand can wait. What's your plan, Miguel?"

"Hitomi's here," Miguel said. "Celia won't be far off."

"Capture her?"

"Yes."

Alejandro clapped his hands and stood. "Suits me," he said. "At least it'll get you all out of my room."

Her father was dead.

The words might have been gibberish.

Her father was dead, murdered by an agent sent to kill Andre Rand.

Kara Lloyd felt cold, empty, alone.

Her mother had died seven years before, leaving just her and her father. Kara was soon to venture off Mars for a position as a security field agent for a mining conglomerate in the Belt. She hated the thought of leaving her father, but he urged her to put Mars behind her. The planet was poison, he said, turning good people evil. He would join her in time, when he could.

But now he was dead, victim of a botched assassination. Mayor Rand had personally sent word and given her such details as Lowell Security had assembled. The killer had fled to Utopia where security satellites revealed Celia Fundichely had built an unauthorized base. The implication was clear: Celia ordered Rand's assassination in a bid to seize control of Mars. Kara's father accidentally took the hit.

The communication contained no mention of revenge, no request for Kara to involve herself, but none was needed. Andre Rand had been her father's friend and benefactor. When she was younger, he had been like an uncle to her. He knew her rage, her desire for revenge, because he felt it, too. He wasn't giving her news; he was begging her to seize revenge for them both. His closing line said it all:

Anything you need is yours.

So for her father, for the mayor, for herself, Kara swore she'd hunt down and slay the dragon.

Chapter 23

Light and sound died in the same instant, leaving the Utopia facility in silence deeper than any Miguel had ever known. This was Martian silence: no stirring of leaves on a breeze, no wash of waves on the shore, no hum of insects. It was the stillness of a dead world.

"Everything's shut down." He spoke in a whisper that rang like a scream in his own ears. "Even air circulation."

Alejandro exhaled in disgust. "What's she up to?"

Setting fists to his hips, Jake said, "Maybe she tries to kills us."

"She could have done that whenever she wanted," Alejandro objected.

Miguel agreed with his brother, although he hadn't yet identified much logic in any of this. "We may as well press on," Miguel said. "She's got to be here somewhere."

"Or," Carmen suggested, "we could wait for her to show up." She hung on Matteo Keller's arm as though he'd escorted her to an art exhibit. "If she wants us, she can find us."

"I'd rather not meet her on her terms."

"You think you have a choice? She doesn't offer choices, Miguel. Andre and I invited her here because she wanted us to. She asked so nicely, but it wasn't a request. It was an order. She'll meet us wherever and whenever she wants."

"Then we should do something unexpected," Matteo suggested. "Surprise her."

"Right," Alejandro said. "'Cause we have so many options."

Carmen and Alejandro had it right. Miguel's own path proved it. He had had one place he needed to be, one option for safety when Andre Rand outlawed him, one thought when Nessa O'Clery captured him. And now again, one course of action: find Celia Fundichely. Somehow, she had anticipated everything and drawn them all here. Which meant Matteo was right, too. Their only escape lay in the unexpected.

"Like what?" he asked Matteo.

"Steal a rover. Split up. Hide. Barricade ourselves in. Talk to her. Commit suicide. Anything. She can't have planned for everything."

Carmen laughed. "Suicide is excessive, don't you think?"

"Only if it's real."

This driver was more creative than Miguel had thought. And he'd said just the right thing. "Hitomi told me I'd find what I wanted in Utopia. She didn't mean fossils. Maybe you got it right, Jake."

Jake grinned. "You wants what I wants."

Now that it came to it, he almost couldn't admit it. He wanted his students out of this, his reputation restored, science to be served. All noble motives. Yet underneath all that, a base desire still lurked. "To be remembered," he said.

"And how the hell does that help?" Alejandro demanded.

"I'll ask her for it."

"Ask her?"

"Yes."

In the darkness along the back wall, someone moved and laughed and waited.

Miguel peered at the shadow. Almost imperceptible, it could have been anything from a person to a piece of furniture. But he knew what it was. "Hello, Celia."

"Hello, Miguel." The voice rang like cold metal struck by a hammer. "Would it surprise you if I said you did surprise me for once?"

"So?"

The ice melted, and a little girl spoke. "Wish granted. You'll be remembered as long as I."

Which only half answered the question. "For what?"

"For making Mars mine."

"What do you want with Mars?"

The laugh repeated, followed now by bass thunder. "Not a damn thing."

Carmen broke the nervous silence enshrouding the others. "Then why come? Why insist on my permission?"

The voice half-disintegrated into static. "It's not always clear who my enemies are. Confusion makes a potent defense."

"Andre wasn't your enemy," Carmen objected. "He was a business partner. I wasn't even that."

The shadow laughed again, a strange, hollow laugh.

Celia certainly had generated confusion. "To the point," Miguel said. "How do I make Mars yours?"

"Isn't it obvious?" Celia's false voice acquired the twitter of songbirds. The sound called Miguel home, and for a moment he wondered why he'd ever left Earth. "Make it yours."

He didn't understand. None of them did.

"Don't worry, dears, you'll figure it out. This facility—the seed of a new colony—is now yours. Use it to do what you do best."

A door snicked open and shut. Power hummed in the walls, bringing with it light and fresh air. They were alone in the corridor with only each other and their questions for company.

"Do what I do best," Carmen said. "What's that?"

"Play games," Miguel said.

"I thought you liked me."

"I do. Your husband's another matter."

"I'm not taking her side—or yours, or anyone's—against Andre."

Alejandro rubbed his forehead, turned, spat on the floor. "Hell," he muttered. "This isn't about Andre Rand." He nodded to Miguel. "My genius brother gets it, right?"

He did. It wasn't about Andre Rand, wasn't about fossils or new settlements or even Mars. It was about Celia Fundichely's one and only concern: herself. "We're all decoys," he said. "All of us. A collective proxy for Andre's newest, greatest nemesis. Nobody will question it. Why wouldn't Celia Fundichely want control of a planet? Even she couldn't seize Earth, but to claim Mars, she need only take down Andre."

"I won't be part of that," Carmen repeated. "I refuse."

"Which makes you part of it," Miguel said. "You'll keep us from winning too easily. Or at all. An eternal battle with us doing Celia's dirty work. And as long as it lasts, everyone who wants her dead will know exactly where to look."

"When they comes for her," Jake added, "they gets us instead." He flashed his maniac grin. "Poor them!"

In a great room of pristine desks with embedded panels, most still covered in protective sheets, Martin Ulenga gave the appearance of a businessman. Bent over one of the desks, his fingers flicking across the active panel, he didn't even look up when they entered.

From the set of his jaw, Petrina knew he was tottering on the edge of rage, but his breath pulsed steady, deliberate. He had himself under control, if just.

Approaching him, Quan Linh placed a tentative hand on his. "Martin. It's good to see you again. Are you okay?"

Martin yanked his hand back.

"He will be," Petrina said from hope rather than certainty.

Ricard Fulbert turned on Hitomi. "What's this about?"

"Your destiny. Take a seat, all of you." Hitomi motioned to the desks.

Nobody moved. Ricard waited, unfazed. Petrina and Linh barely breathed. Leah Leaf backed against the wall, arms crossed, a smirk on her face.

"Do as she says," Martin snapped.

Petrina raised an eyebrow, but his attention remained on the panel.

Ricard glanced over his shoulder at Martin. "Seriously?"

"Yes, damn it. Sit."

Ricard shook his head but sat. The rest followed suit, all but Leah, who continued to lean on the wall as though she knew something even Hitomi didn't. Petrina was pretty sure that was an act.

Finally looking up, Martin sneered at Leah. "What the hell's with you?"

Pushing off the wall, Leah approached him. "I'm waiting for the show to start. What's with you?"

"I'm trying to concentrate, which is damned hard with all of you making noise."

"Concentrate on what?" Leah studied the panel. "Geologic surveys? Trust me, there's no gold here."

Before Martin could reply, Hitomi stepped to Leah's side and said, "You should sit before you lose the light."

A chill ran down Petrina's spine. "She's here?"

Hitomi's smile faded into blackness as the lights winked out.

In the darkness, a shadow moved among them. Distant laughter echoed from the walls. They might have been in a cavern.

"It's not *that* funny," Leah said.

"Oh, but it is," the shadow rumbled. "If you know the joke."

"So explain it."

Turning as soft as a mist, the voice answered. "Martin himself is the gold I seek. You all are."

"Don't get your hopes up. I don't work for you."

"Of course you do, Leah. You have no choice."

"I think I do."

Again the laugh, but this time it sounded like grinding rocks.

"Then what's your command, oh mighty goddess?"

"Two things, my dear. You will help someone live, and you will watch someone die."

Leah fell silent. Petrina shivered.

With no trace of alarm, Ricard asked, "Who lives?"

The voice took on a metallic hue. "Me."

"Of course. And who dies?"

The dark silence roared in their ears. Then Celia spoke, but only to taunt them.

"Who do you think?"

A suborbital might be the fastest way from Lowell to Utopia, but it lacked stealth. That's why, after landing on the primitive pad, Kara Lloyd waited for alarms, guards, something. An hour she waited, but nobody emerged from the facility. A scan of the building revealed no armaments, no surveillance, no defense of any kind. The heat signatures within were too faint to reveal population. It didn't look like much, but the structure must have been well-insulated.

Suiting up, Kara left the ship and made the trek to the airlock, which opened at the touch of a button, leading her into a seemingly deserted building. She shucked the envirosuit and stashed it in a nearby locker before beginning a quiet reconnaissance. She carried a rhewgwn, a compact assassin's handgun firing ultracold ice darts which left no trace but the wound. It wasn't ideal for headshots, but it could blow open a major artery or, with a clear shot between the ribs, do fatal damage to the heart. And she had marksmanship skills.

The place seemed oddly dark and quiet, as though it had been abandoned once built. Yet in his roundabout way, Andre Rand had assured her Celia Fundichely would be here. Andre wasn't about to make it sound like a contract, but Kara knew he wanted Celia dead. They both did. Kara wanted Celia dead twenty times over, a hundred times, a thousand.

The first level proved empty, but on the second she heard voices. Without making a sound, she crept toward the murmur, slipping from light into darkness, silent, feeling rather than seeing her way, passing closed door after closed door until her fingers wrapped around the edge of an opening. The voices rang in her ears now, clear, distinct, a group of people talking circles around each other. Kara listened to the conversation, paying no attention to the words, paying full attention to the soundscape, mapping everyone's locations, figuring out who was important and who was not.

"And who dies?"

"Who do you think?"

"Us."

"Why would you think that?"

"What do you really want?"

"My dear, I told you."

"Why don't you show your face for once?"

"Because she's afraid. She's afraid she's the one who might die."

"We aren't killers."

"Two of you are."

"Leah Leaf, maybe, but not the rest of us."

"Hasn't Ricard told you about his adventures?"

"Ricard?"

"Oh my yes, Ricard can be ruthless when his lady love needs protection. I admire that in a man."

"What's she talking about, Ricard?"

"Enough! Turn on the lights. Let's see your face."

"She never shows her face. She's afraid to."

"She revealed it to me."

A little girl's laugh silenced them, then a whisper suffused the darkness: "Ah, she's here. Let's welcome our angel of death."

A blaze of light left Kara momentarily blinded. As her eyes adjusted, she found the others with hands thrown over their faces in a vain effort to fend off the glare. Only one faced the light with eyes full open: a woman with jet black skin and a brilliant grin that nearly split her face in two. She pierced Kara with that mocking smile as though daring her to pull the trigger.

This was Celia Fundichely. It had to be. But why was she smiling? Didn't she realize she was dead? Kara wanted her to know it, willed her to know it, demanded that look of triumph turn to terror.

It didn't.

Kara drew a bead on the demon's heart.

Celia silently laughed.

The others dropped their hands, eyes still batting at the light, and then they saw Kara, saw the weapon, looked at her with blank, befuddled eyes, and still Celia watched, waited, drew herself up as though presenting her heart as a target.

Was it a trap, or was the woman insane?

It didn't matter. Kara's father was dead. Celia was the reason. Kara squeezed the trigger. She squeezed it over and over and over until the cryochamber was empty and tears stung her eyes and a dozen red stains spread across the grinning woman's chest as her body toppled, her teeth still flashing in the light while blood pooled about her on the floor.

Someone screamed.

Gasping for breath, blinded by tears, Kara fled. She ought to kill the others, ought to rid herself of witnesses, but she didn't know who they were, she was out of rounds, she couldn't think, couldn't kill people who might be as innocent as her father. She ran, expecting pursuit, but no footfalls dogged her. She made it to the first level and scrambled into her envirosuit, watching over her shoulder, yet nobody followed. She hit the airlock and bolted into the fading Martian evening, across the scraped rock to her suborbital, a cloud of blood-red dust marking her passage, and still nobody pursued. She fumbled through the launch sequence and rocketed into the thin atmosphere, alone.

What the hell was going on? Who were those people?

Gradually, her heart settled into normal rhythm, her breathing slowed, her shaking hands stilled. What should she do now? All those people, all those witnesses. But no, that wasn't her concern. Andre Rand had hired her. He would protect her; he would clean up the mess. It would be days, maybe a month or more before word made it back from Utopia. Kara only needed return to Lowell and grab the first flight to the Belt. Nobody knew her. Nobody would be looking for her. She was nothing, just a neophyte security agent on her way to employment in the Belt.

Or maybe not. Not anymore. Word would leak out. Not even Andre Rand could stop that. Security agent was Kara's cover now. She was an assassin, and not just any assassin. She was the assassin who took down Celia Fundichely. She'd be famous, infamous, sought after for contracts, marked for death. What kind of life would that be? She didn't know. She only knew everything had changed the moment her father died. She could never be with him again, never have a normal life again. But most of all, she could never have the thing she craved most: to watch Celia die again, again, again, a thousand times over.

Kara wept and couldn't stop until the ship touched down in Lowell Colony.

Chapter 24

Andre Rand poured a glass of champagne, tested its flavor, and found it good. He poured one for Carmen. "To world domination," he said. He smiled like a demon who had successfully corrupted a soul, and they drank.

It was the day after her return. Alejandro Carrasco had piloted the suborbital back to Lowell's spaceport and informed the skeptical port authorities that the first lady had been on an exotic vacation in the Martian wilderness. They didn't buy it, but how could they argue with Carmen Rand's personal pilot? Now Andre and Carmen were at the window in his office, admiring the stark beauty of the rusted desert. A distant storm yellowed the horizon. Carmen thought her husband looked more pleased with himself than usual. He didn't yet realize how little had gone his way. He'd be in for some nasty surprises in the coming months, and she wasn't sure how she felt about that. Normally, she'd let him fend for himself, but now…

Now he needed her, although he'd never admit it.

"Where the hell have you been?" he asked, but not in anger. He didn't care that much. Not yet.

"My driver seduced me. He was so damn good, I let him drive me all over the planet."

Andre laughed. "*He* seduced *you*? That's a new one."

"Variety is the spice of life, my love." She leaned into Andre and kissed his lips. He pulled her close and didn't free her mouth for a brief, endless minute.

"I don't know why I let you run around," he said.

"Sure you do. Sex isn't what gets you off."

"Sometimes it does."

"Sometimes," Carmen agreed. "But mostly it's power, and I'd just be in the way."

"Not so."

"Just so."

Andre ran his fingers through her hair and gazed into her eyes with more affection that he had for a long time. "Videographers eat you up. The public eats you up. That gives me power. Ergo, you give me power. Ergo, you're not in the way."

"You do love me, after all."

"You know I do."

They drank without breaking eye contact.

"Why're you in such a good mood?" Carmen asked. "What happened while I was under the influence of my driver?"

Andre smiled.

"Come on, I told all. Now it's your turn."

"Not all, I'm sure. But let's just say…" He swirled his glass and gazed into the liquid. His eyes shone as bright as the sun. "I understand Celia Fundichely has left Mars for good."

This was the stupidest thing Alejandro had ever heard. "Body doubles," he said. He'd returned to Utopia after delivering Carmen home and making a quick stop to offer Nessa O'Clery a chance to expand her operations to Utopia on Miguel's behalf. She expressed cautious interest in the proposition but made no commitments. Not yet. Now Alejandro was wondering why he'd bothered to come back. He should've jumped the next passenger ship bound for the Belt.

Mudiwa stretched her beautiful dark form in his face, flanked by Petrina Ulenga and Quan Linh. She draped her arms over their shoulders as though the three of them were sisters. Damn beautiful sisters, though nobody would mistake them for kin. "That's right," she said, grinning unnervingly like Jake.

"For a dead woman."

"Quick, isn't he girls? Almost as smart as that scientist brother of his."

Petrina and Linh weren't as enthused as Mudiwa about their new situation. Alejandro figured they'd rather be digging up rocks than impersonating the dead. Yet it was oddly the same, wasn't it? Dead life on Mars. Strangely poetic.

"What's the point?" Alejandro demanded. "You're inviting assassins to dinner, and for what?"

Petrina looked away. "To keep people guessing."

"And get paid," Mudiwa added. "A hell of a lot. We're set for life."

"Sure," Alejandro agreed. "A very short life."

"She gave us a security team," Linh said. "Your job—you, Jake, Ricard, Martin, and Leah—is to keep us safe."

Alejandro didn't point out that Celia had assigned Ricard and Martin two jobs. They were expected to oversee technology development as well as security. Petrina and Linh were given double duty, too, as natural resource managers. "Which leaves my largely useless brother."

"He's not useless," Petrina said. "Dr. Hernandez is in charge."

Alejandro snorted. "Is that supposed to make us feel better? What exactly is he in charge of?"

"Everything. Running the base. Building out the new colony. He's an experienced administrator. He has contacts with settlers and smugglers who can supply materials and labor and technical expertise. And he's adept at countering Andre Rand."

Adept wasn't the word. Besides, none of that answered the real question. "What the hell's the point?"

Mudiwa shrugged. "She didn't tell us. Who cares? We're rich!"

"Rich slaves," Alejandro said.

"I've been a slave," Linh snapped.

"That was to protect you. I told you I'd come back, which I would have, had you stayed put."

"Point is," Petrina said, "we have jobs and no choice but to do them. She kills everyone who fails her."

"Damn it, she's *dead*!"

Mudiwa grinned at him. "She's right here in your face, babe."

An hour north of the facility, a low ridge snaked across the plain, pockmarked by craters. The wind whipped a streamer of dust from the crest of the ridge and blew it eastward. It sailed overhead like the tail of an otherwise unseen dragon. Just below the rise, a rover halted, all systems but life support killed. It stood alone, disconnected from everyone in the universe.

Inside, Miguel swiveled the pilot's seat to face the rear. "You don't need darkness anymore," he said.

A brilliant smile flashed from the heart of a shadow.

"I've seen you," he said. "I've seen your twin. And here, it's just the two of us."

"But games are fun," Celia Fundichely said. "I live for games. Massive wealth can be so tedious."

"How did you know Andre planned to assassinate you?"

"Everyone plans to assassinate me. In Andre's case, I made sure of it. It wasn't hard. I only had to make him nervous. He despises competition, and here I am." The shadow rose, moved into the light, and there indeed she was, arms spread wide like an entertainer, her black body clothed in a skin-tight black outfit. In the dim light, she almost looked naked.

Miguel swallowed and looked away. "You were convincing. Everyone bought it, even me."

"The blood was real. It just wasn't mine."

He didn't ask whose. "You weren't breathing. Your heart had stopped."

"Certain drug cocktails do remarkable things."

"We about buried you behind the facility."

"Why didn't you?"

"Mudiwa asked to take care of your body, alone. Long-lost sister. We could hardly refuse." Miguel laughed. "She was in on it."

"Only at the end. I had Hitomi fill her in."

"And now the solar system believes the great Celia Fundichely is dead."

Celia shrugged. "Or not. Andre will spread the word and take credit without taking credit. My trio of doubles—is that an oxymoron?—will be a plague on Andre, ensuring the reverse is known. Nobody will know what to think. They'll target Utopia, of course, over and over, but I won't be there. I'll be safe."

"Will your sister and my students?"

"If everyone does their jobs. So don't disappoint me."

"And what does a dead empress do?"

She approached Miguel, slowly lifted a hand, palm open so as not to alarm him, and stroked his cheek. "Goddess, Miguel my dear. Goddess. I'll enjoy myself. Death is liberating, for those with life left in them. I might even find a companion. It could be pleasant to wake up to a warm partner."

Miguel wondered what she'd do if they all left Mars, vanished into the Belt or the outer systems. Science still beckoned. He and his students could still get their names into the history vids. His face must have broadcast the question, because she leaned into him, kissed him lightly on the lips, and whispered in his ear. "Careful, my love. I've killed men for less. With my own hand."

He waited until she backed off to say, "I'm not your love and don't want the position."

"Yes, you want Carmen, and who could blame you?"

"We're not together anymore."

"You will be."

Miguel didn't see any hope of that. He and Carmen had used each other too badly. Whatever real feelings he might have for her, she had only contempt for him. Besides, Matteo was the better man if she needed more than Andre could give.

"Trust me," Celia said. "How do you think I made all this work? I know most people better than they know themselves. Take you. You think you want fossils and fame and a future for your surrogate children. And of course, you do. But deep down, all you really want is to live again, to reclaim what you threw away. Carmen may not be Mona, but she's damn close, no?"

No. Maybe. He hadn't consciously considered that. "I've lost Carmen, too. Why would she come back?"

"God, Miguel, I can't tutor you in a single afternoon! You're supposed to be smart. Figure it out."

His smarts were in science, not people.

"Time for me to go." She tapped the center of her chest, and something black oozed up from the neckline of her clothing to engulf her head, leaving a clear space around her face. The clear space took on a sheen, and Miguel realized with a start that the substance had formed into an ultrathin helmet.

"That's an envirosuit?"

"Took you long enough."

"But it's almost not there."

"Just like me, in more ways than one: tougher than it looks, one of a kind, and way too expensive. Maybe someday it'll be commercially viable. Meanwhile, it sure looks good on me, doesn't it?"

It did.

She cycled the airlock open. Before she stepped in, Miguel asked, "And that's it? You're done with everything? Fame, fortune, the Belt, Mars?"

Celia turned an enigmatic smile on him, and with another step and a tap of a button was gone.

Miguel watched the viewport as her black form shimmied up the rise and vanished beyond the top of the ridge. Ten minutes later, a sleek craft ascended into the sky from the far side of the ridge and diminished to a point. When it winked out, Miguel pondered the sky for a long time.

They had no fire, real or simulated, no stars overhead, only seats around a conference table and dinner trays filled with reconstituted vegetables and simulated beef. Not bad for such a remote outpost, but not what meals had been in Lowell Colony. Only one thing bothered Miguel: he wasn't sure he recognized his students anymore. Martin and Petrina, Linh and Ricard—their eyes had hardened, their playfulness had vanished, their enthusiasm had faded. He'd tried to protect them, tried to get them away before it was too late, but he'd failed. He'd lost a lot, but the thing he most regretted losing was them.

Linh cocked her head. "Why so glum, Professor?"

"Am I?"

"Uh-huh."

Yes, he was. "You shouldn't be here. You should be out there." He waved vaguely at the ceiling. "Making discoveries that change how we view ourselves."

"That's certainly changed," Ricard said. "Have you ever been to the Belt, Professor?"

Miguel shook his head. "The Martian wilderness was the extent of my travels."

"It wasn't what I expected. I don't think Ganymede would have been, either."

But it would have been a chance, a new start away from Andre Rand and Celia Fundichely and their ilk. Miguel twined and untwined his fingers and stared at nothing.

"Neither is Mars," Martin said. "Mars isn't what we grew up thinking it was."

Linh reached across the table and took Miguel's hands in hers. Her touch was feather-light. "I don't believe you meant to teach us that, but we had to learn it eventually. Mars is the Belt, socially if not astrographically. It's wild and ruthless and full of opportunity if you don't care who you hurt. You don't mean to be callous, but you fall into it. You end up caring too much about yourself, too little about others."

Miguel squeezed her hand. "I care about you. All of you."

Petrina scoffed. "Is that why you fucked Carmen Rand?"

Unable to meet her eyes, he looked at the table. That wasn't the word he would have used.

"Don't tell me it was for love."

"She isn't looking for love," Miguel objected.

"That's not an answer."

"Petrina—"

"Don't obfuscate and don't lie. Give it to us straight for once."

What could he say? He hardly knew himself, anymore. Celia may have been more right about him than he thought. "We both had our needs," he said. "We used each other's to satisfy our own."

"There you go," Martin said. "Reciprocal treachery. That's Mars. That's the Belt. That's us. We've lied and cheated and even killed to keep our heads above the sand. And now…"

When his voice faltered, Petrina picked up the thread. "Now it's easy."

Linh released Miguel's hand. "Don't you see? This was her plan. She didn't just lure us here. She trained us to be what she needed."

Hell, Miguel thought. *That's what Celia meant.* Carmen would come to him not for love or lust or old times' sake. She would come to protect Andre and to escape him. Miguel would take her back to undermine Andre and to feel Mona nestled in his arms. They'd exchange friendly fire over and over, waging cold war in hot blood, against each other and against themselves. They'd love and hate each other for it. They'd love and hate themselves for it.

Celia wanted them warring to eternity.

And so would they.

Thank you for reading! Please leave a short, honest review wherever you purchased this book. I greatly appreciate it, and it will help others discover my books.

Acknowledgements

Throughout my long training and modest career as a writer, I've benefited from the kind assistance of many, many people. Some of their names have faded from memory, but their influence lives on in my stories.

For the present novel, I owe special thanks to my daughter Andrea Bullock, who edited the manuscript; Veronica Mui, whose insightful ideas transformed the storyline; and Kat Sidhom-Yarborough, who ensured I got a key female perspective right. And of course, my eternal gratitude to my late wife Kathleen, who enriched my life without measure and without whom I would never have written anything publishable.

Dale E. Lehman is an award-winning writer, veteran software developer, amateur astronomer, and bonsai artist in training. He principally writes mysteries, science fiction, and humor. In addition to his novels, his writing has appeared in *Sky & Telescope* and on Medium.com. He owns and operates the imprint Red Tales. He and his late wife Kathleen have five children, six grandchildren, and two feisty cats. At any given time, Dale is at work on several novels and short stories.

Visit https://www.DaleELehman.com to find out more about Dale's books.